W9-BON-666

IAN McDONALD

BE MY ENEMY

an imprint of **Prometheus Books**
Amherst, NY

Published 2012 by Pyr®, an imprint of Prometheus Books

Cover illustration © John Picacio
Jacket design by Grace M. Conti-Zilsberger

Inquiries should be addressed to
Pyr
59 John Glenn Drive
Amherst, New York 14228–2119
VOICE: 716–691–0133
FAX: 716–691–0137
WWW.PYRSF.COM

16 15 14 13 12   5 4 3 2 1

Library of Congress Cataloging-in-Publication Data

McDonald, Ian, 1960–
    Be my enemy / by Ian McDonald.
        p. cm. — (The Everness series ; bk. 2)
    ISBN 978–1–61614–678–8 (hardcover)
    ISBN 978–1–61614–679–5 (ebook)
    I. Title.

PR6063.C38B4 2012
823'.914—dc23

2012018572

Printed in the United States of America

To Enid, as ever.

Author's Note: There is a Palari dictionary
at the back of this book.

1

The car came out of nowhere. He thought it might have been black in the split second that he saw it. Black and big and expensive, maybe German, with darkened windows and rain drops like oil on its polished skin. All in the moment, the moment before the impact.

School had finished for Christmas. Games in the morning, then a half day. Rain with an edge of sleet mixed in had been blowing diagonally across the football pitch. Sometimes it had been so heavy that he had to squint to see the action at the other end of the pitch. The rain had driven the cold deep into him. He was all alone on the goal line, banging his gloves together and jumping up and down to try to keep the cold from reaching all the way in to his bones. The pitch was like a plowed field. The players were so muddy he could hardly tell Team Gold from Team Red. He hadn't had to make a save since the twenty-fifth minute and the ball hadn't been in his half of the pitch for ten minutes. Figures moved across each other, a whistle blew, arms went up, cheers, high fives. He squinted through the rain. Goal. Team Gold's goalkeeper picked the ball out of the back of the net and kicked it up the field, but her heart wasn't in it and the wind caught the ball and swerved it right across the pitch and over the side line. Mr. Armstrong blew his referee's whistle three times. Game over. Team Red and Team Gold, whose players looked like members of Team Mud, trudged off to the changing rooms. Three nil for Team Red over their only serious rivals in the Bourne Green Year Ten League was a crushing victory, but he was tired and wanted to be off for the holidays, and he wondered whose dumb idea it had been to hold a match on the last morning of the term, but most of all he was cold cold cold. The hot showers couldn't drive out the cold. The festival lights for Christmas and Diwali and Hanukkah couldn't warm him. Mrs. Abrahams, the head teacher called everyone into the stifling heat of the assembly hall and wished them a Happy Holiday and See You All In The New Year, but he was too bone cold to appreciate the heat. He had forgotten what it was like to be warm.

After school, he trudged, head down against the stinging sleet, along the alley known as Dog's Delight, dodging the turds. Not all of the turds had been left behind by dogs. He continued across Abney Park Cemetery. The Victorian headstones and monuments were glossy with rain. The stone angels wore small, lacy collars of frozen sleet. Trees branches lashed wildly in the wind, and clouds, low and dark, raced across the sky.

One more Christmas present to get, and it was the hardest. It was a guy thing; none of his friends at Bourne Green had any idea what to get their Mum's either. Vouchers were popular and easy: a couple of clicks and you could print them out at home. Spa treatments, things to put in your bath, and general pampering goodies all rated with the guys. Mums loved those kinds of things. He considered those lazy gifts. This year, Laura needed something special, something chosen by him, for her, with thought and care. The last time he had been in the city to do sushi with Colette he'd passed a new yoga shop. The window was full of mats and exercise balls and healing tea and pale cotton stretchy stuff. He hadn't been thinking Christmas presents then. He hadn't been thinking at all. You don't think when someone who has been the pillar of your life dies. You react, slowly, painfully.

The bike had cost four thousand pounds. It was a forty-first birthday present that his father had given to himself. Tejendra had shown him all the engineering details: the lightweight carbon-fibre frame, the Campagnolo gear train, the aluminium and chrome headset. But it hadn't looked worth the money Tejendra had paid. Laura's eyes had widened at the cost, which would have been enough to cover a family holiday in Turkey. Tejendra had assured her that it was at the bottom end of the carbon-frame range. They went up to eight thousand. Laura's eye widened even further when she saw Tejendra roll out on to the public roads in tights and hi-viz yellow. MAMIL: Middle-Aged Man In Lycra.

"You're going all the way into college on that?" she'd asked.

"And back again."

And he did, for five months, all through the spring and summer, and even Laura had to admit that her husband started to look trimmer and slept better and had more energy. Tejendra announced that he was even thinking of the hundred-mile Thames Valley Sportive; the physics department was entering a small team.

Then, three days before sportive Sunday, Tejendra came up on the inside of a Sainsbury truck at the traffic lights on Kingsland Road. The truck turned left and knocked Tejendra under the wheels. He had placed himself in the driver's blind spot. Tejendra, a reputable fine physicist and a brilliant man, had forgotten about something as simple as that, and it had killed him. "I couldn't see him," the truck driver said over and over and over. "I couldn't see him." The bike's carbon-fibre frame had shattered like bones. Tejendra had died instantly, in his helmet and yellow hi-viz and bike shorts. It took the ambulance half an hour to make it through the morning rush-hour traffic. Not even the Moon could save him. Up there they could send probes between stars and open gates to parallel universes, but they could not bring humans back from the dead. Maybe they could; maybe they just didn't care about humans enough.

"Up there you can step from one universe to another," Tejendra had said. "Makes you wonder if there's any physics left for us to do." From one universe to another. From world to world. From alive to dead. One step, one moment, was all that separated them. There was no warning, no reason, and absolutely no arguing with it. Dad to no Dad.

He'd been sent to Mrs. Packham, the school counselor. He

played head games with her. One session he would be angry, the next remote, the next sulky, the next plain insane. He knew she knew he was playing games. He didn't want to be an official victim, a Bereaved Pupil. The truth, the things he felt in his heart, the sense of disbelief, the slow understanding that death was forever, that what had happened to Tejendra was insane, an offense against the worldview his Dad had nurtured in him—that the universe was a rational, organized place that followed unbreakable laws—all these he told to Colette. She had been Dad's research colleague and a family friend almost as long as he could remember. An unofficial aunt. She listened, she said nothing, she offered no advice and no judgements. She bought him good sushi and Japanese tea so hot it scalded the taste buds off his tongue.

Dad had died three months ago. The seasons had turned, a new school year had begun, and now Christmas hung over the end of the year like a great shining chandelier, all glints and lights. At the top of the year they would start again. In the long night of the short days, they would move on.

So, he needed to buy presents, good ones. Through the cemetery gates he could see a huddle of people at the bus stop, pressed together out of the rain. He pulled out his phone. The number 73 bus was due at the stop in thirty-eight seconds. Rain smeared the screen. He waved his hand. A map appeared showing the bus as a little animated character ambling along Northwold Road to the terminus. He could see it, one of the new double-deckers looming over the little scuttling cars and the white vans, shouldering its way into the bus lane. The traffic was so quiet since the new fast-charge, high-capacity batteries had come down from the Moon and made electric vehicles cheap, quick, reliable, and must-have. Stoke Newington High Street purred where once it had growled. A double baby buggy crossed his path. He skidded, almost went down. The woman, short and stocky, with dark, lank hair, glared at him.

"Sorry. Okay? Sorry."

For once there was no one parked illegally in the bus lane, and the bus was swinging along. He had to get it. Timing was everything. Miss this one bus and he would miss the shops. The crossing was a hundred meters up the road, but there was a gap in the traffic. It was all about judging relative velocities. Like goalkeeping: ball, goal line, body. The traffic opened. He darted out between the parked Citroen MPV and the old gasoline-powered builder's van.

So he never saw the car come out of nowhere. And when he did see it—black car, black raindrops on its polished nose—it was far too late: it hit him harder than he had ever been hit in his life, hit him up into the air. The car kept moving, and he came down on the top of it, and this second impact now was the hardest he had ever been hit in his life, so hard it knocked everything but sight and consciousness out of him. The car continued forward, sending him tumbling into the street, and that was the hardest of all; it knocked every last sight and thought out of him. Black car, black rain. Black.

Black into white. Pure cold white. He smashed up through the white with a cry, like a diver coming up for air. He was in a white bed in a white room, beneath a white sheet, staring up at a white, glowing ceiling. He sat up, gasping. Since Dad had died, he had been waking up in the middle of the night not knowing where he was, what house, what room, what bed, even what body he was in. After a moment his mind would catch up with his senses. Safe. Warm. At home. This was not one of those moments. If he went back to sleep again, he would not wake up in his bed in Roding Road. This was real. He was here. He hugged himself. He was freezing. The cold was embedded in the hollows of his bones.

Opposite the bed was a window. It was the width of the room. It was black, scattered with lights. The view was like being in a skyscraper at night, looking across at another city skyscraper, a huge skyscraper that filled the entire width of the window. It seemed to curve toward him at the edges. A white object, fast, hard, and shiny, dropped past the window, almost too quickly for his numb brain to process the movement. It looked like an insect. A plastic and metal insect, with windows in it. It was huge, the size of a Boeing at least.

Alarmed, he dived out of the bed. Instead of crashing to the floor, the sudden movement took him up and all the way across the room in a slow-motion dive to bang hard on the window. He dropped slowly, softly to the soft white floor tiles. His memory flashed back, from white to black, from soft floor to hard street, from strange white flying machine to the hard nose of a black car, the raindrops quivering.

"Where is this?" He stood up. The action carried him half a meter into the air. Again he settled slowly and softly. "Whoa." An experiment. Be scientific about this. He was wearing shorts and a T-shirt, white like everything else in this perfect room. He pulled off the tee, balled it up, held it out at arm's length, and let go. It dropped as slowly as a feather. "Low gravity. Okay." He went to the window and pressed his hands to the glass. His head reeled again. He was not in a skyscraper. This room was on the inside of an immense, dark cylinder. The windows curved away on either side of him. The cylinder must be a kilometer across, he estimated. He looked up. The windows rose up, ring upon ring. Far, far above was a black disk. He made a circle out of his thumb and forefinger and held it up against the disk. He was that far down. Now he looked down. The rings went down. He lost count after forty levels, and still they went down. He could see no end to them. "A bottomless pit," he whispered. "No. Can't be. It's logically impossible. This is engineering." And he knew where he was. A second white insect machine was rising out of the depths of the pit. "I'm on the . . ."

The cold rushed into him. The strength drained out of him. His knees buckled. He put out his hands to steady himself against the glass. And his arms and hands opened. Rectangular patches on the backs of his hands lifted up on plastic struts. Long hatches opened on his upper and lower forearms. The back of each first finger joint flipped up. There were things inside. There were things *inside . . . moving*. Things not his flesh. Things not quite living but not quite machine. Things unfolding and extending and changing shape. He saw dark empty spaces inside him full of aliens, pincers and grippers and manipulators and scanners reaching out of his body.

He screamed.

"Peace." A little old woman stood in the middle of the floor. She closed her right hand in a fist and the panels and hatches in his skin closed. There was no sight of a seam or a scar. "I am sorry," the little old woman said. He hadn't seen her arrive. He suspected no one ever saw her arrive. She had a round face, her hair was pulled back and tied in a bun, and the creases at the corners of her eyes and her mouth made her look as if she were smiling. She wasn't smiling. Neither was she as old as she looked. Her skin was a pale grey with a pearl sheen; she seemed to shimmer. She wore a plain dress and very sensible shoes. Her hands were now folded one over the other, like a new kind of praying. She looked like his Bebe Singh, but this was the most famous little old woman in the world. This was the Manifestation of the Thryn Sentience, Avatar Gracious Interlocutor for the Felicitous Communion of Sentients. Known to the world as Madam Moon.

"Greetings, Everett M. Singh," she said. She spoke with a distinct sing-song accent, maddeningly familiar but unlike any accent of his world. "It is the eighth day of Christmas and you are on the dark side of the Moon."

2

The fat little cherub rode the dragon like he was in a rodeo, one arm in the air, the other holding tight to the dragon's mane. This was a Chinese dragon, as lithe as a stoat, capering in the air over a city of crystal skyscrapers. The cherub's fat little face was wild with glee. The card spun in the air, end over end, fluttering down through the cathedral-sized space of LTA *Everness*'s interior. It looked like a single flake of snow. Bent over Dr. Quantum, Everett Singh glimpsed the movement out of the corner of his eye. He reached up and caught the card. A chubby angel on a luck dragon. *Yubileo*.

"What does it mean?" he shouted up into the vaults between the gas cells. "Yubileo?" An object detached itself from the industrial grey nanocarbon engineering and hurtled toward him. Sen Sixsmyth plunged headfirst down a drop line from the high catwalk. Her head was tilted back, her arms were pulled in like falcon wings. The line shrilled through her drop harness pulleys. She was an unlikely grinning angel. She came to a halt a meter above Everett's upturned face. She looked down at him.

"*Yubileo*. Jubilee! Jubila! Jubilation! Rejoice rejoice!" Her breath steamed in the air.

"Aren't you cold?"

Sen was dressed in a clingy grey knitted top, ribbed tights, a pale fur gilet, and pixie boots and seemed perfectly comfortable in the freezing air. Everett had on two T-shirts, two pairs of leggings, and two pairs of socks under his dock shorts, and an old Air Navy great coat Mchynlyth had liberated from his time on His Majesty's Air Ship *Royal Oak*. Still, Everett was pale, anxious, and growing stupid with the cold. He had cut the ends of the fingers off his knitted woollen gloves. The cold seeped into them through the icy screen of Dr. Quantum. After half an hour of coding, each keystroke was as painful as a hammer blow. He kept missing the keys, miscoding, making mistake after mistake, worrying that he was too thick with the cold slowly seeping through the airship's hull to know that he had made a mistake.

"Me? I's never cold. That's cause I's always moving, always doing something. Cold ain't got the time to catch up with Sen. Sit-down work, brain work, that makes you cold. All the blood rushes to your head. That's a well-known fact. All work and no play makes Everett a dull boy. And a cold one. Yubileo! Let the bona temps roll!"

Everett held up the card. Sen snatched it away and, upside down, folded it into her tarot deck one-handed. Her agility astonished Everett. He could think in multiple dimensions, but she could move in them. As a goalkeeper, he had been cat-quick, but she was like wind and lightning. Someday he would ask her to teach him the ways of the ropes and lines and pulleys. Someday when he wasn't busy saving the *Everness* and all who flew in her. Sen twisted and tumbled upright in one graceful twist and landed lightly on the deck. A flick of her fingers and the Yubileo card was between them. She slid in under the shoulder strap of Everett's borrowed greatcoat. He understood that the cards were an extra language to her—her third language, after English and the palari dialect of the Airish, the airship people. There were things only the Everness Tarot could say. She talked through them, and she talked to them. Everett had heard her whispering to the cards, in the big, echoing spaces of the *Everness*. There were plenty of places in an airship where you could imagine you were alone. He had seen her kiss the deck of cards with fast-flashing joy, then again with the slow love of a lifelong friend. They were sisters and friends, she and her face book of wolves and travelers, angels and queens and cherubs on dragons. And planesrunners. She had made a card for him: a boy stepping from a gateway, juggling worlds. She made new cards when she sensed the pack needed them. But she hadn't incorporated the Planesrunner card into the deck. It was his, to use when he needed it most. The card, not Everett, would know when it was the right time.

"You need a break."

"I got us into this. I have to get us out."

"How you going to do that if you's seeing all them bijou letters double? Take a break with Sen."

Everett had to admit that he needed a break. He had been up long before the dawn turned the great ice red, even before Ship's Engineer Mchynlyth, a famous bright and early riser. He had brought Captain Anastasia Sixsmyth her breakfast in her latty. When he knocked, she answered with bleary eyes, muffled up in three cardigans and bedsocks, frowning. For once she hadn't seemed overjoyed to see a plate of his cooking. Everett might be planes-runner, head coder, and the only way of getting *Everness* and her crew off this random parallel Earth, wherever in the Panoply of the mul-tiverse it might be, but he was also ship's cook. The Airish, Captain Anastasia constantly reminded him, were a people of appetite.

"Mchynlyth's got the snipships to work. Wanna take a varda?" Sen asked.

Everett wanted very much to take a look at the drones. When he had pulled the trigger on the stolen jumpgun and dropped *Everness* out from under the guns and fighters of Charlotte Villiers and the Royal Air Navy into a random parallel Earth, everything inside the Heisenberg field had gone with them. Including two state-of-the-art Royal Air Navy remote drones—snipships connected by an invisibly thin but incredibly strong nanocarbon filament. Moving as a team they could use the nanocarbon monofilament line like a cheese wire to slice off *Everness*'s impeller pods and carve her up like a Christmas goose nineteen different ways. Cut off from their mother ship in another universe, they had gone into automatic hover mode. For the first two days, *Everness*'s crew had been too busy working out where they were to notice what else had come through the Heisenberg gate with them.

"Well, I'm not leaving good Royal Navy technology sitting out there dish deep in snow for whoever comes trolling along," Mchynlyth declared. Until he said that, no one had thought that there could be a "whoever," out there. He had trudged out with First Officer Sharkey through the shrieking, scurrying snow. The cold was so intense that his fingertips flash-froze to the metal. In the six days they had been in Engineering, Mchynlyth had taken them apart and rebuilt them to his own specifications.

Sen was already halfway to the central staircase. She looked over her shoulder.

"You coming, omi?"

Everness trembled. Sen seized the handrail. Everett pushed his technology to the safe side of the table. The vibration was deep and huge; every part of the ship and everyone on her was shaken to the core.

"I hates it when it does that," Sen declared. Since tying down in its mooring, the ship had been shaken by irregular but deep tremors. Not from *Everness* herself, but from deep in the ice. "What's doing it?"

"How would I know?" Everett said.

"You's the scientist."

"Yes, but . . ." There was no arguing with Sen. "Let's go."

"I bets its some big ice monster, deep down there," Sen said. Everett thought a moment about explaining how scientifically unlikely it was that a giant monster could exist in the ice. Pointless. At least there might be some heat in Mchynlyth's dim, electricity-smelling, junk-stuffed cubbyhole.

It was the eighth day of Christmas, on the great ice that in another universe was the North Sea, twenty aerial miles from the airspace of High Deutschland. In the Airish version of the song, on that day my true love gave to me "eight breezes blowing." Wind, hard, unceasing, and icy, had been a constant since Everett had triggered the Heisenberg jump into this white world. Wind shrilling over the hull with a hiss like knives. Wind drawing long moans like the songs of alien whales from the guy lines. Wind pulling and tugging and worrying at every rough or protruding feature, ice fingers seeking for something they could hold on to, work at, tear free, and strew across the ice. Wind shaking *Everness* like a dog with a rat as Captain Anastasia navigated her away from the jump point. If Everett's theory was correct—that every Heisenberg jump left a trail behind it—she didn't want special forces dispatched by the Order arriving on top of them, or even inside the ship. E3's Heisenberg Gate technology was sophisticated enough to follow that trail and open a jump point right on the bridge. The wind shrieked over the hull as Everett made Christmas dinner up in the galley, every pan and pot and piece of cutlery rattling as he skinned and gutted the pheasants and made naan dough. *Everness* held her nanocarbon skin close and tight against the icy wind. Captain Anastasia had brought her down to a handful of meters above the great ice. Mooring lines, driven hard into thirty thousand years of ice, held the airship against the titanic draft of air rushing down out of the north. *Everness* creaked and strained and shivered at her anchors, but the anchors held.

"Now," Captain Anastasia declared, "we eat."

Everett carried the red gold and green saris he had bought from Ridley Road Market back in Hackney Great Port to the tiny galley table and spread them out. He lit little candles in empty jars. Sharkey gave a long and magnificent grace in the thunderous language of the Old Testament. Then Everett served: pheasant makhani with saffron rice and naan bread, which he puffed up on the end of a fork over a naked gas flame in a piece of kitchen theatre. To follow was his festive halva—Captain Anastasia's favorite—and his signature hot chocolate with a spark of chili. The tiny cabin was bright and fragrant with Punjabi cooking, but the spicy dishes could not win over the mood of the crew. Everyone ate elbow to ribs, knee to knee, in silence, looking up at every creak of the ribs, every change in the shirr of wind-whipped ice across the ship's skin. Snow piled in the porthole window. Everett looked out of the frosted porthole and thought, *my dad is out there.* When Tejendra had pushed Everett away from Charlotte Villiers's jumpgun the weapon had fired him into a random parallel universe. Everett had done the same thing when he jumped *Everness* out from under the guns and fighters of the Royal Air Navy. There was a chance that Tejendra and Everett had been jumped to the same universe. There was always a chance. Everett understood probability, he could work out odds. Flick a pencil up into the air: what are the odds that it will come down on its point and balance upright? There's a chance, a very small one. Now, do that a hundred times in a row. That was the probability that father and son had been jumped to the same universe. And even if that slim possibility had come to pass, no one could survive unprotected out there for more than minutes. The last time Everett had seen his dad, he'd been wearing Canterbury track bottoms and a T-shirt. But he was out there, somewhere. *Tell yourself that. Don't think that he was on the forty-second floor of the Tyrone Tower when Charlotte Villiers banished him to the same point in another universe.* Reality is marvelous, that was one of the first lessons Tejendra had taught him. They had been camping in the Dordogne in Southwest France. One still, clear night Tejendra had roused Everett from his bed and taken him out into the dark. "What are we looking at?" Everett, aged almost six, had asked. His dad had just pointed up. Far from the light and roads, the sky blazed with more stars than Everett had ever seen in his life. They were beautiful. They were brilliant. They were terrifying. He looked up into infinity. It called him, it touched him, it changed him. "I wanted you to see this," Tejendra said. "We used to get skies like this in Bathwala when I was your age. You look up, and keep looking. This is the heart of all science: wonder." Tejendra was out there. Everett would find him. It was Christmas all across the multiverse. He watched the snow pile up against the porthole, flake by flake.

Blue electric lightning flashlit the interior of Mchynlyth's engineering bay. Sen banged on the wall.

"Is it safe?"

"My engineering keeps your ass in the air and you're worried about a few wee sparks?" a Glasgow voice bellowed from within. "Come into my parlor. Dinnae touch anything. Live cables." As Everett had hoped, the room was warm. It smelled of overstrained wiring oil and Mchynlyth, mostly Mchynlyth. Captain Anastasia had shut off the water to the showers, partly to stop the pipes from freezing, partly to conserve dwindling supplies. After eight days on the ice, everyone was getting stinky. Sen masked it with ever-larger dashes of her unique, musky-sweet perfume. Mchynlyth pushed his welding goggles up onto his brown forehead to frown at Everett.

"Should you not be getting our sorry dishes out of here?"

"Omi needs a break," Sen pleaded. "One mistake and that could be us, kablooey. Bits everywhere."

You're closer to the truth than you know, Everett thought. *Scary close.* The deeper he delved into the mathematics of the Infundibulum—the map of all the parallel worlds of the Panoply—the more complexity and delicacy he saw. His dad had worked a staggering piece of mathematics. It was as fine and intricate as jewellery. The further in he went, the bigger it got. Everett felt he was swinging around with a sledgehammer among these shimmering walls of finely worked code. One mistake, one slip in transcribing the code, and the next Heisenberg jump could send each and every atom of *Everness* and her crew to different, separate universes. They would all die instantly.

"Should you not be building that power supply?" Everett threw back at Mchynlyth. The idea was simple. Simplicity was a fundamental of physics, like mass and charge and spin. The more simple a thing is, the more likely it is to be true, Tejendra had once said. The jumpgun was a pocket-sized Heisenberg Gate. The Infundibulum was a control mechanism. All that was needed to turn them into a fully programmable go-anywhere machine was a way of hooking them together. Everett could hack the operating system in his tab computer to interface with the jumpgun—Mchynlyth had even custom built cables and connectors—but the jumpgun spoke a language unlike anything he had ever seen before. Deep down, it was the same—it must always be the same, a universal computer language of ones and zeroes—but getting the devices to talk to each other meant going down into the code and rewriting every line, digit by digit. Code by code, Everett was turning Dr. Quantum into a translator between two computer languages that were so different that they might have come from alien worlds. Everett suspected they had. What it meant was slow, painstaking labor, with the cold seeping through the ship's skin into his fingers, his bones, his brain.

Mchynlyth grinned.

"All done and dusted. I just need some power to hook it to. But tell me, what do you think of these beauties?"

The two drones hung from cables hooked to the engineering bay's grid roof. They swayed slightly as *Everness* shifted in the wind. They were white bug machines, four propulsion fans held out like dragonfly wings above a stubby body holding sensor pods, communications, and power. Mchynlyth had rigged a drop line harness under each one, and he'd welded long handlebars to the propulsion-fan mountings. To operate the machines, the pilot would sit in the harness and grab the handlebars that reach down on either side to steer.

"I can see what you're thinking Mr. Singh. It's look a wee touch brute force engineering. Weld a bit of pig iron on and have done with it. It works. It's simple. Let go and the thing will go into hover. Simple. Safe."

"Bonaroo," Sen said. She ran her fingers over the metal, dewed with condensation. "Can I have a go?"

Mchynlyth slapped her hand away.

"Dinnae touch what ye cannae afford. If we havenae the power for a hot shower, we certainly haven't enough to send you gallivanting all over the sky, wee polone."

Sen thought about looking hurt and sulky and realized this would cut no ice with the ship's engineer.

"How fast?" she asked brightly.

"Well, I had to rejig the power-to-weight ratios," Mchynlyth said. "They were never designed to carry lard arses like you."

Everett thought, *I would have asked about the battery life.* That was the difference between him and Sen. One of many, many differences.

"I'm going to call them bumblebees," Sen declared.

Mchynlyth stared at her in horror.

"Hedgehoppers," Everett said. He didn't know where the name had come from or where he had heard the expression; it was just there on his tongue. It felt right. Mchynlyth nodded, weighing the name in his head. It was sticky, it clicked. Everett could see that it had even stuck and clicked with Sen. She glared at Everett.

"Shouldn't you be working on getting my dolly dish out of here?" she said fiercely and snatched the Yubileo card out of Everett's shoulder strap.

Alarms bells sang out the length of *Everness*'s two hundred meter hull. Mchynlyth threw down his welding gun and bolted from the cubby. Sen was on his heels.

"What is it?" Everett shouted over the din of a dozen competing alarms.

"Call to quarters!" Sen shouted over her shoulder. "Come on come on."

"There's only one thing'll get Sharkey pealing the bells like that," Mchynlyth shouted. "Something's come through the Heisenberg Gate."

3

He could see no end to the white. There were no sharp angles, no clear joins between floor and wall, wall and ceiling. The light came from everywhere. It even seemed to shine from his own white clothing, a simple, soft sleeveless T-shirt and baggy cotton track pants. He held his hand up. His skin looked very dark in the white glow that came from everywhere. He thought he could just make out the lines in his hand and on his forearm where he had been put back together again. There was no pain. But the cold was still there, coiled inside him. He knew it would always be there. The old lady beside him saw what he was doing and turned to look at him. She said nothing. She might have been smiling. He found her emotions hard to read. His skin, the grey lady, and the upright black circle in the center of the room were the only things that weren't white. The white robbed the room of any sense of size. It could be kilometers across or he might be able to reach out and touch the opposite wall. But he sensed that the black ring was big, bigger than human sized.

The center of the ring suddenly blazed with light, whiter than white, painfully bright. Two men in dark suits stepped out of the light. The first was a sharp-faced white man with fair, curly hair. The second was the prime minister. Their steps, begun on another world, carried them a long way in the Moon's low gravity. The prime minister lost his footing for a moment but recovered with dignity. Madam Moon stepped forward to meet them. A nod indicated that he should do the same. He had worked out a way of walking on the Moon that didn't send him bounding into the air looking stupid. It was a kind of low shuffling. It was not very elegant, but it kept him on the floor. The fair-haired man had the trick of it but the prime minister did not. Every stride took him up into the air and down again.

The fair-haired man bowed to Madam Moon. She cupped her pearl-grey hands together in a gesture that was half prayer, half Indian namaste. Then he shook hands with Everett M.

"Mr. Singh, I am E4 Plenipotentiary to the Plenitude of Known Worlds. My name is Charles Villiers."

"Pleased to meet you."

Then it was the prime minister. His handshake was firm and his look direct.

"Everett. Good to see you."

"Thank you Mr. Portillo."

"The prime minister would like a few words with you in private," Charles Villiers said.

Madam Moon dipped her head. The slightest turn of a hand opened a door in the white. Beyond it was a small conversation room. A padded white bench ran the length of the circular wall. He followed the prime minister through the door and his breath caught in his throat. The little room was roofed with a transparent dome. Above the dome was the black of space. Hanging in the center of it, huge and impossibly blue, and so close he felt he could reach up and pluck it like fruit, was the Earth. One step had taken him right through the center of the Moon. The prime minister looked up for a long moment at the shining Earth.

"The mind rebels," he said. "We can't trust what we see any more. It's all Photoshop and Hollywood special effects. The mind rebels, but the body believes. My body says, this is lunar gravity and I believe what I feel. The body doesn't lie." Again he looked up at the full Earth. "They say that people who see the Earth like this, so far away you could blot it out with your hand, never see it the same way again. They see it as small and very beautiful and fragile. They see it as one thing, one world." He sat down across the conversation pit from Everett M. "Extraordinary. The car takes me to the Shard, I take the lift to the Plenitude Embassy on the sixty-fifth floor. There's London Bridge, there's London Bridge Station, and the Tate Modern,

St. Paul's. You can see for forty miles, up there. I step through the Heisenberg Gate and I am on the Moon, looking up at the Earth, and I can see for two hundred and fifty thousand miles. They're everyday miracles now. Your generation grew up with them, Everett. For you, there has always been a Woman in the Moon. I was ten when they came."

No, Everett M thought. *I'm the generation that never had a "What Were You Doing When?" moment.* His mum always told him that if he hadn't been so comfortable and lazy inside her he would have been born on the day Princess Diana died. As he was, he waited until after the funeral to come into the world, which meant that Laura had been able to watch the national grief unroll across the BBC News uninterrupted for days on end. When the news had broken that the fast German car had crashed under Paris, that the Queen of Hearts was dead, the women in the maternity ward had all gathered together around the television in the day room, though they each had their own pay-TV screens. It had been a shared thing, a "What Were You Doing When?" thing. What was Laura Singh doing the day Diana died? Having you, Everett M.

It seemed to Everett M that prior the arrival of the Thryn, history had consisted of shared "What Were You Doing When?" moments. What were you doing when President Kennedy was assassinated? What were you doing when they landed on the Moon? What were you doing when John Lennon was murdered? What were you doing when the nuclear plant at Three Mile Island exploded? What were you doing when Margaret Thatcher was blown up by an IRA bomb? What were you doing when the secretary general of the United Nations announced that Earth had been in contact with alien intelligence? That it had been in contact with it for twenty years? That the aliens weren't thousands of light years away in space but right next door, on the Moon? That NASA had sent men to the Moon partly to make physical contact with these aliens? That the aliens had arrived in the Earth/Moon system in 1963, three months before the assassination of President Kennedy?

That, Everett M thought, gave older people big problems: making a "What Were You Doing When?" moment out of something that had been kept secret for twenty years. August 27, 1963: What were you doing? Anything to mark that date as different or extraordinary? Was it your birthday, a first date, a bank holiday? Was it the last good day of a great summer before you had to go back to school? Or was the day the aliens came just a day like any other? You went to school, to work, to the shops while at the back of the Moon the Thryn ship came out of sleep after thirty thousand years of travel and turned its senses on the blue world beneath it.

The size of a coffee can: that was what everyone knew about the Thryn probe. The size and shape of a coffee can. Coffee hadn't come in cans for years; now more people knew what a Thryn star-seed looked like than a coffee can. It was kind of small for a spaceship carrying aliens, but it was as big as it needed to be: the spaceship *was* the alien. Long before the probe had started its journey, the Thryn had passed from biological intelligence to a machine intelligence. The star from which the probe came—Epsilon Eridani—was not even the Thryn home world. They no longer had a home world. The probes were seeds, blown between the stars like dandelion down. Each contained all that was necessary to build a new Thryn Sentiency. Some fell on fertile worlds and sprouted and took root and grew a civilization. Some fell forever between the stars and never felt the tug of a sun's gravity to wake them up. Seeds were cheap and plentiful. But the seed waking up in the Earth/Moon system and searching for raw materials to convert into another Thryn Sentiency discovered a thing no Thryn seed-ship ever had before. It reached out with its intelligence and touched another intelligence. An intelligence that was not Thryn. This was something other, an alien intelligence.

The world of 1963 was a world on armed watch, of rival superpowers with daggers half drawn from sheaths. The United States and the Soviet Union eyed each other with spy planes and satellites and early warning radars, each wired to a hair trigger that could launch enough nuclear warheads to smelt the surface of the planet to glowing glass. The Thryn probe's sensor sweep triggered alarms in both American and Russian early warning radars. It looked to each like the other was launching a strike. Panic cascaded upward. In the White House and the Kremlin fingers hovered over "launch" buttons. The world came within a breath of nuclear war. Then both the US and the USSR learned, like the Thryn, that this was something other.

Out at the Moon, the Thryn Sentiency saw what it had triggered, and hesitated. The Thryn Sentiency pondered. The Thryn Sentiency deliberated. The Thryn Sentiency thought deep and hard and long— long for a machine intelligence. In human terms, it was something in the region of three minutes. The Thryn Sentiency spoke.

The world of 1963 was nervous, paranoid, bad tempered—adolescent. It would have broken at the revelation that alien intelligence had arrived. The USSR, the USA, and the other permanent members of the UN Security Council made a deal with the Thryn Sentiency. Six years later, when Neil Armstrong and Buzz Aldrin stepped onto the surface of the Moon, what the camera did not show was the figure waiting there to meet them, the figure of a little lady with kind eyes and grey skin. She wore no heavy space suit, her skin was bare to vacuum. Madam Moon, a construct of the Thryn Sentiency. She watched them plant the stars and stripes and salute it, but the Moon was not theirs. In the six years since the agreement, the Thryn coffee can had unfolded into replicators and fabricators and constructors and had dug deep into the dark side of the Moon, sending tendrils of Thryn technology down through the rock like a fungus. Solar collectors opened like mushrooms on an autumn morning all across the South Pole–Aitken Basin. By 1983, the agreed date for the conspiracy to end, the Thryn Sentiency had converted the entire far half of the moon into a terrifying warren of spires and pits and webs and fans that looked a little bit like a science fiction movie city and a little bit like a dead, white coral reef, but most of all like nothing anyone had ever seen or even imagined before. All the way down to the Moon's cold, dead core.

Laura and Tejendra had not been born when the Thryn star-seed arrived. In 1983 Laura had been in Year 9 at Rectory Road Comprehensive, writing *Duran Duran* and *Spandau Ballet* on her pencil case in felt marker. Tejendra had been choosing his A-Levels for Oxford while his mum and dad begged him to go to Imperial because it meant he wouldn't have to live away from home. August 27, 1983, twenty years to the minute after the Thryn seed-ship sensors almost touched off a nuclear war, that was the "What Were You Doing When?" moment. The great deception was exposed. There were protests and riots and outcries, but they died down, as they always do, and people realized that the alien was on the dark side of the Moon and quickly forgot about it. Out of sight was out of mind. And the occasional piece of Thryn tech that made it down and onto the streets made up for looking up at a huge harvest moon and never quite seeing it the same way. History stopped. There were no more "What Were You Doing When?" moments.

No, Everett M thought. There are no more big moments like that, when everyone shares history. But there are small ones, private ones. What were you doing when your dad was killed in a stupid, needless traffic accident?

"It's always been like this for me, sir," Everett M said.

"You don't need to call me sir," the prime minister said. He paused. He seemed to chew over the words he was about to speak, as if they had an unpleasant taste. "Is there any pain at all?"

"I just feel cold all the time."

"They—Madam Moon—has done an extraordinary job."

"She told me I should be dead. She rebuilt almost every part of me." Everett M turned his face up into the Earthshine. There was no warmth in it. "Mr. Portillo, why couldn't they save my dad?"

"I know what happened, Everett. I don't know why Madam Moon couldn't save him. The Thryn Sentiency can work wonders, but it can't work miracles. It can't bring back the dead." Again, he chewed bitter words. "Everett, the man who came with me is very powerful. You know what a Plenipotentiary is?"

"It's an ambassador of our entire planet to the Plenitude of Known Worlds."

"That's right. He's much more powerful than I am—but don't let him think that. He'll be talking to you soon. He will ask you to do a thing for him. It's a big thing, but only you can do it. Everett, I need you to do what he asks. Everyone needs you. It will sound strange, but he wouldn't ask you if there was any other way. And I want to tell you, Everett, that I, and the whole government, we will support you. We will look after your mum and your sister, your dad's family—don't worry about any of those. Mr. Villiers is going to ask you to be a hero. Not just for the country, not even for the whole world, but for all the Known Worlds. Can you do it, Everett? Will you do it? For all of us?"

Everett M felt a touch of air on the back of his neck. He turned his head to see that the door back to the gate room was open. Madam Moon and Charles Villiers stood side by side, waiting for him. Prime Minister Portillo lightly touched Everett M on the shoulder as he let him go first through the door.

"Good man," he whispered. "I know you can do it."

"There is not one world," Charles Villiers said.

"There are many worlds. Yeah, I know," Everett M said. They stood on a balcony overlooking the great pit that Everett M had seen through the window of the room when he first woke up on the Moon. Madam Moon had opened another of her jump doors and walked through with them onto this high ledge.

Charles Villiers's face was soft, his skin soft, his voice soft, and Everett did not believe any of it. "I am Plenipotentiary from our world to the recently contacted plane E10. Have you heard about it, seen anything online?" he said.

"My dad worked in multiverse research."

"Of course. Forgive me, Everett. Then you'll know that it is very similar to our plane, with the major exception of the Thryn Sentiency."

"I heard that." He looked over at Madam Moon, standing by the wall where she had opened the jump door. Always smiling, hands folded just so. Was it the same little old lady who had met Armstrong and Aldrin on the Moon forty-two years before, the frail little old lady who could stand the hard vacuum and a sleet of harder radiation? Was it even the same little old lady who had come to him when he woke in a panic as his body opened up and expanded? Were there many Madam Moons? Did the Thryn Sentiency create and annihilate its manifestations as it required?

"They're talented," Charles Villiers continued. "They developed Heisenberg Gate technology without Thryn assistance. We might possibly have done that ourselves, but they've gone one step further. They've done what no one else in the Plenitude has done. They have a working map of the Panoply. You know what the Panoply is?"

"All the worlds, not just the ones we know about." Everett M's dad had been working on exactly that project in this world. Working was not a strong enough word. There must be a word for work that is incredibly hard and at the same time filled with joy, work that tests the best of you and strains you to your limits but so fills your mind that everything else seems pointless by comparison. Work that drives you without pity, but that you love with all your heart. Work that you can't do, no one can do, but that you absolutely must do. That was the kind of work Tejendra had been doing all last summer. His adventures on the Middle-Aged Man bike had been part of the same rush of energy. At the end of the summer term, in the quiet after the students went, he had made a breakthrough. Not a solution, but a way to a solution. Thinking about how to think about the problem. Then, the random meeting with a Sainsbury truck turning left at a traffic signal.

Something Charles Villiers said snapped Everett M out of his memories of that last summer, when his dad had been alive, totally alive, head full of mathematics. "You said, working map?"

Charles Villiers smiled. It was the softest of all the soft things about this elegant, well-dressed, and thoroughly groomed man, and it sent ice deep into Everett M's heart.

"There are many worlds," Everett M said. Charles Villiers hadn't completed the phrase. "There is not one you . . ."

"There are many yous," Charles Villiers finished. "Everett, this must be hard to hear, but in E10, your father completed his work. He has a fully operational map of the Panoply. With it, and a Heisenberg Gate, he can jump to any point in any world—even within a world, like the jump that took Mr. Portillo and me from London to here."

"You're talking about many Tejendra Singhs," Everett M said. "You're not talking about many Everett M. Singhs."

Charles Villiers sat back, startled by the anger in Everett M's voice.

"There is a danger that the map—the Infundibulum—may fall into the wrong hands."

Everett M shivered as cold air spiralled up from the depths of the pit. His arms were bare, his feet were bare, his clothes were light and thin, he understood nothing. He remembered what his dad had said, when you understand nothing, you ask questions. Why is there a pit ten kilometers deep on the Moon? What are all the windows for? Why are there balconies, why is there even any air? What does Madam Moon need air for? Why did Madam Moon, the Thryn Sentiency, need all of this, any of this? Was it just stage dressing, Hollywood movie CG, projected right into his brain? He didn't doubt that the Thryn could do that. And if they could do that . . .

"Ask the Thryn Sentiency to give you another map," Everett M asked. "They're thousands of years ahead of us, that's what everyone says. So why bring me here? Because they can't give you another map, can they?"

Charles Villiers softly clapped his hands together in delight.

"You are a very clever young man," he said. He dipped his head to Madam Moon. She pressed her hands together in her half-greeting, half-blessing. "Humanity has been studying the Sentiency closely—probably more closely than anything else—for almost fifty years. Thryn technology is not thousands of years ahead. It's five, maybe four hundred years, at our current rate of technological development. And, all due respect to Madam Moon, the Thryn are not really a Sentiency at all. How can I explain this?"

"You don't need to," Everett M said. "I think I get this. They got enough technology to be able to build a machine that could reproduce their civilization. After that, they didn't need to invent anything. So they didn't."

"Clever, Everett, clever boy. The Thryn Sentiency is not really sentient in our understanding of the word—it's not self-aware. It doesn't have to be. It just has to work. We look at all this and think that there has to be a guiding mind behind it, but the reality is, it builds itself from simple, blind instructions. The Thryn Sentiency is more like an immense, complex, high-tech plant—a flower, a tree—than what we would call a civilization. Every Thryn Sentiency is a clone of the others. It reproduces itself perfectly, and that is why humanity will be greater than it. It allows no mistakes. Everything great about us comes from mistakes. Evolution has stopped for the Thryn Sentiency. Not for us. And that is why we will be greater than it in the end."

Everett M looked again at Madame Moon, her kind face, her folded hands, her patient expression, her eyes that, now that he knew what was behind them, were the deadest things he had ever seen.

"We need you to be an agent, Everett," Charles Villiers said. "A secret agent. James Bond. James Bond junior."

"Mr. Villiers, who is *we?*"

"The Plenitude. This world—our world. There are forces beyond the Known Worlds more powerful and more dangerous than you can imagine. Forces that make even the Thryn look puny. And there are forces inside the Plenitude as well. I've said too much already. Suffice to say, if they gain control of the Infundibulum, we are all in danger. Even your family, Everett; your friends, everyone you care about. We need you, Everett. Only you can do this."

They had him. He was on the Moon, alone, in the hands of one of world's most powerful men, a man to whom even the prime minister dipped his head, a man who knew his family, knew where they lived. It had always been the last shout from the bully at Bourne Green School: *I know where you live.*

"What do you need me to do?"

Charles Villiers gave his horrible, soft smile again.

"Be yourself, Everett. Just be yourself. But first, Madam Moon has a few more . . . alterations to make."

What? Everett started to shout, but Madam Moon opened her hand and it seemed to unfold before him, and close around him, and he fell into endless, soft grey.

4

The wind in her face was made from flying shards of glass. Not a centimeter of Sen's skin was exposed to the freezing air—it would have frostbitten her flesh in an instant, peeled it down to the bone—and the wind seemed to resent it. It looked for any opening. It clawed at the edges of her goggles. It tugged at the fur-trimmed hood of her Baltic survival suit. It tore at the edge of the scarf she had wrapped over her mouth and nostrils, and it studded the scarf with diamond-sharp ice crystals. To breathe that killing air was to inhale a lungful of daggers. The wind screamed at Sen Sixsmyth from every line and strut and spar on the hedgehopper. Sen Sixsmyth screamed back at it. She pushed the handlebars forward and sent the little flying machine swooping down toward the endless ice plain.

White below her, white above her, white before her, and white behind her. In her hi-visibility Baltic survival suit, she was the only speck of color in the endless white. She was the only speck of life. In the mythology of the Airish, in the Everness Tarot, part of which she had inherited, part of which she had built over time as needs called forth new cards, white was the color of death.

"Yay!" she yelled to the knifing wind as she tugged the throttle cable. The fans pushed her harder, faster against the wind. Mchynlyth had promised something more clever and responsive on the next refit, but from the moment Sharkey's radar had picked up something in the middle of what had been nothing, it became clear that all flight testing would have to be done in action. It worked. She had a couple of jerky, scary moments down on the cargo hoist when she almost threw herself at full speed into a bulkhead, and again when she nearly gave herself whiplash after another of the mysterious tremors shook the ship, causing her hand to slip on the thrust bar.

34

The controls were sensitive, quick, and immediate. A touch too hard and the hedgehopper, like an unbroken horse, would try to throw you. After *Everness*'s slow, gentle, subtle controls, this was fierce, fast fun. You could fly forever, and that was the trap. There was no sense of scale, nothing to judge how close you were to something, nothing to distinguish one thing from another. It would be very, very easy to fly your hedgehopper straight into the ice at full speed. She felt at once very big and very small.

Sen looked up. She could barely see the white of the drone against the white sky. She could imagine she was flying entirely alone. It was a feeling as thrilling as the fast, mad flight over the great ice. On *Everness* you could be away from people, but you could never be alone. The ship was her family and her friends, her home and her world. It surrounded her, it enclosed her, it was the walls of her universe. She often wondered what it would be like not to have the curving skin of *Everness* around her, to walk away from Mchynlyth and Sharkey and Mom and just be Sen—not Sen Sixsmyth, not Sen of *Everness*. Just Sen. It might feel like this: fast, fun, cold, and thrilling. A bright dot of color in the middle of nothing. And as she thought that, a bright dot flying in a gale of ice, she realized that to be truly alone, to have no family, to have no friends, to have no home, no world—to be like Everett—was not fast and fun and thrilling. It was terrifying. To have nowhere, no one. *No*, Sen thought, *you got me*. The thought made her feel fierce and glowing inside.

A bright orange speck moved into the edge of Sen's vision. Of course she was not alone. On the big ice, to be alone was to die. She glanced to her right as the second hedgehopper slipped in beside her. The pilot raised a thickly mittened hand from the steering bar and made a "pull-back" gesture. Sen replied with a palm-up "what?" gesture. Again, the mitten made a "slow down, draw back" movement. Slow down. Preserve battery life. Mchynlyth had been a little vague about how the hedgehopper batteries would perform in the extreme conditions on the ice.

"The numbers go everywhere," he had complained. "Anything from five hours to five minutes. Now, if you could lend me a real mathematician . . ."

"Everett is otherwise engaged," Captain Anastasia said.

"Could you even give me a wee loan?"

Captain Anastasia had widened her eyes in that way that every crew member quickly learned to recognize: *I am the captain.* The power situation was critical. Even guyed down *Everness* was burning charge to keep her head turned into the endless wind. And how much Everett would need to open the Heisenberg Gate when he finally figured out how to get the jumpgun and his dally comptator to talk to each other, well, that was anyone's guess. She had kept a close eye on the power meters as Mchynlyth charged the hedge-hopper batteries.

Out over the ice, a plug crackled in Sen's ear.

"Slow down."

"Aw, Ma." Sometimes Annie could be no fun at all. The earphone went dead. Even communications consumed power. Use too much now and there wouldn't be any for when you really needed to talk. Sen eased back on the throttle cable and dropped back into formation with Captain Anastasia. The ice reached out beneath her feet and merged with the sky.

Somewhere out there was the thing. Sharkey's radar had revealed no shape or structure, only that the thing that had come through the gate to hunt them was big, and fast, and would be on top of them in a very few hours.

"Do we have Einst . . . Heisenberg Gates that big?" Captain Anastasia had asked as the entire crew huddled around Sharkey's radar monitor. The glow shining up through the magnifier lens lit their faces green.

"You don't," Everett had said. "I mean . . . we don't."

"The Thing from Another Universe," Mchynlyth had said, and at that moment an ice tremor had shaken *Everness* like a November leaf on a tree, drawing a great moan, like a whale dying, from the lines and cables.

The monster, Sen had mouthed silently.

"Nonsense," Captain Anastasia had snapped, breaking the spell. "Mr. Mchynlyth, get those little flibbertigibbits airship-shape. I want a varda at what's out there. Ignorance kills. Sen, with me. Mr. Sharkey, keep an eye on that thing. Mr. Singh, crunch numbers."

At last, Captain Anastasia had something to captain. Crunching numbers, building machinery, scanning for threats, these were not things that needed her. Sen had seen her become bored and edgy and fidgety. She didn't like to depend on other people. Other people depended on her. Sen had grown fidgety with her.

Now they were zipping low over the ice in rickety harnesses slung beneath pirated air drones, just the two of them, her and Ma, doing the thing that no one else could do. Sen glanced over at Anastasia flying along beside her. Anastasia caught the glance, returned it with a nod of the head. Sometimes, Sen thought, they were more like sisters than mother and daughter.

Memory by memory, Sen was losing her mother—her birth mother, her real mother. The voice had been first. She could remember words but not the voice that spoke them. Then things like hands, and how tall her Ma had been, and the exact color of her hair. Now her face was vanishing. All Sen could remember was her mother's smile, her eyes, the tiny diamond stud in her nose. Details. Little by little, memory by memory, her real mother was disappearing. Someday she would vanish completely, blow away into ash like the *Fairchild*, burning up in the sky.

Tears froze painfully in the corner of each eye. Sen flicked them out with her fingers, and she saw something. Something in the ice, a dark streak, barely visible, moving in line with her, ahead. It could have been meters or miles deep. She saw it for only in instant, then another object grabbed her attention. Dead ahead. Right at the edge of her vision, where land merged into sky, white on white, a movement. It looked like a whirlwind of glitter. The white ice and the white sky took away any sense of scale: this new object too could have been kilometers away, or right in front of her. Sen waved to catch Anastasia's attention, pointed forward. Anastasia gave her a thumbs-up. They both pulled on their steering bars and swooped the hedgehoppers up to surveillance height. Anastasia stabbed a mitten at Sen. Sen nodded. She let go of the throttle cable and reached into the knitted sock. The gloves made her fingers thick and stupid. She could barely grasp the object inside. It was as slippery as wet glass.

"Come on," she hissed at the thick gloves, the dumb fingers, the freezing wind. "Got you." She held Everett's crossplanes telephone. He'd trusted her with it before, when she wore it to send images back while she infiltrated the Tyrone Tower. It was a bonaroo piece of E10 tech and it was the only camera they had. He'd shown her how to use it. Tap here for still photographs, here for video. Slide that bar up and down to zoom. It focuses automatically. Tap to take a picture. Easy. *Easy for you, Everett Singh.* He wasn't swinging in a sling beneath four ducted fan engines, with the wind driving needles of ice into his face so he could hardly see, one hand needed for steering and only one hand free to operate the camera, a hand thick and numb with the cold, like there's a frozen cod there instead of a hand, flying headlong into something completely unknown. *Yeah, easy Everett.*

The flying ice storm was close, and it was big. Sen glimpsed a dark heart to it, something huge, half seen, relentless. The Dear, but it was fast. What was that thing?

Captain Anastasia circled her hand in the air, then pointed at the storm thing. *Going in.* Sen made sure her hand had a firm grip on the phone, pulled the steering bar back, and swooped in. She could see the dark at the heart of the ice blizzard. It was big, it was fast, it was scary. It was a hovercraft. She'd seen the Thames hovercraft, nifty little flitters that shuttled those poor people who had to go to jobs in offices, in buildings attached to the ground. This was nothing like those. This was one hundred and fifty feet of armored death on a cushion of air and shattered, scattered ice. It was a tank that could do ninety miles per hour. It was a battleship for a frozen ocean. It had not just one gun turret but three, two facing forward, one covering the rear. As Sen zoomed across it, phone shaking in her hand, hatches opened in the armored upper deck and missile arrays slid out. Chain guns turned this way and that on their mountings, tracking her. Click click click click click. The turbulence from the big fans engines sent her rocking dangerously in her fragile hedgehopper. The phone slipped. Sen shrieked and caught it.

Captain Anastasia glanced over, shook her head, and made a cut-throat gesture. *Cut and run.* Sen shook her head in reply, swung the hedgehopper so that she banked almost horizontally to the ground, and went back for a second run. Her gloved thumb danced over the tiny, fiddly controls. Video video video. She had it. She held the cameraphone out and shot a long tracking shot over the back of the leviathan. The guns tracked her as she zipped over the great battle-craft. She shrieked with the joy of fast movement and at her own cleverness, weaving and dodging between the propellers. They would shred her faster than thought, turn her into a red spray in the cascade of ice and snow thrown up by the aircushion, but Sen Six-smyth was too fast and clever and cute for that. At the last moment she pulled up and over the command bridge, boot toes scraping the communications aerials, then she pushed the hedgehopper into a dive and turned around in her harness to take a shot of the crew behind the glass. They wore very smart frock coats and tightly wound turbans. Then up and away with a laugh and a dirty Airish finger gesture.

Anastasia crackled in her ear.

"You finished?"

"One more."

"You're finished. Let's get the hell back to the ship. If that thing catches us on the ground it will cut us up like Deutscher sausage.

Where did Charlotte Villiers find a dally toy like that? It's almost as fast as we are. I'm going to call Sharkey and tell him to make ready for lift."

"Ma!" Sen yelled as something fast and dark shot across the farthest edge of her vision. Captain Anastasia reacted with the speed and three-dimensional instinct of a Bristol-born Hackney-reared Great Port air-rat. A flick of the hand sent the hedgehopper peeling away from the fast, dark object that roared out of nowhere behind her. Sen saw the object come to a halt and spin with impossible agility. It had turned away from Captain Anastasia, and now it was coming directly at her. She pushed the steering bar all the way to the limit. Whirring rotor blades slashed so close to her feet that she could feel their updraft tugging at her Baltic suit. Sen fought to control the hedgehopper and went into a hover. She looked frantically around. There, standing off a hundred yards away. The air machine was shaped like a brass coffin standing upright in midair. The upper half of the coffin was a bubble of ribs and impact plastic. Inside was a man with a leather flying helmet on his head and a microphone to his lips, the pilot. What held him aloft were two sets of rotor blades, one on the right of the air coffin, the other on the left. Engine and fuel tanks were mounted on the rear of the coffin. The machine was brass and dull green, the lettering and numbering looked like Arabic. The symbol of two crescent moons, back to back, was the giveaway. Behind it, the hovering battleship drove on through its self-generated blizzard of ice shards.

"Fly!" Captain Anastasia shouted into Sen's earpiece. Sen did not need telling twice. She spun the hedgehopper in midair, yanked the throttle cable, and swung dangerously in her harness as the four fan engines kicked in. Captain Anastasia slid in alongside Sen. Her voice spoke in Sen's ear through the wind shrill, the whine of the fans, the clatter of the helicopter-coffin. "Sharkey. Get the ship airborne." No *Mr. Sharkey*. No *airship-shape* or *Hackney-fashion*. Sen was scared now. She glanced over her shoulder.

"He's coming for us."

The pilot had dipped the cockpit of his strange craft and angled the rotors; he was beating down on them at terrible speed. Sen could not take her eyes off the threshing death of those rotor blades.

"On my mark!" Captain Anastasia said, looking over her shoulder. "Three, two, one. Go!"

Sen peeled right, Anastasia peeled left as the gyrocopter came barreling through in a roar of engines and rotors. Sen looped high, looking for Captain Anastasia. She was the navigator. She knew the way home to *Everness*. The gyrocopter went into hover and pulled itself upright. Machine arms, needle tipped, unfolded from grooves in the shell.

"Oh the Dear," Sen whispered.

"Sen," Anastasia said. Her voice was clear as a blade of ice, clean through the clatter and fear. "Get the pictures back to Everett. You must do this. Keep on this heading. Sharkey will find you." Then she went looping high into the sky and Sen could see what she was doing, like a bird decoying a hawk from a nest. "He's gasoline powered. He can run our batteries into the ground. I'll buy you time."

"Ma, no!"

"I order it so, Miss Sixsmyth. Steer for home." The hedgehopper soared away until Captain Anastasia was an orange fleck beneath it. Sen checked the little compass Mchynlyth had glued to the underside of the drone's body. It was their only navigation instrument. The needle jumped and quivered in the constant vibration, but it held true to north. Sen looked around her. There. At the peak of its climb the hedgehopper seemed to hang in the air. For a long moment it hung, the air frozen around it. Sen's earphone crackled. "I'll be bona, my love. There's not a ground-pounding E2er can outfly Anastasia Sixsmyth." Then the crazy little flying machine spun and went plunging down in a dive, straight for the gyrocopter. And the gyrocopter answered, arms unfolding an array of claws and cutters and fingers as complex as an insect's mouth. They charged at each other. It was a game of midair chicken.

"Ma!" Sen screamed.

At the last minute the gyrocopter dived under Anastasia's hedgehopper. The E2 pilot was good. He skimmed the ice, pulled up to a safe altitude, turned instantly, and charged again. Sen saw Captain Anastasia glance over her shoulder, see the gyrocopter behind her, and pull the throttle cable hard down. Sen though she saw her raise a hand as the fans swiveled in their mounts and threw the hedgehopper away. The brass machine leaned into the wind and followed. Anastasia would never get away. She was in a rickety kite bodged together by Mchynlyth with a welding torch, some wiring, and a glue gun. The pursuer was in a fast, clever piece of E2 engineering, built to hunt. She had batteries. He had oil.

Sen watched them dwindle into the huge white. She understood lonely now, Everett-lonely. The compass told her one course to follow. Her heart told her another. Then she saw the thing beside the compass, a red bulb the size of her fist. The monofilament, the weapon of choice when the hedgehoppers were twin slice'n'dice attack drones.

"Ma!"

"Save your power," Anastasia hissed.

"Ma, no. We can beat him. We's not helpless."

"Get to *Everness*."

"Ma, I's got the line. The cutty line. The one what cuts through everything."

A pause, filled with wind in the wire and the shrill of blown ice.

"I'm coming in."

It was silly and it was obvious and the last thing that should happen when you are engaged in desperate battle with an implacable enemy, but Sen's heart leaped in her chest. She felt the glow of warmth spread through her, to her face, fingers, frozen toes. Way out, where ice and sky met, she saw the orange speck that was Captain Anastasia stop getting smaller and start getting bigger. But the gyrocopter was behind her and it was bigger and it was stronger and it was faster. Anastasia would never make it. Sen swung in her sling, tilted the steering bar to the left, and banked toward her mother.

"Cut you!" she screamed into the protecting scarf, stiff with ice crystals. "I's gonna cut you to pieces, you bastard! I hates you, you needs to die!" All she had seen of the gyrocopter pilot was a glimpse of goggles and helmet but she hated him. She hated that his flying craft was bigger and stronger and faster. She hated that he kept coming and coming and coming, that he would never stop, that he would never go away. She hated that he did not care who Sen or her mother were, that he did not care to care, that to him they were just targets. She wanted to cut him. She wanted to wrap him in monofilament and snap it tight. She wanted him to fall from the sky in bloody, quivering chunks to the ice. "I hates you more than anything!" she screamed.

Anastasia was coming in low and fast. Sen pulled the red handle free and felt the weight of it in her hand. She swung the steering bar and put herself on a course that would take her past Anastasia, fan blade almost to fan blade. This was the difficult bit. She would have one shot, one only. No. It wasn't difficult. It was impossible. The closing speed was terrifying. Behind Anastasia was the gyrocopter, closing fast, and the wind was snatching and shaking Sen's hedge-hopper. She squinted through her goggles, hefted the handle. Closing. Closing. And now. She threw the handle and caught a glimpse of Anastasia swerving to catch it, then Sen was past, the gyrocopter in front of her. She pushed hard on the steering bar, making the hedgehopper climb. Sen pulled her feet up. Her boot toes barely cleared the gyrocopter's rotor blades. She looked up. The monofilament was shrieking off the reel. Anastasia had it. Sen pulled the hedgehopper round into a slow curve. Out in the sky she saw Anastasia mirror the same maneuver. They weren't prey any more. They were armed. They were the hunters. But Sen could see how she was in danger from her own weapon. Steer wrong, cross the line of the monofilament, and it would carve her as readily as it would carve the gyrocopter. The two hedgehoppers looped around in the sky until they were in formation, side by side, a hundred yards apart, the gyrocopter dead ahead.

Sen snarled with rage as she bore down on the gyrocopter. On this course the monofilament would hit it dead center, cut metal and man and machine clean in half through the waist. Her earpiece crackled.

"Sen. Go high."

She ignored the voice and pulled on the throttle cable. She wanted him dead. She did not care who he was. He had no name, he had no face, he was just a part of the machine. But he had tried to kill her, he had tried to kill her, and now Sen could kill him, kill him a way he would never guess, he would never know, kill him so fast he wouldn't realize how stupid he had been, how clever Sen had been.

"Sen. Go high. Take the blades!"

The aircraft leaped toward each other. One moment they were half a sky apart, the next they were staring at each other.

"Sen!"

She saw the pilot. She saw his eyes. She imagined him leaping apart in two neat halves, the gush as all the blood and all the bowels and organs and bones of his body dropped out into the air. She saw herself kill a man.

"No!" she cried. At the instant of contact she pushed the steering bar forward. The hedgehopper climbed. The monofilament sheared clean through the rotors blades without even a jolt. She heard engines scream. A shard of carbon-fibre blade shot past her, fast and deadly as a missile. The gyrocopter, shorn of its rotors, dropped. She saw the pilot's eyes go wide and wild. Sen raised a hand to him. Then the front of the gyrocopter blew open. The pilot ejected in a burst of launch rockets, and a parachute opened above him. The dead gyrocopter beat him to the ground. It exploded in orange flame. Fire on the ice. The wind caught the pilot and carried him away.

"Reel it in Sen," Anastasia said. "Reel it in and set course. We're going home to *Everness*."

5

The gate was a ring of neon, green inside blue inside red. Through the gate and he was out, and the last soldier was down. There was nothing between him and the white light. He didn't know how he sensed the soldier pop up behind him. He saw nothing, heard nothing, felt nothing, but he knew the soldier was there, and he spun, rolled, came up on target all in one thought. The paint ball whistled past his ear and splattered in mashed-insect green on the maze wall. He used a single thought to fire a dart from the gun that emerged from an open hatch in his arm. The dart took the model soldier clean between the eyes. Everett held the dart gun on target, swept the maze with it, once, twice. Clear. Up and out.

Charles Villiers waited in the antechamber. He applauded softly. The hand claps were very light and dry in the huge white room. A woman stood at his side. She was so like Plenipotentiary Villiers that they could be twins. Everett M suspected they were closer than that. She was dressed in what looked to him like 1940s-style clothing— tight skirt, fishnet tights, jacket nipped at the waist but wide at the shoulders, a small, dapper hat with a lace veil that covered her eyes. Her lips were very red, vampire red. She could only be from E3, that weird parallel earth with no oil.

"My alter, Charlotte Villiers," Charles Villiers announced.

Alters creeped Everett M. They were the many yous that Prime Minister Portillo had carefully avoided talking about. Sometimes they were the same sex, sometimes, like Charles and Charlotte, they were not. Everett M knew the urban legends about alters—that they could share thoughts across universes, that many famous people had been replaced by evil alters without anyone ever knowing, that they should never meet because if they did they would annihilate each other in a colossal explosion that would destroy everything inside ten kilometers.

Charlotte Villiers extended a gloved hand. With a flicker of thought Everett M retracted his weaponry. The hatches in his arms closed without a seam. He took the offered hand. Charlotte Villiers's grip was strong, but with the Thryn enhancements, he could crush it like an origami bird. He could crush any hand. He hardly needed to think about the weapons Madam Moon had put inside his hands and forearms, the grip she had put in his fingers and the agility in his shoulders, the speed in his legs, the sight in his eyes that went way beyond normal vision, the super-sharp hearing, the new sense that was not quite sight and not quite hearing, more like a radar in his head. They were as much a part of him now as the lungs and heart and brain he had been born with. But could he even trust those? Just because he couldn't see them didn't mean they had not been touched by Madam Moon. There might be no part of him that had not been rebuilt by Thryn technology.

"Impressive, Mr. Singh," Charlotte Villiers said. "It's almost second nature to you. Thought and action one seamless whole. I think you'll soon be ready for what we need you to do. Soon."

"I don't quite understand what you mean ma'am." Everett M had learned that Plenipotentiaries expected to be addressed respectfully. Shake their hands. Bow to them. Call them ma'am and sir. He did so, even though he mistrusted Charles Villiers and mistrusted his cool, arrogant alter even more.

"Paintballs, Mr. Singh. Really, what are they? A small sting and a stain that quickly washes out. The real world does not fire paint, Mr. Singh. The real world fires lead. Dare you face a live-fire run, Mr. Singh? Safeties off. No paint. Lead. Hot lead. That's a test worthy of what we've had done to you."

"That's a big ask, Ms. Villiers." Despite the veil, Charlotte Villiers could look Everett M clear and straight in the eye in a way that her alter, Charles, could not. Everett M could look straight back.

"Yes it is, but I couldn't ask it if I were not prepared to do it myself. A race, Mr. Singh. First out of the gate wins. Live fire. Are you up to it, Mr. Singh?"

"Ms. Villiers, I don't mean to be rude, but I've been fitted with Thryn technology."

Charlotte Villiers snapped open her bag. She took out a small gun. It was as pretty as jewellery, with an ivory handle, a barrel engraved with twining flower patterns.

"St. Xavious's School Shooting Champion 1996; Cambridge Ladies Sporting Pistol and Revolver 1997, 1998, 1999; All-England Women's Small Arms 2000, Empire Games Gold Medal 2001. Charles, be a darling, set up a doubles course."

"Ms. Villiers, I don't think . . ." her alter said.

"Charles, my mind is set."

Charles Villiers went to the control panel, a black oval on the top of a white cylinder that was the only feature in the white antechamber. White on white was the colorless color of the Thryn, but Everett M knew by the tug of gravity that this training facility was not on the Moon. Where it might be, he had no idea. He had walked through a doorway, and in one step he'd felt the weight on his bones grow six times. Charles Villiers's finger hesitated over the touch panels. His alter snapped him a freezing look. Charles's fingers danced over the glowing lights. Everett M heard subtle machinery whir beyond the big, white wall with the glowing exit portal. The floor trembled. He was learning this about Thryn tech: it consisted of massive transformations hidden behind perfect, seamless surfaces.

"Thank you, darling."

Everett M's eyes went wide as Charlotte Villiers shook loose her skirt, let it fall, and stepped out of it. She unbuttoned her jacket and slid it off. Beneath she wore a leotard and fishnet tights. Her body was as lean and wiry as a whippet. From her bag she took a pair of light ballet pumps, kicked off her shoes, and pulled them on. Last of all she removed her hat, straightened the veil, and handed it to her

alter. She kept her gloves on. Charlotte Villiers shook out her curling
fair hair and glanced over at the control panel. Again, that glare of
ice. "Charles. I said, safeties off." A fingertip skimmed a switch. A
light went from green to red. Entrance gates opened on either side
of the exit portal, black holes in the white. Charlotte Villiers walked
up to the gate on the right, moving as lightly and confidently as a
hunting animal, her gun easy in her hand.

"Will you play, Mr. Singh?"

Everett M gave her a small bow and took his place in front of the
left gate.

"Whenever you're ready."

Charlotte Villiers smiled.

"Count us down, Charles."

A thirty second clock appeared over the gate. Everett M looked
down deep into himself, felt the depth of the Thryn technology
inside him, touched it, woke it. Strength, speed, alertness gushed
through him. He felt the weapon systems under his skin come to
life. He willed away the tranquilizer darts, the concussion field. Live
fire was live fire both ways. *Nano-missiles and finger lasers online*, he
thought, and he felt them stir inside him.

The counter ticked down, twenty to ten to five. Klaxons blared.
The gate was open. Everett M leaped forward. Beside him, Charlotte
Villiers sprang like a pouncing cat.

When the first soldier sprang up straight in his face within two strides
of the entry gate, Everett M knew this was not the same maze. He
ducked under the targeting laser, pointed his fingers, and swept it across
the machine. His own laser sliced the dummy into two smoking halves.
Melted plastic dripped from burn line as the severed top half wavered
and then fell to the floor. It hadn't even had time to pull its gun.

Cold gripped Everett M but he pushed on. The fingers lasers
drew on the energy of his own body. Each shot drove the cold deeper
into him.

The corridor doubled back on itself in a sharp S-shaped bend. An obvious and easy place to defend, with pop-up soldiers, one in each corner, covering the approaches and the angles. Running the mazes had taught Everett M to notice hairline cracks in the floor, the edges of the trapdoors and hatches from which the soldiers sprang. He edged carefully around the corner. Too far and the sensors would spot him and the soldier would pop up and shoot. It would not be paint they were firing this time.

He heard a muffled gunshot. That would be from the other maze. He didn't think it was the dummy soldier. A television-screen-sized area of the corridor wall blurred and turned into an image: Charlotte Villiers in her maze, pressed up like Everett M against the same corner. Her gun was pressed against her cheek, ready to swing on to the next target. Everett M didn't doubt that Charlotte Villiers was watching him on a similar screen.

But I can see things that you can't, Everett M thought. With his new Thryn sense, he looked into the hairline cracks in the floor and felt out the mechanisms in there, the ones he could see and the ones he could not see directly. He could sense how they were connected together and how they would operate. *I see you now*, Everett M thought, willing power into his finger lasers. He took a breath, then rolled. The soldiers at each end of the corridor came up, their guns swinging. He took their heads clean off, one with the left laser, the other with the right, before they could take aim. Again he heard gunfire, but he followed the roll through, underneath the arc of fire of the third soldier at the far end of the double-back. As the soldier tried to track him, Everett willed the panel in his forearm open. The nano-missile he fired took out the soldier instantly. The blast was deafening in the confined corridors of the death maze. His Thryn-augmented hearing moderated the noise to a safe level.

Did you hear that, Charlotte Villiers?

Everett M moved into the next section, a screen that was clearly Thryn technology following him as he moved. He watched Charlotte Villiers take the pop-up soldiers cleanly out, one shot each. She walked like a cat down the corridor, calmly and efficiently reloading her gun.

The next section was a long, straight run of corridor. It was clearly a big, obvious trap. Everett M scanned it with his Thryn sense—he had come to think of it as *longsight*. He longsaw nothing. But that didn't mean that there was nothing there. There could be traps inside traps, traps beyond the range of his longsight. Maybe there were no traps, and that was the trap. Maybe the maze was designed so that you would edge forward, always expecting something to spring on you, but nothing would, until you were so tense with expectation that when the real trap sprang, you would fall right into it. Everett M armed weapons, slid them out of the hatches in his arms, and walked forward. And walked. And walked. The screen kept pace with him, Charlotte Villiers matching him step for step. His evil twin, his alter. This section of the maze, Everett M thought, was that last kind of trap.

At the end of the corridor the maze turned sharp right. Here was where the trap would be sprung. Everett M willed power into his legs. Accuracy and firepower are good, but speed is best. Speed is life. He launched himself forward. And walls, ceiling, floor opened up in soldiers and turrets and swivel-guns. A sweep of his left-finger laser took out three soldiers, pin-point shots with the right took out the turrets springing out of the floor. As he ran and jumped and dodged, he launched nano-missiles from his forearm and sought out and killed the ceiling guns. He hated using the missiles. They were single-shot weapons that could not be replaced. But there was so much, coming from everywhere, all at once. He made the next turn of the maze. Behind him the corridor was a mass of burning, smoking, melting plastic and circuitry.

Everett M was panting. He was freezing. He had pumped a dangerous amount of energy into the lasers. And he did not know how much more of this there would be. He looked at the floating screen.

He had been too occupied with the cacophony of gunfire and explosions on his side of the maze to pick out the pistol shots that rang out from Charlotte Villiers's side. On the screen she stood calmly, steadily reloading her gun. A single bead of sweat ran down the side of her face.

A section of wall opened. A new corridor curved out of sight. Everett M clenched his fists and felt the power channeling into the Thryn biotech lasers. And again. And again. He darted through tunnels that switched back on themselves and went over and under themselves and perhaps even through, each turn guarded by soldiers. He fought through a maze of panels that slid and rearranged themselves, sometimes opening false corridors, other times exposing entire batteries of automatic weapons. He slid down shafts that suddenly opened under him, fired between his feet at the gun turrets opening up deadly iron flowers before him. And every time he looked, Charlotte Villiers kept pace with him—cool, elegant, and relentless. Not a blonde curl was out of place.

Behind him, Everett M Singh left smoking wreckage. He was shaking with the cold now, and he'd grown ravenously hungry. His own lasers could kill him just as surely as any soldier's bullet, sucking the heat out of him until hypothermia came creeping into his bones, with its sly, evil suggestions: *Slow down, lie down, rest a little, go to sleep.* But he kept pumping energy into the lasers. He had to keep the nano-missiles in reserve for when he really needed them. Adrenaline burn kept him going, kept his Thryn senses sharp and fast and deadly. He seemed to have been running this maze for hours. He thought it might be rebuilding itself behind him, turning him back on himself and sending him through the same loop again and again—the same, but rebuilt into something different every time. He might be on Earth, but this was not human technology. He was sure of that. And then he saw it, a glimmer of neon. The exit gate. He paused to lock his longsight on the glow. Suddenly, a ring of soldiers sprang up around him. Everett M crossed his arms and yelled. A spread of nano-missiles shredded them. The gate was in sight. He could afford to use missiles now. Everett M willed power into his legs and charged for the circle of white light. Soldiers leaped up in his path. He cut them apart with laser fire even before they had completely deployed and unfolded. He glanced at the moving screen. Charlotte Villiers was three paces behind him. The Thryn technology had turned Everett M's natural body sense—the same body sense that had made him such a good goalkeeper at Bourne Green—into something almost like a super power, but Charlotte Villiers moved like a trained athlete. Senses, thought, action amounted to one thing—*instinct*. Everything was instinct, every move the minimum effort for the maximum effect. And her little evil gun never missed.

There was nothing between Everett M and the exit gate. A quick dash would win him the race. Then he remembered. *Look behind you.* He turned just as the soldier bounced out of the floor. A nano-missile blew it to shards of flying plastic and metal. As he turned to the gate, he saw Charlotte Villiers running for her own glowing exit portal. He saw the soldier pop up behind her. He saw it unfold and level its guns. He saw that she did not see it.

Thought and action in unity. Everett M took a visual fix on the soldier in the other maze. He fed targeting commands to his Thryn systems. With a yell, he loosed his final nano-missile. It blazed out through the gate in front of him, then turned. *Go go go!* Everett M willed at it. The nano-missile entered Charlotte Villiers's maze through the exit gate. On the screen, he saw Charlotte Villiers's eyes go wide in shock as she dived out of the missile's path. *You think I'm trying to kill you*, Everett thought. You'll find out the truth in three, two, one . . . He could hear the explosion through the maze wall. Charlotte Villiers looked behind her. In that glance, she made up her mind. She ran for the exit gate. In his own maze, Everett M sprang forward. But he was so cold, so drained. He watched Charlotte Villiers pass through her exit gate two steps ahead of him.

She stood beside her alter, hardly out of breath. Everett M could read the look on her face. It was not triumph. It was something he had never seen before: hatred. *I saved your life*, Everett M thought. *You owe me, you will always owe me, and you hate that. You hate that and you hate me.* With a thought, he powered down his lasers and closed up the weapon ports Madam Moon had put into his body. *I have an enemy now.*

6

Frost clung silver to the decking and to the nanocarbon-fibre struts. Everett's breath froze as it left his mouth. He carefully wiped the ice crystals from Dr. Quantum's screen. A careless touch and he could erase a key line of code. Days of work, with the temperature dropping around him as Mchynlyth tried to conserve power, could be undone in an instant. And he couldn't even be sure that there wasn't a mistake in there, some unnoticed slip of fingers so cold they hurt. Everett remembered the sports teacher at Bourne Green School who had arranged to end the Christmas Term one year by holding a football tournament. Sleet had blown horizontally from a weather front straight down from Greenland. Within ten minutes Everett's fingers had been so numb that he couldn't grip the ball. A kick, a punch, a dive between the ball and the back of the net was the best he could do. The teacher-referee finally, mercifully, blew the whistle. In the shower at home Everett had almost wept with pain as the hot water brought life painfully back to his frozen hands.

This was worse.

Everett blew on the fingers of his right hand, breathing a little warmth and movement into them. Done. It was done. It had been a long, painful grunt job. There had been no moments of revelation, no blinding insights that ignited and inspired him to work beyond the limits of exhaustion and hunger. It hadn't been like the night, two universes away, when he had discovered how to turn the data in the Infundibulum into a map of the multiverse. Unlike that night of breathless insight, this project had been nothing but the hard slog of translating one bit of code into another, finding a way for the Infundibulum and the jumpgun to talk to each other. And it was finally done. He would have loved a day—even a few hours—to debug the code. But he had only twenty minutes. That was the lead time Captain Anastasia and Sen had over whatever they had found out there on the ice. Sharkey's radar had picked up three contacts: two that were small, fast, and fleeing, and one that was big and fast.

Everett didn't believe in a god, so he couldn't send up a little prayer. And he didn't believe in luck—he knew how probability worked and how people liked to make coincidences into patterns. So he just said "Okay, go,"—a geekboy's prayer—and tapped the *run* button. Code scrolled up the screen. Everett watched, his breath steaming and freezing. The code rolled on and on and on. Had it looped? Just as he was about to hit the *cancel* button, the screen went black, then cleared to show the desktop and an *install* dialogue box. He clicked *install*. The green bar filled. Everett realized that he was holding his breath. The screen went black again. Then the Infundibulum opened, along with his own piece of code: the Jump Controller. Everett had designed it from his memories of the control system for operating the Heisenberg Gate in his own world, hidden down in the abandoned Channel Tunnel exploratory diggings, buried deep under chalk. Operating the Jump Controller was simple. You dragged a multiverse address code from the Infundibulum into the *destination* panel. Then you hit the big *JUMP* button. The interface fed code to the jumpgun, which opened a maximum-aperture portal around *Everness*. And in an eye blink you would be somewhere else.

It took Everett three goes to get his numb fingers to drag a piece of multiverse address into the destination box. The *JUMP* button went from grey to green. He looked a long time at the long string of numbers. The way back. The code for this exact geographical location in his own world. He felt no sense of achievement, no exaltation, no need to punch the air or rejoice. Job done. The road home was open. Then he slipped Dr. Quantum inside his many layers of cold-proof clothing and ran up the frost-slippery stairs to the bridge.

Sharkey came from the communications desk to peer over

Everett's shoulder while Everett connected the special USB cable to the jumpgun. Mchynlyth had built Everett his own station, beside Sen's flight control desk. He had wired it and cabled it and had built a cradle for the jumpgun so that it didn't look like what it was: a handgun that shot people into another universe. Everett carefully docked Dr. Quantum and hooked up the power. He stroked the screen and it came alive with a haunting, hypnotizing visual display of the dimensions-within-dimensions folds of the Infundibulum.

"'He telleth the number of the stars; he calleth them all by their names,'" Sharkey said softly. Everett did not like him so close. He had not trusted him since they had made their run for the border of High Deutschland, trapped between two pursuit frigates and the fighters of HMAS *Royal Oak*. Sharkey had called for Captain Anastasia to hand Everett over to Charlotte Villiers. He'd wanted to surrender the Infundibulum to save the ship. *You quote the Bible*, Everett thought, *but do you live by it?*

Sharkey looked up suddenly. He went to the great curving window of the flight deck. He pulled down a magnifier from in front of one of the ceiling-mounted computer monitors and moved it on its angle-poise arm over the glass until it was focused on the thing out there in the white glare that had distracted him. He pulled down a microphone on a scissor arm.

"Mr. Mchynlyth, the prodigals return."

Everett felt a vibration run through the airship, through the decking, up through his feet. In his brief time as stowaway, cook, planesrunner, and now as a transuniverse navigator, he had learned the many shivers and shudders and twitches and tremors of *Everness*. This low hum was the cargo hatch lowering. He would not feel the hedgehoppers landing, they were too light and clever to make a heavy footfall, but he could feel the bridge shake to other feet, two sets, coming fast up the spiral staircase. He didn't look up. He worked on, steadily, surely connecting Dr. Quantum to the jumpgun in its cradle.

"Mr. Sharkey, Mr. Mchynlyth!" Captain Anastasia made every entrance voice first. "Prepare for flight." She strode onto the bridge, pulling off her sheepskin-lined gauntlets. "I want us up up and away from that thing." Every time she spoke, Captain Anastasia's tone of command made Everett jump. He had always had problems with authority, whether school teachers who insisted you play football in a Christmas sleet storm or E3 Hackney Great Port Airish airship commanders. Everett turned away so that Captain Sixsmyth would not see his smile of relief—and affection. It felt like pride to see her back where she belonged, standing at the great window, hands clasped behind her back, in command. Sen pulled off her flying helmet and shook ice crystals out of her amazing pure-white afro. The crystals rang from the decking like little bells. She pinched Everett as she slipped behind the piloting console.

"I's back, Everett Singh. Glad to see me or what, omi?"

Everett looked away, embarrassed. She was so direct, so cheeky, so aggressive. She scared Stoke Newington Everett, but she was irresistible to Punjabi Everett. Sen wiggled out of her orange Baltic suit and took the Everness tarot from its place next to her heart. She kissed the deck and set it on the control panel.

"Mr. Singh!" Captain Anastasia loomed over Everett's console. She held the smartphone up for him to see. The screen showed a blurred image of what looked like a hovercraft from hell, armed and armored and adorned with the back-to-back crescents of Alburaq, E2's strangely displaced Britain. "Have you ever seen anything like this before?"

"No, ma'am."

"Thought so. Me neither. In your professional opinion, can we fight it?"

"Ma'am, not a hope."

"Thought not. That thing is ten minutes behind us. Thank you, Mr. Singh. Is the Heisenberg jump operational?"

"I think so."

Everett saw Sharkey glance over.

"Mr. Sharkey," Captain Anastasia shouted, without ever taking her big, deep eyes from Everett, "cast off double quick. Get you up on that hull with a skinripper and cut us free."

"Ma'am . . ."

"Double quick, sir." Without another word, Sharkey rose from his seat and went to the companionway. Everett saw a quick backward glance, saw the set of his shoulders, the way he pulled the skinripper—the Airish knife designed to cut and repair airship nanocarbon—from his boot top. Captain Anastasia pulled down a microphone and thumbed the talk button of the palari-pipe. "Mr. Mchynlyth, I have two questions for you. Can we fly? Can we make a Heisenberg jump?"

Mchynlyth's Glasgow accent was flat and hard as a spade in the charged atmosphere of the bridge.

"We can fly, we can jump. We cannae do both."

"I need both, Mr. Mchynlyth."

"I dinnae have the power, and even if I did, the impeller pods are frozen solid. And that's before I get on to the steering gear. And the ballast; it's ten tons of solid ice in there. I cannae work miracles."

"I'm afraid nothing less than a miracle will do, Mr. Mchynlyth." Captain Anastasia turned her gaze to Everett. "Mr. Singh, two questions for you. What is the difference between 'think so' and 'know so'?"

"'Think so' means the power hookup mightn't work. We fire up the jumpgun and go nowhere. Or the interface mightn't mesh, and we'd go nowhere. Or there could still be a bug in the system and we wouldn't go nowhere, we'd go everywhere. Each atom would be sent to a different universe. Like *vammm*! So fast you wouldn't even know it."

"My next question: how long until we get from 'think so' to 'know so'?"

"Ten, fifteen minutes."

"That thing will be on us in five. We were lucky once, we will not be so again. Sen, on my command. Mr. Singh, bona speed."

"Ma'am."

As Captain Anastasia turned back to the window, Everett saw Sen slyly turn up a card from the Everness tarot. She saw him see. She showed it to him. It was not one Everett had seen before, but that did not surprise him. He was beginning to suspect that Sen owned many, many more cards than she carried in her deck at one time. The picture on the card, drawn in ink, was of a flock of crowned butterflies—or were they moths?—chained together wingtip to wingtip, flying up to the smiling moon. The name of the card, written in very old, beautiful, faded handwriting, was *Powdered Wings*.

What does it mean? Everett mouthed silently.

"They travel together to a far goal, and that can be like a big hope thing, or a completely hopeless thing," Sen whispered. Everett had noticed that Sen's voice, the words she used, the structure of her sentences, changed when she spoke of the Everness tarot. Who had taught her the voice of the cards? How had she come by the cards? "Or, they want to fly free, but they never can. Always two meanings." She folded the card back into the deck. She turned away from Everett to her flight controls, but he could read from the set of her shoulders and the tension in her arms that she was troubled by what she had read in the card. She would never tell him. He was not Airish, so he would see bright Sen, sassy Sen, feisty Sen, brave Sen, smart Sen, but he would never see scared Sen. Her fears, her dreads, these she would always keep closed up with the cards, next to her heart. Forced to live close to each other, the Airish built subtle, strong walls around their lives. It made him sad. When Captain Anastasia had asked him his professional opinion, he had glowed with pride. He was respected, accepted, one of the crew. Family. Now, in the way Sen turned her back and turned her face to a mask of *everyday* and *busy work*, *nothing wrong* and *don't ask*, he saw that there were places in the lives of all these people around him where he could never go.

The power hookup lit green on Everett's control console. Lights came on in the handle and barrel of the jumpgun. They shifted red to orange to yellow back to red. What they meant he had no idea. But when he touched the jumpgun, it felt warm, it felt charged, it felt alive and powerful. He dragged a multiverse address from the Infundibulum into the Jump Controller window. The code sat there, the JUMP button remained grey. Everett hissed a *shit* through his teeth and went down into the code. From the corner of his eye, past Captain Anastasia, who was once again at her accustomed place by the window, he could see what looked like a blizzard on the forward horizon.

Everness shook. *Everness* shook hard. Loose fittings rattled. Dust and dead, dried spiders fell from the many cavities and crannies of the ceiling. Everyone on the bridge looked up from what they were doing. *That's the biggest one yet*, Everett thought. He looked over at Sen. She silently mouthed the words *I's seen it. It's real. The thing in the ice.*

Captain Anastasia pulled down the palari-pipe.

"Mr. Sharkey, how close are you to cast off?"

Sharkey's voice came through a shriek of ice wind.

"Two more, Captain. 'He casteth forth his ice like morsels, who can stand before his cold?'"

"Spare me the word of the Dear, Mr. Sharkey. Inside now."

"There are still two—"

"Cut a hole in the skin if you must, but I want you in now, Sharkey."

There was a dark eye in the heart of the coming ice storm. As it bore down on *Everness*, it grew in resolution, from shadow to the vague outline of a machine to something with ducted fan engines and artillery turrets and machine-gun pods and missile racks. What the photograph had failed to capture was the size of the thing. This was a battleship riding a cushion of air. This was a killing machine. He tried the JUMP command again. The button remained greyed out. Back down into the set-up menu. *Everness* trembled again to the strange vibration.

"Mr. Mchynlyth, I need everything you have to the engines," Captain Anastasia cut her engineer off before he could complain. Everett had learnt learned this about Mchynlyth: he would moan and gripe and complain and invent a thousand reasons why any request was unreasonable, illogical, impossible, but then he would deliver, every time. "Sen. Take us straight up."

"Bona, ma'am." Sen swiveled the impeller-attitude control, turning the engine pods into lift mode, and pushed the power levers all the way to the end of the slot. "Power is at—"

"I am aware of the power situation, Miss Sixsmyth."

Everness lifted by the nose. Two mooring lines held her down by the tail. Everett grabbed Dr. Quantum to stop it from sliding off the console. The deck tilted higher. Every centimeter of *Everness*'s two hundred meters creaked and strained.

"Trying to code here!" Everett shouted. The airship shook again to another of the strange vibrations that seemed to emanate from deep inside the ice. Then the deck lurched with a jolt that knocked everyone from their feet and rolled the ship to the left. The right rear mooring line had snapped. *Everness* was still held to the ice by the single left rear line. Sen climbed back to the helm and tried to balance the lift and thrust controls to bring the ship on to an even keel.

"Half the impellers is meese and the ballast's froze solid," Sen hissed. Slowly, slowly, *Everness* rolled on to the horizontal. "Go on polone!" Sen yelled, playing the levers like a musical instrument. *Everness* strained at the remaining anchor line like an animal tugging at an ankle trap. The main communication board crackled.

"Attention airship, attention airship." The voice spoke in the oddly accented English of E2. It was not these people's native language, Everett remembered. There was no English language, there were no English people. They were a mixture of Moorish and Hispanic. Plenipotentiary Ibrim Hoj Kerrim—Everett always thought of him as an ally—had learned his English through an implant plugged directly into his brain. People who possessed the technology to do that would have no difficulty destroying *Everness*. "We are targeting you with numerous and overpowering weapons systems. Land immediately, land immediately." *But you won't use them*, Everett thought. *You daren't risk destroying the Infundibulum.* But they would know that theirs was an empty threat. They must have secret, smart ways of crippling an airship.

"Are we there yet, Mr. Singh?" Captain Anastasia asked.

A single button glowed at the center of Dr. Quantum's screen: *this change requires a restart*. "I'm rebooting the system." *My TV-Tropes moment*, Everett thought as the application shut down and the screen went blank. *The Last Minute System Reboot*. Another jolt: the final line parting. Sen gave a small shriek as *Everness* climbed rapidly. Her hands danced over the board, trimming and stabilizing and balancing impellers.

"Land immediately E3 airship, land immediately," the loudspeaker demanded. Captain Anastasia stood at the window, looking down. She spoke no word, she did not move.

"We can't get away from them," Sen said.

"It's not them I'm getting away from," Captain Anastasia said.

The noise was so huge, so terrible that it broke through the whine of the straining impellers, the groans of *Everness*'s stressed airframe. It was an endless tearing shriek. It sounded like the world cracking open. It was the sound of a million miles of glass shattering at once. Everett and Sen rushed to the window. *Everness* was high now, enabling them to look down at the pursuing battlecraft, almost directly under them. Directly under the hostile ship, the surface of the ice was cracking in a web of lines and fissures that followed the direction of the hovercraft. Everett held his breath. From *Everness*'s bridge he could see what the crew of the hovercraft could not, a dark crack opening in the ice behind them, racing toward them, under them like jagged lightning. The ice wrenched apart. At the last moment the hovercraft pilot saw the peril and tried to steer out of it, but it was too late. The crevasse widened into a chasm, a canyon in the ice. The hovercraft wavered on the slip, then went down, end over end.

"Oh the Dear," Captain Anastasia said. "Those men, all those good men, those poor men." Then Everett saw the bottom of the crevasse. It was vast and dark and it moved.

"Ma, when we was out, I saw . . ." Sen's voice trailed off as she searched for the words to describe what she'd seen.

"I saw too," Captain Anastasia said in a voice Everett never wanted to hear again. "Return to your posts." Everett tore himself away from the horror. Whatever was down there—something huge, something ancient, something that had been awakened by the vibrations of the hovercraft over the ice, something that could swallow *Everness* whole—it was moving.

"Status, Mr. Singh."

Dr. Quantum had rebooted. Everett's fingers flew over the touchscreen, opening apps.

"I'm getting the Jump Controller up."

"Mr. Mchynlyth!" Captain Anastasia bawled into the microphone. "Whatever power we have left, divert it to the jump gate. Sen, all stop impellers. Mr. Singh, we are in your hands."

Infundibulum open. Multiverse address up. The jump code to get out of there had been entered. But *Everness* had moved from the position that Everett had originally calculated as their exit point, and the ship was now drifting in the wind. Every jump began at a specific code and ended at another. Everett had to find his location in this world and then link it to the destination code. And the code he'd need to jump out of this world was changing by the second.

"Dundee, Atlanta, and Sweet St. Pio," Sen said. Sharkey's family curse. But there was no rage or hate in Sen's voice, just an ice-cold numbness. Everett looked up. The thing in the ice had risen, the eater of the hovercraft, the destroyer of worlds. It towered up from the chasm, taller than *Everness* was high, a worm, a dragon, a snake, an ice monster, all of these and none of these. Metal. It was made of metal. Metal and swollen, sun-starved flesh. Its blunt head weaved in the white sky, sensing with organs and abilities unknown to humans, questing, hunting. Finding. The head turned to look down on *Everness*. It was studded with brass portholes. The head opened. It kept opening. Everett had seen one of the drilling machines used to dig tunnels for the London Underground. It had been equipped with rings and rings and rings of teeth and grinders and diggers. The head of the Ice Thing opened like a flower, a flower all blades and grinding wheels.

"Mr. Singh . . ." Captain Anastasia said.

There. Everett grabbed the code and slid it into the Jump Controller. Then he opened up the destination window and dragged in the destination code. The button was grey. The button was grey. The button couldn't be grey. The button *could not* be grey. Grey was death. He glanced up. The death mouth of the Ice Thing was descending on them. The glance distracted him, made him able to see the thing he hadn't seen for looking too hard: a dialogue box.

Is this your intended destination? Accept/cancel.

Accept.

Sen shouted something in a language Everett did not understand. Captain Anastasia was a black shadow against a universe of blades and fangs and swirling teeth. The button went green. *Jump.* Everett hit it. The world went white.

"Where is we?" Sen's voice said, somewhere in the white. Then the white turned to blue, with clouds, clouds that weren't made of teeth, clouds that didn't want to eat you, clouds that were just clouds. Little fluffy clouds. Beyond them, an airplane glittered in the sun.

"Home," Everett said.

He came out of the white into gloom so thick that he could not see. Then Everett M remembered that he could do something about that. He could do something about almost anything since he came back from the Moon. A thought opened up the image-amplification system Madam Moon had inserted into his brain. Every minute, it seemed, Everett M discovered some new Thryn improvement or enhancement or augmentation. The scale of what had been done to him was terrifying, like suddenly discovering yourself on the edge of a very tall building, looking down. They had opened doors in every part of him. At home—wherever home was now—there had been an Advent calendar on the kitchen wall, beside the signed photograph of radio 2 DJ Chris Evans and some of Vickie-Rose's splodge drawings. Twenty windows opened, five still to go. Beneath each window, a picture, a snapshot, a glimpse of a surprise. He was like that, with alien weapons and superpowers rather than snow scenes and robins and wise men pointing at a star.

The gloom brightened. He was in a dank, damp chamber. The Heisenberg Gate stood at the center of a ring of workstations, and beneath his feet was a metal grating. Above him was a rough rock roof, lined with runs of power cable and studded with light brackets. He faced a line of soldiers in black. Soft caps and hard guns. Their guns were aimed at him. What did they think he was going to do? Everett M stepped on the ramp. The guns twitched but remained trained on his heart.

White light washed out their faces. The Heisenberg Gate had opened. Everett M's Thryn senses learned fast: do a thing once and they never forgot. The image enhancement circuits moderated the light to a comfortable level. Charlotte Villiers stepped out of the gate and the white light vanished.

"At ease," she said. The soldiers sloped their weapons. A man stepped through the ring of soldiers, a shabby man, with thinning hair, in a raincoat and a suit that didn't look right. His tie wasn't straight.

"Welcome to Earth 10, Everett." The man extended a hand, but he hesitated when Everett M reached out to grasp it. "Goodness. How extraordinary. I'm sorry . . . I never imagined . . ."

"For God's sake Paul, it's only an alter," Charlotte Villiers snapped.

"I know, oh I know," the dowdy man said. "It's just . . . I'm sorry Everett, I knew—know—your alter so well, all his life. I was—am—a close family friend, almost an unofficial uncle."

"I don't know you at all," Everett M said. "Maybe you didn't work with my dad in my world. Maybe you weren't at Imperial." Maybe you never even existed.

The dowdy man came to the same conclusion. He mumbled his name—Paul McCabe—and shook hands limply, but Everett M could see that he was shaken. Then Everett M saw the second civilian, behind the ring of soldiers, and it was his turn to be shaken.

"Colette?"

She heard his voice say her name and she winced. Everett watched an array of emotions play across her face as she looked at him, emotions that did not belong together. Recognition and confusion. Memory and betrayal. Affection and horror.

"So you want me to hunt him," Everett M had said at the gate from his own world.

"No no no Everett," Charles Villiers had replied. "We want you to *be* him."

"Come along Everett," Charlotte Villiers said now. Her heels rang from the metal flooring. "Don't stare." The soldiers parted. Paul McCabe visibly cringed away from her. Everett M followed.

Beyond a heavy security door was a long rock-cut tunnel, lit with bulkhead lights and flickering fluorescents. Nothing could have been further from the white, slick, Thryn-built jump rooms of Everett M's world.

"Where are we?"

"Worldgate One," Paul McCabe said. Everett M tried to place his accent: yes, Northern Ireland. *You hate me now because I've told you that in my world you're nothing.* "We paid a branding company quite a lot of money to come up with the name. Rubbish, isn't it? You're in the old Channel Tunnel test drilling from the 1970s. You have the Channel Tunnel in your world?"

"We have three," Everett M said. "All maglev." *Stop trying to sound like you are still my unofficial uncle,* he thought. Everett M glanced over his shoulder. Colette Harte walked behind him. She caught Everett's eye. *I see hate there,* he thought. *But it's not for me. You didn't hate him so you can't hate me. It's for her, Charlotte Villiers, and him, Paul McCabe, but most of all for yourself. They've made you do something, become something you hate more than anything.*

A black car waited at the end of the tunnel, in front of a colossal set of metal doors. It gleamed like liquid in the harsh fluorescent light. Everett M had seen that glint before, from the polished hood of another black car, the moment before it hit him and knocked him into another life. The Everett M from before the collision and the Everett M he'd become were so different that they might as well be separate people. In a way it had killed him, that other black car. He shivered.

"Are you cold, Everett?" Paul McCabe asked.

"I'm always cold."

Charlotte Villiers sat beside Everett M in the back of the car. Paul McCabe rode up front. The driver was a big, shaved-headed man in a suit. He looked more like a movie thug than anyone Everett had ever seen. *But I can own you,* Everett M thought. Colette Harte had remained at the facility. She had not spoken one word to

Everett M in his short transit through Worldgate One, but he felt that her emotions had gone from revulsion to suspicion to sympathy. He felt sure that he could count on her to be an ally.

Winter sleet was clearing from the sky over the South Downs as if swept from the sky by a giant, impatient hand. Low winter sun was breaking, turning the wet road to a glaring blade of light. The black car whisked Everett M past long lines of trucks bound for the Channel Tunnel. It was all so familiar. It was all so strange.

"We need an agent on his world," Charles Villiers had said under the white lights of the Panoply training facility a universe away. "We need someone who can get up close, into his friends, into his family."

"Someone like me," Everett M had said.

"We took terrible liberties," Charles Villiers had said. "We did things to you without your permission, Everett. But we couldn't pass on an opportunity like that."

"What, I'm supposed to be grateful for you turning me into RoboEverett?"

"Everett, Everett, so cynical. You would have died. We saved you."

And so I owe you, Everett M thought now, as the black car merged into the never-ending wheel of traffic on the London Orbital motorway.

"We need you to be him, Everett. We're going to put you into his family. We've written a cover story, it'll stand up. We've a dossier on his school, his friends, his family. A lot of it overlaps, of course. The people on E2 have put it onto a memory implant, but there will still be holes, so the story is you suffered a brief fugue state. The trauma of your father's disappearance made you have a bit of a personality breakdown."

"My father's dead," Everett had said.

"Yes, yes, of course. Sorry Everett. Your alter's father. The story: you had a personality breakdown, you went missing, the police missing person's unit found you. You're still suffering from memory loss. Your mother—his mother—has been notified, the police will bring you back."

Everett M peered out the window now. Paul McCabe had stopped trying to make conversation with him. Charlotte Villiers had not even attempted to talk. She sat neatly and properly. From time to time she checked her make-up in her compact mirror. Everett M studied this world into which he had been pushed. The differences were in the details. The cars looked the same, but in this world they burned oil products. Same with the power station at Dartford: the smoke stacks spat out the exhaust from hydrocarbon fuel. So different from the clean hydrogen fusion plants that powered Everett M's world. But these people had developed the Heisenberg Gate—and the Infundibulum, the gateway to the entire Panoply of universes, which no one else in the Known Worlds had done. No. Not these people. His father.

"He'll come back. He'll come back for his Mum and his sister."

"Laura and Victoria-Rose," Everett M had said.

"Victory-Rose," Charles Villiers had corrected. "In this world, your little sister is Victory-Rose. He'll come back, and we need you to be there when he does."

"What do you do when he does?"

Charles Villiers had looked genuinely astonished.

"Why, take the Infundibulum from him."

"And these weapons?"

"He travels with a crew of pirates," Charles Villiers had said. "Villains—bad people, they wouldn't hesitate to cut down anyone who gets in their way . . ."

For the first time in the mission briefing, Charlotte Villiers had spoken.

"Oh, for God's sake Charles, this is not a theme park ride. Everett, he is your enemy. He doesn't know it, but he is. He doesn't know what he has, the damage he can do without even thinking. For all our sakes—and the sake of your mother and sister, and even his mother and sister, we must have the Infundibulum. There are forces out there that are a threat to all of us. If they get the Infundibulum before us, it will be the end of everything we know, on all of the Ten Worlds. We must have security."

Remembering those words, Everett M looked over at Charlotte Villiers beside him. Her lips were thin but vampire red beneath the veil of her hat. *The threat, you say*, Everett M thought, *the threat that will destroy everything we know. You never say what it is. But the threat to Mum and Vickie-Rose, I know what that is. It's you.*

He knew by heart the landmarks they passed now, the buildings and places that mapped his life. The chimney of the Lea Valley incinerator, the Olympic stadium, White Hart Lane. Everett M looked around. These shop signs, he recognized them, The Egg Stores. Konoc Polish Supermarket. Sofa King. This was Stamford Hill. There was the gate to Abney Park Cemetery. Where it had happened. Even the bus stop was in the same place.

"Stop here." Paul McCabe looked round, startled by Charlotte Villiers's voice after so long a silence. The Obvious Thug driver pulled the black car in without comment or question. He opened the door for Charlotte Villiers. She stepped onto the pavement.

"Careful in the traffic, Everett," she said as he got out in the road. "We wouldn't want history repeating itself."

"Why have you brought me here?" Everett M asked. Stokie was bright with hard January sunshine. He shivered with cold. Charlotte Villiers took a pair of round-eye sunglasses from her bag and put them on under her veil.

"I want to tell you about your enemy, Everett. He's your alter, but he's not you. He's smarter than you. He's a lot smarter than you. His Dad may have discovered the Infundibulum, but this Everett turned it into a working map. He's the important one. You, well, you're the raw materials we had at hand.

"There are no accidents, Everett. There are no coincidences. It wasn't your bad luck you were run down by a car on this spot in your own Hackney. We arranged it. It's easier if we make it look like an accident. We would still have had to take you apart and have Madam Moon put you back together again. So much simpler than a kidnapping. Kidnapping, I've found, does attract the wrong attention. A carefully rehearsed accident, a cover story to your family, it's all so much less fuss.

"So, don't flatter yourself, Everett. It's not about you. It's never been about you. It's about him. Because of him, everything that happened to you happened. Because of him we put Thryn machinery into your body. Because of him, you're here. Not because of you, because of him. Remember that when you see him. You're just the alter."

She raised a gloved hand. The driver opened the door for her. Everett M stood blinded by the low winter sun. He felt as if the black car had hit him a second time. Everything was knocked out of him. Home, family, friends, his entire world, his sense of self, his dawning teenage sense that he was unique and special: all smashed to pieces and left lying on the side of the road. The Thryn technology inside him felt vile, like ashes in his blood. He wanted it out, he wanted to claw the hatches open and rip out the circuitry that was half machine, half living flesh.

Charlotte Villiers took off her dark glasses and stowed them in her bag. *I saved your life*, Everett M thought. *But that doesn't mean anything to you. Nothing about me means anything to you, except that I'm his alter. I'm just a body draped around these things you put inside me. An avatar.* Against his will, Everett M felt the Thryn weapons systems powering up inside him, drawing on his horror and rage. He wanted to slash the black car into glowing chunks with his lasers, melt those chunks with his missiles, blast everything to burning slag. But he would still be in this world, and his mum and Vickie-Rose would be in his world, and between them, the people Charlotte Villiers worked for. He clenched his fists, forced the hatches to stay closed, powered down his weapons.

"Come along Everett," Charlotte Villiers said. "God, this is a ghastly little world."

The first policeman was a detective sergeant called Milligan. He had a moustache. *Sergeant Tache*, Everett M thought. The other was a family liaison officer, whatever that was, and her name was Leah or Leanne or Leona. *Leelee*. Everett M had always made up his own names for things and people.

No matter what you've done, or haven't done, if you ride in a police car you will always feel like a criminal. *Skoda*: he'd never heard of that make of car. Everett M had never been in a gasoline-powered vehicle before. It smelled funny, spicy and dizzy, and a little dangerous. The fumes caught him at the back of his throat. He'd noticed that people on this world were always coughing and clearing their throats. How could they live in this reek?

It would be a left onto Northwold Road. Roding Road was the second left. On cue, the Skoda turned left. There was something in Everett M's stomach that the Thryn had not put there. The houses were the same color, had the same aerials and satellite dishes, the same cypress trees and paving in front, the same trampolines sheathed in safety netting at the back. Only the cars were different. There was the house, his house. The door was open. His mother, Laura, Mum, was on the front step, looking down the street. *Not my mum*, Everett thought. *His mum. Not my mum.* But she dressed like his mum in a sweater dress and black leggings, and she wore his mum's big beady necklace and bangles, and her face had the lines of worry and frustration like his mum's, and she twisted her left foot on its toe because she was impatient in the same way that his mum did. Then Everett M's understanding turned on its head. It was not this Laura Singh who was wrong, not this street, or this world; it was him. He was the fake, the alien. He felt sick. He wanted to throw up everything wrong with him, every piece of alien technology that had been put into him.

Now she saw the police car. She put her hands up to her mouth. For a moment she didn't know what to do. Then she started to run. And Everett M knew what he had to do. He hated doing it more than anything he had hated before, but he had to play the role.

"Stop the car!" he shouted. "Stop the car!"

Sergeant Tache pulled in, startled. Everett M jumped out even before the car had stopped. He ran toward the running woman. She was waving her hands in astonishment and joy and relief, and Everett M ran toward her and felt none of those. She fell on him and wrapped him in her arms, her hair, her smell, her warmth. All of them Everett M knew. They raked his heart. Her it was her. *No, it's not her.*

"Oh, my Everett, oh my boy," Laura said. She was crying. Her cheek was wet against his. All the doors on Roding Road were open, those neighbors at home were on their doorsteps, smiling and applauding and dabbing tissues to their eyes. Everett M knew them all. Every single one of them.

"I'm sorry," he said. It was part of the script.

Sergeant Tache and Leelee had got out of the car. Leelee looked sniffy. Sergeant Tache looked like there were official things he was meant to say but would say later.

"Oh, everyone's looking, and me without a dab of slap on me," Laura said. "Come in, come in."

The hall was decked with Christmas cards, standing on parade on every flat surface, those that weren't occupied by tea-light holders. It even smelled the same: coffee and garlic and a permanent undertone of pine toilet cleaner from the downstairs lav. In the front room the sofa and the chairs were in the same place—the front room, the good room, not the den room with the old leather sofas and the books and the flatscreen television and the games consoles. This version of it carried the same vague smell that Everett M had never been able to place in his own universe but always thought of as *vacuum cleaner*. The Christmas tree stood in the same place in the bay window that it did in Everett M's world. It looked bare and spare of ornaments and random collected things that people hung on real Christmas trees. Everett M's mum—his real mum—almost hadn't put a tree up this year at all. "What's the point, love?" she'd said. "He always used to do it. Physicist and he could never get the lights to work." Everett M wondered what the excuse was in this world.

"I cleaned up as much as I could," Laura said. "I kept the presents—what was left of them."

"Mum, would you mind?" He wanted out of this room. It was a shrine to two kinds of loss: in this world, and in his world.

"What? Oh, sorry . . ."

"No. I'm sorry." He wasn't. From the top of the stairs he called down, "Where's Vickie . . . Victory-Rose?"

"At her Bebe Ajeet's. She's bringing her over tonight, when it's a bit quieter. She's so happy you're home."

She's so happy at anything, Everett M thought, *if she's in the least bit like my Vickie-Rose.* A plastic bag rattling in a tree, a postman wearing shorts, a dog with its head out a car window. Anything.

He opened the door to his room. *His* room. Tottenham Hotspur hit him from every wall. Delphic, Enter Shikari. Megan Fox in cut-offs. Marcus Fenix from *Gears of War*. Hubble Space Telescope images. Exactly the same, in exactly the same places. The books on the bookshelves, the comics, the video games—everything he liked in all the same places. Everett M opened up the laptop on the desk. A password prompt came up. Everett MEverett M. entered his own password, a complex string of numbers and letters, upper case and lower, that no one but he could even begin to remember. It worked. Straight in. *There has to be something between us*, Everett M thought. *Some atom of difference. Something that makes him the genius ten worlds want to get their hands on and me just the body double.*

E-mail password, Facebook password: both the same. There was a hole in the postings. It was the same length as the gap in his own entries. Of course. Some of the postings and comments were different, but that didn't matter. It was just social stuff. Ryun Spinetti. Everett M knew the name from Bourne Green. He had been on the football team, not a bad striker though he'd never got anything but a penalty past Everett M. He'd moved away—family broke up, something like that. They were never close, certainly not best friends like him and this world's Everett.

Everett M opened the closet. The shirts were hung on the left, the pants on the right. Neat, of course. Shoes in the bottom. Everett M lifted a football boot. It sat in the palm of his hand. Clean—of course—but this Everett had missed some tiny flecks of mud and blades of grass stuck to the studs. A friend gone and a dirty football boot. That was all the difference.

Everett M threw the boot at the poster of Gareth Bale. The studs tore a small hole in his face. Everett M took the torn edge and ripped it down, ripped the stupid, grinning picture of the tall Spurs striker off the wall. Then he turned to Roman Pavyluchenko and Danny Rose, tore them down, tore strips from the wallpaper where the Blu-tack stuck to the wall, tore those faces into shreds. The bands, the games, the movie stars, the science prints: torn from the wall, torn to pieces. He couldn't stand the sight of them. He hated them for being the bands he loved, whose music moved him, rocked him, kept him close like a friend, and also for being all those things to *him*. The books, the comics: he kicked the piles of comics and sent them flying like dry leaves; he overturned the bookcase and spilled the bright spines of the paperbacks onto the carpet. He couldn't look at their covers. Each would be a love betrayed. He stamped on their spines, snapping them, like breaking the back of a poisoned, dying seagull. Finally he took the laptop and smashed it across the edge of the drawers, smashed it and smashed and smashed it until it snapped, two halves dangling from a web of colored wiring and broken circuit boards.

Then the rage failed and he saw himself standing ankle deep in the wreck of that other Everett's life. Precious things, valuable things, good and useful things that could never be made whole again. Things that he loved. He remembered when his dad had taught him about entropy. A broken egg never unbroke itself. A burned book never went back from ashes to being paper and print again. A torn face of Gareth Bale never stitched itself back together again and jumped back onto the wall. But that impossibility of going into reverse was what made the universe work: water ran from high to low and never low to high, heat from hot to cold and never the other way. The universe was running down, very slowly but very surely, like a clock. In the end, there would be no high, no lows, no hot or cold, no difference that would allow a thing to flow from one to another: equilibrium. Then time would stop, because there would be no difference between before and after, because there could be no before or after, no change, ever. *Entropy* was the name physicists had for this quality. It was a huge and terrible truth of physics: entropy allowed life to happen, but only on the promise that everything would go cold and die. Every universe, known and unknown, would end up indistinguishable from all the others. And because there were no differences between them, they would become one.

Everett M stood among entropy in his alter's room. He wished, he wished, he wished he hadn't done so much damage. But it could not be undone, and so he must live with it.

Laura stood at the door.

"Everett?"

She looked scared. He hated to see her scared. She didn't deserve to be scared.

"Sorry."

"It's all right, Everett. It will be all right."

"I'm so cold."

8

"**P**aris?"

"About forty miles Nor'nor-west," Sharkey said. "'Can this cockpit hold the vasty fields of France?'"

"I thought you didn't do Shakespeare," Everett said. He had studied *Henry V* the previous term. His English class had gone to see it in the round "O" of the Globe Theatre. The girls had adored it. All the way back on the tube and train they'd been pouty and theatrical. Everett had thought it sort of wrong to see a play in daylight, half outdoors.

"Never said that, sir," Sharkey said. "What I did say was that psychos, freaks, and sociopaths quote Shakespeare. Take your pick of them."

Everness's crew crowded around the magnifier lens pulled over the green display screen on the radar binnacle. Outside, the great clouds tinged with the pink and yellow of snow ran on a wind from the north. *Everness* ran with them, her power exhausted, only enough power in the batteries to operate the bridge controls and hold her on a stable heading.

"Can I see a map?" Everett said. Sharkey raised an eyebrow; Captain Anastasia lifted her chin: *do as he asks*. The charts were stowed in tubes on a vertical conveyor belt. Sharkey pulled the chain and drew the loop of maps down and around. He unrolled the chart on the map desk, clipping the ends under brass rods.

"Where are we?"

Sharkey placed an emphatic finger. The names, the cities were the same, the features were very different. This map showed a smoke ring of power plants surrounding Paris, just as one encircled London.

Beyond that wall of chimneys and cooling towers, furnaces and steam turbines, train lines and coal conveyor belts, the map depicted a landscape that was gouged apart with mines. Opencast mines the size of towns had been scooped out of the plain that ran from Paris to Belgium and Germany in Everett's world—High Deutschland on this map. Hills had been turned into pits; forests into ash-colored craters. This was a land stripped to the bone for coal. Everett tried to compare the outer Paris shown on the map with his memory of outer Paris, the time Tejendra had decided to take everyone in the car through the Channel Tunnel shuttle to Disney Paris. Tejendra and Laura had been fighting before they even got out of the Eurotunnel terminal at Sangatte. It had been one of those we-have-a-long-way-to-go-with-the-kids-in-the-back-listening kind of arguments, composed mostly of sullen silences.

"I think we're right in the middle of the flight path into CDG," Everett said.

"Your acronym Mr. Singh?" Captain Anastasia asked.

"CDG. Charles de Gaulle. Europe's second busiest airport. Between Paris, Amsterdam, and Frankfurt, this is the highest density of aircraft movements in Europe. In fact, with the wind in this quarter, it'll take us right over the main runway."

"How do you know this?" Sen asked.

"I'm interested in this sort of thing."

"Aircraft movements?" Sen had a variation on a look, a very slight tilt of the head, that turned puzzlement into complete incomprehension, as if she were looking at something dragged up from the thickest silt at the bottom of the darkest lake in the deepest cave.

"I do know that we'll be setting radars off from here to Berlin," Everett said. Captain Anastasia's eyes widened.

"Mr. Sharkey!"

He was at the radar monitor before the final syllable of his name was spoken.

"The sky is full of metal," Sharkey said with wonder. "It's like a storm made of flying tin." In the same instant the communications board came alive. A dozen voices hailed *Everness*. Everett had never been good at French, but he could hear the anger.

"Belay that racket Mr. Sharkey," Captain Anastasia commanded. "I can imagine what they're saying." She pulled down a microphone and thumbed for engineering. "Mr. Mchynlyth, any chance of motive power?"

"I havnae the power to make a cup of tea, let alone gallivant us all over the sky," came the voice from the speaker. "That jump drained the batteries, or do you no remember that wee detail? I can just about keep our head in this wind."

"I'll take that as a no."

Stupid, Everett thought. *I forgot that the ship had moved. I plotted a straight point-to-point jump, identical locations in different universes. I should have thought, should have taken the time, should have made the calculations right.*

He felt a warm touch brush the back of his hand, which rested atop the map spread out before him. It was fast, it was fleeting, it was gone before anyone else could register it.

"You got us away," Sen said. "We was dead back there."

Can you read my mind? Everett thought. It was not the first time Sen had said exactly what he needed to hear without asking what he was feeling. Everett believed in an ordered and predictable universe. Sen and her insights and her comments and her cards that spoke to no one but her upset that calm and rational universe.

"French air traffic control is asking us to identify ourselves," Sharkey said.

"Tell them we are an advertising blimp for an international circus," Captain Anastasia said. "We've slipped our moorings and are drifting on the wind. Advise them to warn all aircraft."

"Cirque du Soleil," Everett said. "It's a real circus in my world. This world. I mean, here."

Sharkey raised an eyebrow. Captain Anastasia nodded: *make it so.*

Sharkey's French was fast and good. Had he picked that up on his adventuring, or was it the heritage of the Lafayette part of his family? Everett was less sure than ever about how much of Sharkey's legend was true, and about how much he could trust the man who spun it.

"French air traffic control again," Sharkey said. "Didn't wash. They telephoned your Cirque du Soleil or whatever you call 'em. They ain't even in the country, let alone missing a blimp. The military is launching fighters."

"Shit," Captain Anastasia whispered. "We need answers here."

And it came to Everett in a flash, a rush, an instant, whole and complete and needing no working out, no testing, no evaluation, just like the night he had seen the shape of the Infundibulum floating in seven-dimensional space in his mind and all he had needed to do was to take the reality in his hands and shape it to his imagination.

"Ma'am, I have an idea."

"If it's anything like your last one—" Sharkey said.

"Enough, Mr. Sharkey," Captain Anastasia cut in.

"'The wise shall inherit glory: but shame shall be the promotion of fools,'" Sharkey muttered.

"I can hide us in plain sight," Everett said. "Right under their noses." He was bristling with excitement. Listen, he wanted to say, this is brilliant, this is simple, this will work. "But first I need to make a Heisenberg jump."

"I don't want to go back to that ice universe," Sen said.

"We're not going to another universe," Everett said. "Don't you see? If I can open up a gate between universes, I can open one up *inside* a universe. It's all just coordinates in the Infundibulum."

Captain Anastasia raised an eyebrow.

"I have multiple contacts," Sharkey said. "Flying tin, on intercept courses."

"Continue, Mr. Singh."

"That's it. I can jump us out of here to somewhere no one will even look twice at us."

"I'm not hearing any other feasible plans," Captain Anastasia said.

"Well, sorry to piss on your chips, but maybe it's just that you're deaf rather than dumb." Mchynlyth's voice rattled from the speakers. "We dinnae have the power. Shall I say that again, more slowly and a hell of a lot more loudly? We dinnae have the power."

"What I do know, Mr. Mchynlyth, is that we can't stay here."

Everett's mind whirled. Ideas churned and boiled like a storm cloud. *Storm.* Captain Anastasia had told him how she came to be Sen's adopted mother. It had been the result of a storm that had sent the airship *Fairchild* falling, burning like a cursed angel from the sky. They had tried to steal lightning. She'd implied that all ships could do this. Everett again remembered his family's trip to Disneyland Paris. They had camped—another money-saving strategy. The second night, the mother of thunderstorms had ripped the sky open and dumped a month's rain on the northwest suburbs of Paris in thirty minutes. When a flash flood of dirty, frothy water washed their folding chairs into the tent, Tejendra had scooped up sleeping bags, bubble mats, and Victory-Rose and bundled everything into the car. Dripping water onto the foyer carpet, Team Singh had booked the last family room at Hotel Cheyenne. That had been August. This was January, as far from lightning season as you could get. Think, Everett. If *Everness* could steal the heart of a thunderstorm, where else could she draw power from? Power lines. Of course. If only he had a map, a map of this world. The revelation was like a physical impact. They'd arrived in his home universe, so he would be able to call up a map on his cell phone. There was once again a world of information at his fingertips.

The on button on the smartphone felt like an old friend. The screen lit. Icons appeared across the top of the screen: mobile network, data network, 3G. An SMS: *You are connected to SFR. You are*

now roaming. Your data limit is 5 megabytes per day. Everett tapped into
the apps and opened up Google Maps. He flexed his fingers,
expanded the screen, again and again. It was slow, so slow. Paris: the
banlieus, that ring of dismal suburbs that was the only thing darker
and more gloomy than the smoke ring of coal-burning power sta-
tions that surrounded that other Paris shown on *Everness*'s maps.
Now, exact location. He flicked on the GPS. Everett imagined signals bouncing up to the ring of satellites orbiting and back again.
An icon appeared. This was him. This was his home world, with him
on the bridge of an alien airship. Here. If he were to drag his finger
across the screen, he would be able to look down on his own home,
in Roding Road, see the blue circle of Victory-Rose's trampoline in
the back garden, the patio furniture on the deck, the chiminea and
the gas barbecue; he would be able to see everything as though it had
been perfectly preserved on that clear August Sunday afternoon
when the satellite had rolled through the sky and snapped its photograph. A time before panoplies and plenitudes and planesrunners,
before the Infundibulum and the Order.

The idea came so sharp and sudden it was like a needle in his
heart: *call home.* He had the number up on speed dial. His thumb
hesitated. They'll be listening. They had to be listening. He would
betray the entire plan. Everett flicked the number away and it was
physical pain. But he had to call someone, send some message, let
someone know what had happened to him, that he was alive and well
out there in the Panoply of worlds. Colette. She was an ally—he
knew that in the same way that he knew that the elegant and subtle
Ibrim Hoj Kerrim was an enemy of Charlotte Villiers and her Order.
But she was too close to Paul McCabe and his faction—she had saved
him once, when Charlotte Villiers pulled a gun to try to stop him
from fleeing through the Heisenberg Gate to E3. They would be
watching her—if she was still on the Heisenberg Gate project. If she
was still at Imperial. If she was still alive. *Ryun. Ryun Spinetti.* Best
mate. He'd seen those other worlds on the video on the memory

stick Colette had given him that night in the Japanese restaurant. Everett tapped up an SMS. His fingers hesitated over the touch keys. What to say in 160 characters?

Get this 2 Mum: am OK. Dad okay. CU soon. What else to say? What else did he need to say?

"French air traffic control is calling us again," Sharkey said. "Charles de Gaulle airport is warning us not to enter their control space."

"Mr. Singh?"

Send. Everett's phone gave a small beep. Gone, for good or for ill. Then he summoned up the Google Earth image, zoomed in on the little star that gave *Everness*'s current location, and worked it forward along the direction in which the wind was blowing.

"Yes!"

Every head turned. Everett went to the great window and pulled down a magnifier. He dialed up the image size. Captain Anastasia stood at his shoulder. Everett passed the magnifier to her and pointed. The lenses hid her eyes, but Everett saw her lips open a fraction and heard a soft echo of his own *yes.*

"Mr. Singh, you may have saved us." Captain Anastasia tapped the edge of the frame, locking in the coordinates. She lifted the lens array off the swing arm, took it to Sen's navigation board, and swiped the code into Sen's comptator.

"Take us there, Sen, and keep us there."

"What's there, Ma?"

"Power."

"Inch her forward a wee hair!" Mchynlyth's voice called up through the song of wind in wires. "I don't want some stray gust catching me and crossing the lines. I'm no tasty crispy fried." The ship's engineer swung at the end of the power connector, a pendulum weighted with a life. Fifty meters above, Everett looked down at him through the open hatch. Below Mchynlyth were the four hundred thousand volt power lines, and fifty meters below them, the hard surface of northern France. He let go of his left-hand grip on the stanchion and took the microphone from its mount. He kept his right hand on the winch controls. The rising wind eddied up through the open hatch and tugged at his loose shorts. "Don't look down," Sen had said when she took him running over the rooftops of Hackney Great Port. But what if you have to look down? Everett felt queasy for a moment. The world lurched. *Keep it cool, man. Remember when you jumped from the capsized* Arthur P *to* Everness's *boarding ramp when you defeated the Bromley's? You hadn't even been able to see the ground at all then, the weather was so foul. That was the thing: if you can't see the ground you can also believe it isn't there at all. It's when you see how far you have to fall and what's at the bottom of it that you get the sweating, panicky fear.*

"Sen, take her forward. Easy, dead easy."

"Bonaroo."

Her touch on the controls was light and precise, but the sudden motion was enough to send Everett reeling toward the drop. He almost took his hand from the winch control. Almost. The power connector cable amplified the ship's power and sent Mchynlyth swinging across the sky. He was coming very, very close to the power lines. If the cable from the ship touched two lines at the same time, they would short circuit. Twenty-five kilovolts would turn you to ash so fast you wouldn't even know it, let alone feel any pain. But if he let Sen carry Mchynlyth too far, he might miss the power line entirely.

"Dead stop, Sen." There were no brakes on airships. Sen could only bring *Everness* to a halt by applying reverse thrust, and that took distance and time. Distance and time were things Everett could work with. It was all relativity. Everett looked down between his feet through the hatch. Mchynlyth's wild swinging was dying down. Everett knew the physics: simple harmonic motion. A pendulum swing always took the same time: long and fast at the start, short and slow when it wound down. A simple, basic principle—the story Tejendra had told him was that in the sixteenth century Galileo had watched a lamp swinging on its chain in Pisa cathedral, measured it against his own pulse, and shown that the period was constant. Everett had never thought he'd see the principle demonstrated using a man on the end of a power cable swinging from the belly of an electrically powered post-steampunk airship.

Mchynlyth grinned up at Everett. His orange-gloved hand gave a thumbs-up, then he pointed down. *Lower away.* Everett worked the winch, never taking his eyes off Mchynlyth. The engineer was not harnessed directly to the power converter; he rode a drop line that ran with the main cable. He would hook the converter to the line, then ride the drop line back up through the hatch and complete the circuit. Everett's job was to get him within arm's length of the power line without crossing the lines. The hand kept waving, patting air: *lower, lower.* The wind was treacherous, gusting, blowing Mchynlyth far out of reach, then heart-stoppingly close. *Lower, lower*—the orange thumb went up. *Cease lowering.* Everett hit the stop button hard. Now Mchynlyth reached around to unfasten the hooked stick from his utility belt. It was fumbling, clumsy work in his heavy, insulated gloves. One mistake, one slip, and he would drop the stick—the *hotstick*, as it was known among the Airish—and he would have to run the risk of a sizable shock, bonding on to the line himself. Everett understood the physics too well. The circuit was not complete. It would be complete, allowing electricity to flow, only when the earthing cable was dropped, but both the power line and *Everness* had picked up different charges of static electricity, just from the movement of air over the wires, or the movement of a two-hundred-meter-long airship through the air. But those static charges were different, and when Mchynlyth connected ship to line, they would equalize. *Equalize spectacularly,* Everett thought. He held his breath. Mchynlyth lunged with the hook and missed. Well short. Again; again a miss. A third time, and little lightnings ran along the hotstick and cracked between hook and power line.

"Oh the Dear!" Sen exclaimed over the intercom. "He's burning, he's burning! Everett, help him!" Up on the bridge, she, Captain Anastasia, and Sharkey had been keeping one eye on the feed from the hull cameras. The other they kept on Sharkey's radar screen. And the interceptor jets scrambled by the French Air Force were seconds away.

"He's all right, he's all right." Everett shouted into the intercom. "It's part of the process." Mchynlyth had hooked securely onto the line and was hauling himself in. He clipped a carabiner to the power line. He was hooked to the four hundred kilovolts. Everett understood Sen's fear. She had lost one ship, one home, one family to the lightning when the captain of the doomed *Fairchild* had tried to rekindle its batteries from an unorthodox source. Now Mchynlyth was wrestling the power connector over the cable, hitting the clamps that locked the contacts to the live line. *Close to half a million volts are running through that*, Everett thought. Mchynlyth was safe, they were all safe. It was the reason birds could perch on power lines. Everything was safe as long as it was connected to earth. Electricity was flow, high potential to low potential, charge to ground.

Captain Anastasia came on the intercom.

"Are we near charging yet? I can see those airoplans on Sharkey's screen and they're a little too close for my liking."

Everett heard the distant thunder of military jet engines. He glanced down between his feet into the dizzy drop. Mchynlyth had swung from the cable on his drop line. Two thumbs up. Everett hit the button on the drop line. Mchynlyth was jerked away from the power connector, clamped like a brass leech to the line, up into the air. He shot up through the tiny hatch, hit the harness release, and dropped off the line to land light and agile, one foot on either side of the rectangle of empty air. One mistake and he would have tumbled straight down to the ground, screaming all the way. Everett had been a great goalkeeper, and he could think in three dimensions and more, but it would take him years to learn the Airish way, which was to live in many dimensions.

Years.

He didn't intend to spend years among the Airish to learn that skill.

"I thoroughly recommend that as a life experience," Mchynlyth said. "Bein' that close to power lines gives ye a wee tingle all over. Right. Come on. This'll be worth seeing."

With a crook of his finger Mchynlyth beckoned Everett across the hull. They ran, crouched in the cramped access ways between the battery stacks, beneath the low ceiling of the cargo deck. They flickered on the edge of death, Sen drawing the last watts of power out of them to hold *Everness* over the power line. On the far side of the hull was a second hatch in the ship's belly, near where the other half of the power connector was stored. When *Everness* was in port, the charging arm ran underneath her and she was connected by two cables, one the live, the other the ground, allowing the power to run through the charging circuitry. The ship was effectively a giant plug. The ground line hung above Everett and Mchynlyth's heads.

"Before I press any buttons, tell me. Yer sure about this?" Mchynlyth said.

"The standard high-tension voltage in France is 400 kilovolts. I looked it up. Online." That expression was unknown in Mchynlyth's world. "The interweb," said Everett, and Mchynlyth nodded understanding. "The rest was easy, just basic mathematics."

"Aye, you see, it's that last wee bit I'm nervous about, the basic mathematics."

"From what you told me, the step-down transformer should be able to handle it."

"Oh, that's dolly. If we go up like a Catherine wheel, it's all my fault."

Everett was about to protest that the equations were never wrong, but only as good as the numbers they were given. Then the fighters went over. The noise knocked the words, the breath, and all thoughts from him. Everett had never been so close to turbojets before. They sounded like the sky ripping right down the middle, from the edge of space right through the heart of *Everness* to the earth below.

"Right then!" Mchynlyth bawled over the diminishing roar of the French Air Force jets. "That makes our minds up for us." He punched the release button. The hatch opened. The earth connector dropped. Mchynlyth and Everett both craned over the aperture. "Keep your eyes peeled," Mchynlyth said. "This'll be quite a show." The cable unreeled with a hissing shriek from the spool. Then the connector end, falling to earth, erupted in a blaze of lighting. Thunder rocked *Everness*. The railing, the cable, every centimeter of metal and nanocarbon crawled with glowing ghosts. St Elmo's fire, Everett recalled. A name like that you remember. Electricity was arcing across the air gap between the falling cable and the earth. That meant current was flowing. Batteries were charging.

"Aye, you get yer dish up to the bridge and work whatever dally magic you do with thon machine," Mchynlyth shouted. He pulled his goggles down against the hard blue arc light. Everett scuttled back through the maze of access ways to the main staircase. The battery casings seemed to thrum and glow with power. He could feel the energy prickling against his skin, like tiny electric spiders. He could smell the thrilling ozone tang of electricity. It always made him think of fairgrounds and summer. Everything was alive. *Everness* seemed to stretch, as if waking from a long, cold sleep.

"We've blacked out most of Northwest Paris," Sharkey said as Everett arrived on the bridge. The American sounded impressed. Captain Anastasia did not turn from her place at the window.

"Do you think we could manage it this time without a last-minute, cliff-hanger, hairs-breadth escape, Mr. Singh?" she asked. Everett took up his station and opened the Infundibulum. Sen nodded. Her concentration was total, her fingers playing the controls like a musical instrument, her eyes flicking from monitor to monitor, holding *Everness* over the power line. Everett saw a bead of sweat on her lip. He wanted to dab it away with a fingertip. He shook the image out of his head.

"There's some mathematics to do," Everett said. "It's not a simple point-to-point transition, the same set of coordinates in different universes." He did not want to say how tricky the math really was. It involved a Fourier transform. His maths teacher hadn't even known what a Fourier transform was. *A mathematical operation that transforms one complex-valued function of a real variable into another.* There was no way to understand it other than technically.

"They're coming back," Sharkey said. Everett glanced up as the Mathika software, the program he had used to calculate the many-dimensional folds of the Infundibulum, opened on the screen. He saw silver wings flash out there in the winter sky, aircraft turning to make a second pass over the airship. "We're being targeted."

"I'm on it," Everett said. A Fourier transform on non-Euclidean space. He entered *Everness's* present coordinates in this universe. The process was instantaneous, but the results needed interpretation. He had to match the location code with that for the place where he intended to jump the ship, and that involved things like the curvature of the Earth. Get it wrong one way and they might jump in at a height way above *Everness's* operational ceiling, with the ship over-pressurized, and explode. Get it wrong the other way. . . . *Don't think about that*, Everett told himself. *You're good. Like you said to Mchynlyth, the mathematics is always perfect.* He reopened the Infundibulum and called up a search menu. In went the output from the Fourier transform. The veils and clouds of Panoply codes whirled and swirled, the camera plunged through glowing walls of jump points. There. Everett highlighted it, copied it. He pulled up the Jump Controller and dropped the code into the window. The board lit green.

"Heisenberg jump is ready."

"'He delivereth and rescueth, and he worketh signs and wonders in heaven,'" Sharkey murmured.

Captain Anastasia thumbed the intercom.

"Status, Mr. Mchynlyth?"

"We can jump and we can fly."

"Mr. Singh—"

"Now hold on one wee moment," Mchynlyth shouted from the speaker. "I'm going to need my power cables back."

Captain Anastasia bit back a curse.

"How long?"

"Two minutes."

"Make it so. Sen, hold our position. Mr. Singh, on my mark. Mr. Sharkey, how far away are those airoplans?"

"They're here, now," Sharkey said, and the ship shook as three dazzling deadly fighters speared out of nowhere, engines a howl of speed and aggression. Everett ducked. Captain Anastasia stood boldly at the great window.

"Oh, but you are beautiful," she whispered as they knifed over the top of the ship.

"We're being hailed again," Sharkey said. "If we do not land immediately we will be fired upon."

"Cables stowed," Mchynlyth reported. "We can leave any time you want."

"Everett, at your convenience."

Everett touched the jump button. *There should be sound effects*, he thought. There should be a noise like engines powering up. There should be some *Babylon 5* kind of *schwummm* noise, like when the starships came out of hyperspace, or even that *Doctor Who* sound, like a dinosaur in pain, when the TARDIS dematerialized. All there was in a Heisenberg jump was white . . .

. . . and then somewhere else.

"Did you say something, Everett Singh?" Sen asked.

"No," Everett said.

"'Funny, cos I's sure I heard you say something."

"I didn't say anything."

"Well, maybe not so much say something as make a sound."

"A sound? What like?"

"Well, sort of like . . . *voom.*"

"What?"

"Voom," Sen said. "Only long. *Vooooom.*"

"I did not go voom."

"Yes you did you did you did."

"The Heisenberg jump's done something to your hearing," Everett said, but it was a lie. He had made a noise. He had gone voom. *Vooooom.* The kind of noise an airship jumping between parallel universes through a Heisenberg Gate should make. Sen pouted at him in annoyance, but out of the corner of his eye he caught Captain Anastasia smiling.

Voom! she mouthed silently.

Snow had fallen on the city. For a moment Everett did not recognize his London, his Tottenham. Then the shadows and shapes and slumpings of slush and melted snow made a pattern, a pattern he knew. That must be the curve of Northumberland Road, there were the tracks and platforms at Angel Road Station. That dark body of water, like a dead eye, could only be Lockwood Reservoir. There was the plaza off the High Road. He and his dad had walked up that road so many Saturdays. Everett pulled down a monitor and clicked up the belly cameras. Directly beneath the hull were the snow-covered stands and the rectangle of grass between them.

"Yes," Everett whispered. His calculations had been perfect. He had jumped *Everness* right over the stadium.

"Where are we?" Sen asked.

"White Hart Lane," Everett said. He felt powerful, he felt victorious, he felt like he had scored a goal right between the posts on that pitch down there. When Sen looked puzzled, he explained, "Tottenham Hotspur. The one place they won't look twice at an airship. They park them over the stadium for advertising all the time.

Hiding in plain sight. By the time they work out that we shouldn't be here, we'll not be here."

"And why are we here, Mr. Singh?" Captain Anastasia asked.

"Because it's where my family is," Everett said. "And I'm going to get them back.'

9

There ought to be a rule. If it snows on the first day of the term, school will be cancelled. No ifs, no buts, no questions. Automatically. An extra day's holiday. A snow day.

Everett M had been awake long before the strange light that always says *snow on the ground* began to glow through the curtains. He couldn't sleep in this bed. It was hollow in the same places, comfortable on the same side, yielded and was hard in the same way, but it wasn't his. So he lay staring at the ceiling, or at the glowing display of the digital radio, until the curtains became a plane of yellow grey. Light like this is as much reflected up from the ground as it is shining from the sky, Everett M knew. He went to the window and saw the garden, the hedge, the roofs covered with pure untrodden snow. While he'd lain awake in this alien bed in an alien world, it had fallen silent, unseen, deep, snow on snow.

He shivered.

By the time he left for school, the purity of the snow had been broken. Footprints drew paths from gate to gate, car tires had pressed grey, icy tracks into the road. The snow made everyone's destinations and intentions visible. On Stoke Newington High Street the school-run SUVs were nose to tail, windows misted, tailpipes making smog, wheels mushing the snow into greasy black slush. A trail of paw prints across Abney Park Cemetery ended in a red stain and a few feathers. Snow had settled around the shoulders and heads of the stone angels like robes and crowns.

The snowballs hit him as he emerged from the Dogs Delight. Two on the back and one on the side of the head. He whirled, surprised and furious. The fury fueled the technology inside him. Everett M felt the thrilling burn of the lasers charging up. Lines appeared in the backs of his fingers. He willed them shut. Everett M had fantasies of power. Everyone did, imagining that they had super-powers and could avenge every slight and offense and injustice. Bul-lies would crumble, sarcastic adults melt. But no one ever could. There were no superpowers. There were no super heroes. But now there was a superhero. He imagined scooping up handfuls of snow, squeezing them so hard in his enhanced grip that they turned to ice. He could run at them so fast that, try as they might to flee, they would never be able to get away from him. They might try pelting him with snowballs to slow him down, but he saw himself opening up his finger lasers, each one tracking and vaporizing a snowball in the blink of an eye. *Zap zap zap zap.* No matter which way they tried to run, he would hunt them down and throw the ice balls so hard and accurate that they would hurt, really hurt. He would leave a message not to mess with Everett M. Singh. Word would spread around the school: *You know that geeky guy, the goalkeeper? Did you hear what he* did?

No. He could never do that. The first rule of superheroes is *always protect your real identity.*

Jeers and shouts from the bushes.

"Hey, Everett . . ."

"So where did you get to over Christmas?"

"Should have stayed there; better than this hole."

"I'm okay," Everett shouted into the snowscape. "Really." No answer, of course, but it was all right. It was better than all right. It was a welcome back. *Not everyone on this world is your enemy.*

Everett M had been trying to avoid the boy all morning. At assembly, where Mrs. Abrahams—same assembly hall, same head teacher—welcomed everyone back to a new term and got sighs and groans when she announced that the school had heating oil enough for three weeks of snow and therefore would not be closing, he dis-appeared into the crowd. He hurried out of classes, using his Thryn senses to put as many people as possible between he and the boy. He found ways to avoid having to go past the lockers. He hid in the library at break, telling himself that he was just reading the papers, learning what was going on in this world that made it different from his own. The prime minister was Mr. Cameron, not Mr. Portillo. The economy was in bad shape. Spurs were three places further down the league standings. The number one singer was still the crappy winner from *The X-Factor*. In none of the pages in any of the papers could Everett M find any evidence that anyone knew of the Plenitude, or even had any idea that they occupied one of many parallel universes. The bell rang. Everett M turned on his Thryn senses and skulked through the corridors of Bourne Green school. But at lunch there was no escape, shivering and exposed out on the snowy playground. Black on white like an exclamation mark on a page: there was no going unseen. Ryun Spinetti cut a line of footprints across the snow.

"You okay?"

"Yeah, I'm good. Good."

"Well, that's good." They stood, hands in pockets, not looking at each other. "So is everything, like, all right now?"

"There's still some things I don't remember properly."

"Whoa, that's like. . . . Like what?"

"How would I know?"

"Suppose so."

These were easy lies. Everett thought back to the black car that Charlotte Villiers had aimed at him deliberately to turn him into her weapon. What he was telling Ryun were hardly lies at all.

"You sound, I dunno, different."

Everett M's heart beat hard.

"Like I said, there's things I don't remember. It wasn't a good time. Can we talk about something else?"

"Sure, sure. So, are you coming over?"

"What? Where?" Never had Everett M so wanted the bell to ring for the start of class.

"My place, after school. I know it's stupid, but my Mum, well, she was really worried about you. And she wonders if you might be able to help her find something she lost, rings or something. Didn't you get my text?"

"I lost my phone."

Ryun frowned. "I sent it this morning."

"I forget where I lost it, but I haven't had it for days."

"I replied to your text."

"What?" His heart skipped another beat, and there was a tight fear rising inside his chest. Ryun slid out his Blackberry, tapped open the SMS. *Get this 2 Mum: am OK. Dad OK. CU soon.*

"I don't remember sending that."

"It's definitely you. That's your number."

"Like I said, I lost my phone."

"But the date, that's today."

Lie. Lie fast. Lie hard. Lie the best you have ever lied.

"Well, yeah, but sometimes it takes time for a message to go through."

"Yeah. I suppose." Everett M could hear that Ryun was far from convinced. "I suppose that what's the 'Get this 2 Mum: am OK' bit meant. But . . . what does that bit mean? 'Dad OK'?"

"I don't know!" Only anger would stop the questions now. "I don't remember. It wasn't a good time. I don't want to talk about it anymore."

Ryun stepped back from the heat of Everett M's anger.

"I'm sorry, sorry. Enough, enough. So, are you coming over?"

"I'll see you."

The bell was ringing. Dark figures began to move across the snow, funneling toward the doors.

"You coming?"

"I'm just going for a pee," Everett M said. "I'll see you in a moment."

The cubicle in the toilets smelled of cigarette smoke. Mrs. Abrahams had put in smoke alarms, and just like in his world, the school kids of E10 had gleefully vandalized them. Everett M took out his phone, his real phone, the one Charlotte Villiers had given him. His thumb hovered over the call button. No, he couldn't bear to hear Paul McCabe's whining, nasally Northern Ireland accent. A text was enough for him.

He's here.

Send.

The viral went around as the classes emptied. It leaped from phone to phone, tablet to netbook to iPad: *Cool! Must see!* The pupils of Bourne Green heard their phones beep or felt them buzz. The moment they were through the gates, outside school jurisdiction, they rushed to open up the message. *Sick video! Is this for real?* The Bourne Green Harajuku girls were clustered around a screen. Everett M wondered how they could wear such short skirts with snow freezing in the gutters. Goose pimples above the so-cute knee socks. Everett M shivered and turned his collar up. His breath hung in clouds. The late afternoon sky was a deep blue with a yellow horizon to the west. That kind of sky said that the cold would be staying and that a deeper cold would come.

"Hey Everett! Everett!" The boys who had dealt out the welcome-back snowballing that morning were huddled over a Blackberry. "Is it?"

"Is what?" Everett M asked.

"Is it real?"

"Everything's real."

"Yeah smartass. I mean, the thing in the video."

"What video?"

"You didn't get—"

"I lost my phone," Everett M cut in quickly.

The footage was a cell-phone shot, the picture jerky, the zoom crazy, the sound crackly and thin. White Hart Lane football ground—the same in this world as in Everett M's home. There was a blimp hovering over it. Everett M had seen advertising blimps before. This was a monster. It was longer than the stadium. And advertising blimps were a bit saggy and carried *advertising*. This had the killer lines of a shark, and the only artwork Everett M could see was a huge heraldic coat of arms painted on the upper surface of the mean, lean nose. And advertising blimps were tethered like balloons on the end of a string. This had engines. This was a proper sky-faring airship. Everett M knew what it was and where it had come from.

"I mean, it's got to be CG," Abbas, the owner of the phone said. "Some dude wants to get himself a job in some special effects company."

"Noah says he seen it with his own eyes," Wayne said. "Real. Honest. It's still there, right over White Hart Lane."

"It's some advertising stunt, innit?" Nilesh Virdi, the last of the three, said. "Maybe not Spurs, maybe like Nike or something. Remember all that shite for the Olympics?" They all looked at Everett M.

"It's obviously a commercial freight airship from a parallel universe," Everett M said. "Parallel universes always have airships. There's been some quantum leakage between universes and it's slipped through. Probably in its own universe this is all like airship docks and stuff. It's obvious."

Abbas, Wayne, and Nilesh all stared.

"You sure you didn't get hit by something?" Abbas asked.

"You can believe me or not, but that's what it is."

Everett M left them gaping at the screen. *I tell them the truth but it's so incredible they don't believe it. He hides an entire airship in exactly the same way by making everyone think it's a stunt or a trick. You're clever, alter-Everett.* At the entrance to the park, away from all the people he had lied to, he took out his own cell phone. He hated the thought of Paul McCabe's simpering voice, but a text would not do now.

"Hello, Paul. Everett Singh. He's coming, he's close."

"Everett, you hold on there. I can get you back up."

"I can take care of this myself." Everett M cut the call, then said to the dead phone, "It's personal."

10

Where the river made its great bend toward the sea at Wool-
wich, Everett put the hedgehopper into a turn. He looked
down at the snow-covered dome of the O2 arena. He had gone with
his dad to see Led Zeppelin there. Tejendra had got up at dawn the
day the application went online, clicking away, *refresh refresh refresh*,
until he made it onto the draw. When the tickets came, Tejendra had
played the albums on repeat over and over. Everett had loved the
music and the sight of middle-aged men with their eyes closed, deep
in rock rapture. He hadn't smelled so much skunk since the night of
Abbas's party, when the gatecrashers did three thousand pounds
worth of damage. The great dome hadn't looked real then. Now, in
the slanting golden light of a January afternoon, it looked even less
real. Snow made everything new and strange. Snow was a new skin
on a city's bones. But it was more than just snow making his London
look alien to Everett as he cut across the Thames toward the Isle of
Dogs. Beneath the skin of snow, beneath the bones of the city he
knew, he could see another London, the smoky, electric-sparking
London of Sen's world, of airships and stone angels in the architecture. In that world the river turned in the same place in the same
direction, as dark as lead on the snow; some of the streets and buildings were the same; most were not. Beyond that London were yet
other Londons, the one he had glimpsed on the secret memory stick
Colette had given him, Ibrim Hoj Kerim's London. There the Isle of
Dogs wasn't buried under corporate towers and conference centers
and glass and chrome business units but was a green place of parks
and palaces, pools and pleasure gardens. And another London: the
abandoned London he had glimpsed when he accidentally opened
the Heisenberg Gate and almost flooded the secret Channel Tunnel

test drill. And beyond that, the other Londons of the Plenitude of Worlds, and the billion billion Londons of the Panoply. His father was in one of them. Cutting in across the Blackwall Basin, Everett felt that if he looked down beneath his feet, looked with all his heart, he could see through all those other Londons as if they were glass, see all the way to his dad.

I'm coming. I have a promise to keep.

Everett glanced over his shoulder. Sen, muffled in goggles and scarf and fur-trimmed parka hood, flew close behind his right wing. Everett lifted a gloved hand and beckoned her to follow him. *Let's go.* He pulled down the throttle cable and aimed the hedgehopper square at the three towers of Canary Wharf. He heard Sen squeal with delight as she drifted into position beside him, grinning with pure pleasure. Everett's heart leaped.

He recalled their flight preparations. Sen squinting at the light reflecting from the white landscape as the cargo hatch opened and lowered them toward the sacred turf of White Hart lane. She sniffed the air. Her eyes opened wide as she took a deep, full breath.

"Omi, how can you breathe that? It's so *clean* it's like it's not there at all."

And every breath of your smoky, coal-polluted air felt like claws scratching the back of my throat, Everett thought. Frowning, Sen said, "What is that *meese* noise?" Everett couldn't hear it at first. A car alarm, blues-and-twos from an ambulance or police car, maybe a plane coming down into London City Airport. Then he realized that it was no one thing. Sen was hearing was all these things, and more: car horns, truck brakes, buses and vans and cars and motorbikes. She was hearing the breath and heartbeat of London, the traffic that circulated day and night. In her world, vehicles ran on rails or on soft tires, and they were powered by silent electricity. This was the roar of a million gasoline and diesel engines; billions of tiny explosions of hydrocarbons in engine cylinders. One huge, endless rolling thunder.

"Come and I'll show you," Everett said, strapping himself into the hedgehopper. The power dial showed two hours of flying time. His plan had originally been to fly fast and fly straight, leave the hedgehoppers hidden in Abney Park Cemetery, find his mum and Victory-Rose, get back to the cemetery, and call *Everness* for a pick up. Captain Anastasia had forbidden him to take either the jumpgun or Dr. Quantum, but he had his smartphone. And in this universe, his smartphone was smart. Then he realized that his world was as strange and wonderful to Sen as her world had been to him. He remembered the feeling in his stomach when it had first dawned on him that he was farther from home than any human from his world had ever been. It had been scary, like looking at your toes hanging over the edge of an unexpected drop and fighting the dark little voice that whispered *step off*. Along with anxiety, there had been an excitement so huge that it became something like joy, and something physical that he didn't have a name for, something that had felt like he imagined sex did. He wanted Sen to know that feeling, too. Victory-Rose would be at Bebe Ajeet's; Laura would be at work. The house would be empty. There was time to take Sen up to the top of his London. "Come on," he said—him, Everett Singh, who had been the follower in Sen's world—and stepped off the edge of the freight platform into the winter air.

Everett pushed the steering bar forward and took the hedge-hopper down from tower-top height. He steered for clear air between the three skyscrapers. With a whoop, Sen followed. Glass flashed golden winter sun and the plazas and squares were pinkish white with black footways tracked across them. The water in the old docks was deep black. Everett glanced at the offices behind the gleaming windows, wondering whether the workers inside were watching him fly past. Were they thinking, *What was that? Was it a bird, was it a plane? No*, he thought, *it was a planesrunner*.

Over the river now, and following it into the heart of the city. On his right wingtip, Limehouse and Wapping, where pirates had been hanged in chains from Execution Dock. On his left wingtip, the ugly tower blocks of Rotherhithe and Bermondsey. Beneath his feet a tour boat powered downstream to Greenwich. Everett touched the control bar and sent the hedgehopper lower still. His feet almost brushed the glass roof of the cabin. A few brave tourists, wrapped up for unexpected snow, were outside on the observation deck. They looked up and pointed as Everett flew over their heads. A little girl waved. They probably thought it was for a movie. Everett gained height and steered straight upriver. A police boat pushed a moustache of white water before its bow. A cargo lighter, low and heavy, ran down to the sea with the tide. Ahead, Tower Bridge stood across the river. To Everett it had always been the gate of London. *Who seeks entry?* He glanced behind him. Sen was on his right wing, slightly above him. Everett gestured with his hand: *we're going through.* Sen grinned and gave him a thumbs-up. He opened up the throttle, gained a little height, and aimed the hedgehopper at the rectangle of airspace between the road bed and the high pedestrian walkway. And through. The afternoon traffic ground along beneath Everett's feet, churning snow into black slush. The city was open to him now. On his right, the Tower of London wore caps of snow on its roofs and tower tops. To the left was the glass egg of City Hall. He skimmed the radio masts of HMS *Belfast.* Snow was drifted against the battleship-grey bulkheads in precise lines along the tops of the gun barrels. Over London Bridge, trains crossing the river into Cannon Street, their windows lit yellow as the January evening unfolded behind the London skyline. Snow blanketed the roof gardens on Cannon Street Station. Block by block, the street lights came to life along the embankments and up the huge blade of the Shard on the south bank. Over Southwark Bridge, then down to skim the elegant ribbon of the Millennium footbridge. Joggers, walkers, art lovers going to or coming from the Tate Modern stopped and stared and turned to follow with their eyes the two incredible, impossible, magical flying things as they flew over their heads.

"Weeee!" Sen shouted. Everett raised a hand in greeting to the people on the bridge as he banked the hedgehopper to the right over the parallel rail and road bridges at Blackfriars. Sen threw up her hands in a gesture of puzzlement. *Where are we going?* Everett jabbed a finger. *There.* Rising above the crowd of lower, lesser buildings, the great dome of St. Paul's Cathedral. Everett pulled back on the steering bar. The ducted fans answered. The two hedgehoppers climbed over the traffic, wheeling around the interchange at Queen Victoria Street, high above the rooftops of St. Paul's Churchyard. The city seemed more muted under snow. The slush softened the rumble of wheels and the grumble of engines. Snow had drifted in the lees of the great dome's ribs and had gathered at the feet of the columns and in the details of the ornamental stonework. Snow had piled on the tops of the railings and balustrades. Everett circled the dome like a London seagull looking for pickings. He tilted the steering bar, turned, and came down as light as a thought on the very topmost lintel of the lantern. A tap on the harness released the hedgehopper. It climbed to the limit of its safety line. Everett stood at the top of the city. Above him was only the great golden cross. At his feet, beneath the curve of the dome, lay London.

Down Ludgate Hill and along Fleet Street, where the City of London became Westminster. Along the Strand, the way west was lit by a ribbon of light. Evening had filled up the streets and lights were lit, though the sun reached the lantern of the dome and set the great golden cross afire. The only other resident of High London was Justice on top of the Old Bailey, her scales and sword burning in those same rays of winter sun. But she was blindfolded. She had never seen—could never see—what Everett Singh saw from his perch high on top of St. Paul's. London was a city of lights, sparkled from the refreezing snow. A cold mist was settling in the streets and on the darkening river. To the south, the tower of the Tate Modern, lit at the very top like the Eye of Sauron, guarded the south side of the river. Trains crossed the Thames, lines of moving light. To the south-west the Houses of Parliament shone, floodlit; across the river the

London Eye was a wheel of light. To the east was the city proper, the dark shafts of the NatWest Tower and the chaos of the Lloyds building. There was no mistaking the Gherkin, like a friendly rocket to Mars. Across the river the lights of the Shard rose like a steeple, higher than imagining. And beneath him, under his feet, the greatest of London's churches, St Paul's. Did anyone see him? Had any one soul among the thousands streaming around the cathedral on its island in the traffic looked up and seen something up there? Had any of those stopped and looked harder, wondering, *is that someone up there?* He hoped so. He hoped that for one moment, one glimpse, he had put a little wonder into the life of one of those pedestrians winding home on wet feet through the cold and snow to a steamy bus or a smelly tube train. A moment that said, *there is still magic in this city.*

"Fantabulosa," a voice whispered beneath him. Everett hadn't seen Sen land. She crouched on the corner of the next lintel around the lantern, gloved fingers gripping the edge of the stone.

"You took me up to the top of your city, so I'm returning the gesture"

"Nah, that was just getting away from the Iddler and his fruit-boys."

"No, I mean when we rode the zip-line, from the ship down to the Tyrone Tower." Everett picked out the shaft of the Telecom Tower out in the west, in far Bloomsbury. In Sen's world, the head-quarters of the Panoply of Known Worlds had occupied the same spot. A true Dark Tower that, with Heisenberg Gates to other worlds hidden inside.

"Dear, yeah! That was bonaroo fun! Seems like years ago, but . . ." Sen's tone changed. "Oh, I's sorry Everett Singh."

"What about?"

"About your dad."

"I'll find him," Everett said. It was not just this London spread at his feet. It was all the Londons, all the worlds. He had mastery of them all. His enemies were many, and they were subtle, powerful, and clever, and Everett did not doubt that he had only seen a fraction of what they could achieve, but he had the thing they did not: he had the Infundibulum, the jump gate, and the ability to work them both. He was the Planesrunner. Now he understood the sudden impulse to perch at the very top of St. Paul's Cathedral. He wanted to show Sen something magical and moving, and he wanted to show himself that he had no fear of heights and perils, but most of all, he wanted to show the city—and all the world—that he had power.

"First we get my mum and Victory-Rose." It was all clear, all simple. "Remember when they found us back there, on the ice? Every time we make a jump, every time someone opens a Heisenberg Gate, every time someone uses a jumpgun, it leaves a trace. They followed the trace and sent the hovercraft. When Charlotte Villiers shot my dad, it'll have left a trace. I don't know how the jumpgun works . . . but the people who made it do. And I have an idea where they are. I'll find that trace, I'll find my dad. I'll get us all back together again."

"And what then?" Sen asked.

"I take us all somewhere far, far beyond the reach of the Order, and we'll never think about the Infundibulum or the Heisenberg Gates or the Plenitudes and Panoplies. We'll live happily ever after in one world and one world only."

"Yes, Everett Singh, but I meant, what about us? What happens to us? The ship, and Mchynlyth and Sharkey, and Annie and me. Where do we go?"

The brilliance flickered. Everett's confidence wavered. His cheeks burned, not with cold, but with embarrassment.

"I . . . I don't know," Everett said.

"And, 'scuse me for saying, but I think there's a bijou flaw in your scenario. If every jump leaves a trace, wherever you go, they can follow you. Just an observation, like . . ."

She was right. Sen had struck the brilliant plan at its weakest point and it had shattered. The sun vanished from the uppermost part of the cross on top of the cathedral. It didn't look like gold any more. The twilight had come and Everett was very cold.

"But I know you, Everett Singh," Sen said, as if she knew the hurt she had dealt out so casually. "You'll think of something, and it'll be brilliant."

In two sentences, Sen restored him. He would think of something. He recognized then that what he had felt as confidence had been over-confidence. His enemies were powerful and had the resources of ten worlds behind them. But he had one advantage. The Order—whatever it was, whatever its plans and fears—could follow him, but it could never preempt him. Everett would always be one jump ahead. That was enough of an advantage to be brilliant. He was the goal-keeper who always knew which way the ball was coming.

"So, what do you think of my London?" Everett said.

"I think it's magic, Everett Singh."

"Sen, I, uh . . . you know the way you gave me the tarot card?"

Instantly she was defensive.

"What have you done with it? Have you lost it? If you've lost it—"

"No no no no . . ." Everett patted his chest. "It's in there."

"Next to your heart. Dally."

"Well, I made something for you . . . Here, put these on."

Sen frowned at the ear buds but hooked them in.

"I made you a mix." Everett tapped up the playlist. "I can't really give it to you because it won't play on any of your technology, but, well, I just . . ." He stroked the play button. Everett had been working on it for days. It had been a welcome distraction from the hours of coding and freezing as *Everness* shut down more and more systems to conserve power. Mathematics and music use similar parts of the brain, Everett knew. Richard Feynman, the physicist, and one of Everett's geek heroes, had been a world-class bongo player. So making a playlist for Sen had been a rest from coding without let-ting that part of his brain freeze solid. From what he had heard

booming out of the Airish pubs along Mare Street, or blasting from
Sen's latty—"it doesn't use that much power," she had complained,
"and anyway, music's a right, like air and water"—Everett had
picked up an eighties, electro, danceable vibe. Electronic without
being techno. Crunching rhythm guitars. Slap or synth bass right at
the front of the mix. Horn sections, but none of the sax solos that
made Everett wince at 90 percent of his dad's embarrassingly fat col-
lection of eighties music. Foursquare rhythms, without being thud
thud thud. Not a hint of any kinds of anything beat based, like hip-
hop, trip hop, drum'n' bass, or grime. It was very white music.
There was music on his player that hit those same groove buttons.
And he found, as the days wore on and the temperature dropped and
lines of code seemed to sway like tangled snakes, that he looked forward more and more to those moments of careful choosing.

On top of St. Paul's Cathedral, like a lord of London, Everett
Singh watched Sen smile and nod to the rhythm in her ears. Then
her face clouded. She pulled out the ear buds. Everett thought he
saw tears in her eyes.

"I'll listen to it later."

"I'm sorry, I just thought you'd like it . . ."

"Oh I likes it, Everett Singh. I likes it too much. That's why I
can't listen to it, not right now. It sounds like home . . . but it's not
home, savvy? Like this city, it's magic, your London, but it's not home.
And I sees this all, and I hears this, and I thinks, I can't have that, not
ever again. It's gone. I asked you, Everett Singh, what happens to us?
What does happen to us? Does I get to live happy ever after too?"

All that remained of the day was a glow of red along the west of
the world. Everett stood at the center of a web of light, streets and
traffic and railways. With the shapes of buildings lost in the deep-
ening darkness, with London reduced to glowing bones, it could be
any city, anywhere, any world. This was not his home anymore. Sen
and he were outcasts, exiles together. His stomach turned, his breath
caught in his throat. The city at his feet wasn't his anymore.

Everett pulled on the safety line and hauled the hedgehopper down from where he had parked it, hovering up among the seagulls and impertinent pigeons. He buckled the flight harness around him.

"I'm sorry Sen."

"Look, it's not your music . . ."

"I know it's not the music. It's everything. That's what I'm sorry for."

"Don't be." Sen's voice was suddenly fierce. Her emotional weather, always changeable, had grown stormy. "I can live with it. We all can live with it. It's our way. We take what we're given and we live it the best we can. That's what Annie says, and she's right." She reached up and hauled down her own hedgehopper. "Go on then, Everett Singh. I'll be right behind you." Everett held her eyes for a long moment, saw truth there, then pulled on the throttle cable and stepped off the high lintel into the clear, cold night air.

11

They descended out of the deep blue twilight to land on the path between the Victorian tombstones. Everett had circled the landing zone twice to make sure it was clear of dog walkers. They wouldn't look up. No one with a dog on a lead ever looked up. He landed lightly on the trodden snow, Sen behind him. Stone angels stood around them, heads bowed, hands folded. They wore halos of snow.

"Let's get these out of sight."

They towed the hedgehoppers to the back of the chapel. Snow had covered the old condoms and cigarette butts and needles that always pile up around the backs of remote, disused Victorian buildings. Someone had built a smiling snowman, given him a snow arm, and plonked an empty beer can in it.

"Okay," Everett said. "Here's the plan. I go and I get Mum and Victory-Rose. I call the ship. By the time I get them back here, *Everness* will be over the extraction zone." He'd picked up the expression from *Call of Duty: Modern Warfare*. "The captain picks us up and I jump us out of here. We're in another universe before anyone notices. Simple."

"Can I say something? Your plan is good but there's one thing wrong in it."

"What?"

"You said, *I* go."

"That's what I said."

"What do I do?"

"You stay and keep an eye on the hedgehoppers."

"You'll need me."

Everett bit back his exasperation. "This is Hackney."

"This is your Hackney."

"In my Hackney, if you don't nail a thing to the ground, someone will steal it."

Sen scowled.

"Don't like it," she growled. "But all right." Then, without word or warning, she grabbed Everett by the shoulders and kissed him hard on the lips. A head shorter than Everett, Sen had to go up on her tiptoes to reach him. Before Everett could react, before he even properly realized what was happening, she broke. "For luck. And love."

Sen looked very small and lost, a smudge of grey in the snow, part of winter herself. She held up a hand in blessing. Everett's lips still tasted of her—honey, apricots, her strange Sen musk—as he hiked off down the cemetery road beneath the bone-finger branches of the trees.

Home drew Everett. He broke into a fast walk, a run. Stupid and treacherous in snow, but Everett's feet knew every pebble and crack in these paths. He had never been afraid in this graveyard. Ghosts, vampires, undead rising—Everett considered these superstitions to be so stupid as to be unthinkable. The Victorian dead slept deep and very, very sound. They made good, peaceful company. Through the main gate, across High Street, over the railway bridge, along the common, and into Roding Road. He could run the whole way. *The Traveler Hasteth in the Evening*—one of Sen's cards, picture of a determined man in eighteenth-century breeches and hat striding along a path that wound away out of sight. The traveler hasteth because his journey has been longer and has taken him further than anyone can imagine, but home is close, very close. He saw himself at the end of Roding Road, he saw himself at the house. Would he ring the bell or just go round back like he always did? Open the door and just walk in. His mum would be singing the wrong words to songs on the radio. Victory-Rose would be having her dinner. What would he say?

Stop what you're doing and come with me. Get your coats, take some jewellery and some small, portable, valuable stuff you can sell. No you won't need a passport or a phone or money. Come on. You're in terrible, terrible danger.

Why should they move even a muscle?

Because he'd come back. That was enough. *I can explain everything, if you'll just come with me.*

Everett's breath hung in great, warm clouds as he ran along the central path between the snow-hooded tombstones. Then he saw the figure between him and the gate that opened to Stoke Newington High Street and he stopped. The figure was little more than a dark silhouette against the yellow backdrop of streetlights, but the size, the shape, the way it stood, its clothes: everything about it said *be afraid now.* The dark figure stepped into a pool of light from the security floodlights Hackney Council had put up. In a flash Everett understood everything.

"No," he whispered. He turned. He ran. After only a few steps, Everett yelped in pain, clapped a hand to his left shoulder. Something had stung him like a hornet. He smelled burned fibre, burned flesh. Without breaking stride, Everett glanced over his shoulder. The other him, the enemy, the Anti-Everett was following him calmly, deliberately along the path. He aimed his finger like a gun. Everett dived and rolled by instinct alone. Snow is not a soft landing. Snow does not cushion a fall. Snow hides hard things, sharp edges in it. Everett cried out as his ribs hit hard against an edge of broken tombstone. He saw a thread of red light flicker in the dark. A physicist's son knows a laser when he sees one. The beam wavered, then slashed toward him like the blade of a sword. Everett rolled to safety behind the plinth of a Victorian funeral angel. Tree branches fell to the path, precision severed. That first beam had winged him. If it had struck home, it would have burned a hole clean through him, cutting him in two.

A laser couldn't cut through solid stone. *Could it?* Everett decided not to hang around for the result of that experiment. He scrabbled in the treacherous snow, trying to find his footing. His side ached. He'd have an incredible bruise there. He hoped that was all he would have. Go. *Go.* Keep your head lower than the height of the tombstones, if you want to keep it at all.

"I can see you!"

His voice, calling him. Taunting him. His own *voice.* On what world had they found him, this other Everett? What had they told him? What had they promised him? What had they *done* to him?

Everett ducked as the tortured air shrieked behind him. Something streaked over his head, then a blast of white, an explosion, kicked the wind out of him, deafened him, and sent him staggering. Stone splinters ripped the side of his *Everness* Baltic jacket. The stone angel was shattered and smoking. Only the feet, toes still buried in snow, remained.

Go. *Go.*

Lasers fanned across the sky. Branches and twigs fell in cascades of glittering snow all around Everett. He put his arms up to ward off the debris and kept running.

"I can take this whole place down to the ground," the voice called.

Think. Think. Thinking is what will save you. Nothing else. He is me. Everything I know, he knows. And everything he knows, I know. That's an advantage. A small one, the only one. Everett knew he could never defeat his double in open combat. He had to neutralize those weapons, get him onto the street, in public, where he couldn't be seen to use them. Everett moved deeper between the trees, slipping from tombstone to tombstone, taking the long, sneaky way around to the main gates and the bright lights and busy traffic of Stoke Newington High Street.

Missiles streaked in. Everett ducked behind a mausoleum. Through the iron grating that protected the Victorian dead he saw a line of explosions light up the night. Trees were burning. Tombstones were toppled like dominoes.

"Don't think so," the Anti-Everett shouted. Everett saw his enemy advancing through the glowing smoke and mist. *What you think, he thinks. What does he want? He wants the Infundibulum. That means he can't kill me. He can't risk damaging Dr. Quantum. He doesn't know if I have it on me or not. That's his disadvantage. That's my advantage. And I have another advantage. He doesn't know that I'm not alone.*

Slowly, silently, Everett crept away from the cover of the mausoleum.

At the first explosion Sen cried out. Then she saw the red beams sparkle among the treetops and heard wood splinter and fall. She fidgeted and skipped in nervous frustration. Was that Everett's voice? What was he shouting? When the trees lit up with flashes and clouds of glowing smoke rose against the sky, she could wait no longer. She slipped into the hedgehopper harness and snapped it shut. The power meter stood at 20 percent. Plenty enough for flight and for fight. One last thing before she pulled the throttle cable. Sen unzipped the top of her Baltic suit and took out the Everness tarot. She kissed the deck and then, with long-practiced ease, cut the deck one handed and turned up the top card. Two knights, one in black armor and one in white armor, faced each other with shields and spiked maces. *Be My Enemy.*

The greatest enemy, the final enemy you face, is yourself.

Then she opened the throttle, pushed forward the steering bar, and went swooping up around the red-brick spire of the Abney Park chapel. From above the cemetery's treetops Sen took a bearing on the fighting. It was dark down there, with close-packed trees and jagged stone monuments. No problem. She had flown a two-hundred-meter-long airship in tougher conditions than this. Lasers stabbed between the trees. Sen pulled back on the steering bar and dived the hedgehopper down toward the cloud of laser-heated steam.

"Everett!" He stood where paths crossed. Sen pushed the hedgehopper into a hover. "Is you all right?"

Why was he standing in the open? Why was there no destruction around him? Why was he wearing different clothes? Why did he have his jacket off and his shirtsleeves rolled up in the middle of winter?

Wrong here. Very, very wrong. Sen slammed the steering bar hard right as Everett aimed at her. His right forearm opened. Fire leaped toward her. With one hand Sen grabbed the red handle of the monofilament line. In the slowed-down time of ultimate crisis, her racing mind said *find a weapon*. And *get out*. She assessed the situation in the split second before the missile impacted. She hit the harness release and fell toward the bank of ploughed-up snow as the hedgehopper exploded.

Hope it's not hiding anything . . .

Hard . . .

Nothing could have been that painful. There must have been a curbstone or a plinth in that pile of slush. But she had to move. And quick. Sen came up into a crouch. The missile had not struck the hedgehopper dead center. The left fans had been blasted away; the remaining two had sent it into a crazy death spiral. Everett—no, the other Everett, the white-knight Everett to the black knight who was her Everett, watched the wrecked aircraft come down in a cluster of grave markers. For a moment his back was turned. Gritting her teeth against the pain in her side, Sen unlocked the monofilament line. She cracked it like a whip.

The other Everett whirled at the sound and movement. Tree branches fell around him, sliced through by the monofilament. Sen cracked the whip again before the other Everett, the Un-Everett, could turn one of his weird, scary weapons on her. A neat row of birch saplings planted along the edge of the path toppled, felled two meters from the ground. A telegraph pole slid apart, its severed upper third held up by the lines. Sen reeled the line back in and spun it above her head. Branches fell in a circle around her. The Un-Everett ducked under the spinning death line. He pointed a finger.

Sen dived behind a tombstone. The laser sizzled into the snowy woodland. She peeked up and sent her line cracking toward the Un-Everett again. He was fast, as fast and agile as her Everett, her black-knight Everett. She saw the Un-Everett's arm open. Sen leaped for fresh cover as the missile blasted the tombstone to stone splinters.

"Everett Singh!" she yelled. "Everett Singh! What did you have for Christmas dinner?"

Everett saw the hedgehopper flash between the trees like a white stone angel raised from a tomb. Then he saw the brief yellow stab of the missile trail and heard the explosion. He saw the remains of the hedgehopper spiral and yaw crazily before crashing down into the tombs. He almost cried out. Almost leaped up and ran to help. Almost. Everett forced his head down. He forced down the awful sick shock in his stomach and the horror in his heart. Keep down, stay down. He had glimpsed something fall from the hedgehopper in the moment before the blast. He had seen that. He had. Sen was all right; Sen had to be all right. So he forced his head down and peered through the rusted iron bars of the mausoleum, hoping to catch a glimpse of Sen, even though he was almost certain no one could survive that fall.

Then he saw tree branches fall. He saw saplings topple and a telegraph pole slump and bounce on its wires. He saw the lasers sparkle in the shed snow. He saw the flash and felt the blast of a missile strike. Everett ground the numbers in his mind, estimating size, storage capacity, trying to work out how many missiles the Anti-Everett had left. And then he heard the voice call his name twice and ask: *What did you have for Christmas dinner?*

He hadn't felt anything like tears in his eyes when he feared she might be dead, but they came when he was certain she was alive. Everett wiped them away on the sleeve of his Baltic jacket. He gulped twice before answering. He didn't want Sen to hear the tears in his voice.

"Pheasant!" he shouted back. His voice croaked with emotion anyway. He thought, *you clever, clever girl. One question tells you I'm alive, that it's the real me, and where I am.* "Pheasant makhani with saffron rice and naan bread!" And he crouched and ran. He rolled to cover as the missile took out the mausoleum behind which he had been hiding. *One more missile wasted*, Everett thought.

"I'm armed!" Sen shouted. Everett heard trees snap and crash, followed by the shriek and blast of a missile. *Another one gone.* Everett picked up still-warm chunks of blasted stonework, made a run, and pelted them as hard as he could at where he calculated his enemy to be. Lasers cut across the shrubbery, leveling bushes. A young holly tree caught and burned. Everett dropped down into cover behind the headstone of a Victorian sugar magnate and heard a whip crack ring out in the freezing air. Sen must have salvaged the monofilament cutting line from the hedgehopper. That was a hell of a weapon. And she seemed to have a good idea of how to use it. Lasers lashed out crazily. Sen was keeping the Anti-Everett down. It was a stalemate, but it couldn't last. Explosions, firefights in Abney Park Cemetery; eventually the police would come, and they were probably on their way already. *That might suit this Anti-Everett just fine*, Everett thought. He had good reason to suspect that the Anti-Everett had been recruited by Charlotte Villiers. If he and Sen were to fall into the hands of the police, Charlotte Villiers would bring the power of the Order to bear on her political connections, just as she'd done during the police investigation of his dad's kidnapping. Everett needed to get them out, and get them out fast.

Then, crouched behind the stone slab, ankle deep in the snow, he knew what had to be done. It was simple. It was brilliant. It required only the ability to see everyday things in a new way, and it required mathematics. He took out his phone and tapped it on. Signal strength, full bars. When Tejendra had given him Dr. Quantum, the second thing Everett had done was to sync it to his phone. The first thing he had done was take it over to Ryun's to show it off.

"Look, this means I can control it remotely from my phone," he had said.

"You came over here so I can watch you do some recreational coding," Ryun had said. "Even for a brother geek, this is deeply boring."

Not now, Ryun Spinetti. Five taps gave him control of Dr. Quantum, which was on the bridge of the airship hovering over White Hart Lane. He had used the same process to put together his playlist present for Sen—how embarrassing had that been? Now came the tricky part, the bit that required the time to think carefully, time he did not have. He had to open the Infundibulum and access its database of jump points over a slow, expensive, data-limited cell-phone line. The jump point to White Hart Lane was still in the Jump Controller's memory. From that he could work out the jump code for his current location. Everett opened up the GPS. It was horribly hungry for battery power.

Every Heisenberg Gate opened two ways. When he had opened the gate to a street in E2, a scrap of newspaper had blown through from that London. Water had gushed in a torrent from the flooded city of E8. And a Heisenberg Gate didn't have to be big enough to send an entire airship through. It could be as small as two people. It did have to be very precisely fixed though, so that it wasn't ten meters up in the air or three-quarters buried in the ground with the dead Victorians. And fixing the location of the Heisenberg Gate would be tricky, given that Everett would have to do so while hiding from his laser-armed, missile-firing, evil cyborg twin from a parallel universe.

Everett's calculations were interrupted by the cemetery's sudden silence. He looked up. *It's too quiet*, he thought, suddenly alert the possibility of a sneak attack.

Goalkeeper reflexes. The laser tore a searing line across Everett's cheek as he threw himself away from the dark shape that rose in front of the dark trees. It burned. It burned like hell. He scrabbled to find cover behind a gravestone, scooping up snow to soothe his seared left cheek.

The same goalkeeper reflexes saved the Anti-Everett. It might have been the sound of the line singing out, or he might have sensed the movement of air on his skin. He, too, had to dive for cover when Sen's monofilament cracked like a whip, slicing an arm and half a wing from one of the stone angels. Very slowly the angel's head toppled forward and fell. Again Sen cracked the whip. She took the top ten centimeters clean off the tombstone behind which the Anti-Everett had taken cover. Everett saw a figure in an orange flight suit skip nimbly to a new hiding place just as the Anti-Everett popped up, popped open his arm, and took out the little praying cherub behind which Sen had been sheltering.

"Sen!"

"Everett Singh!"

"Give me cover."

"I got his lilly dish, Everett Singh."

Everett pressed his back hard against the cold stone and turned to his phone. His cheek hurt. His cheek hurt like nothing he had known before. He would have a scar there. A real laser burn, not like the fake one Tejendra had claimed. It would forever mark him as different from his double.

He heard whip cracks and missile fire. How many of those things did the Anti-Everett have? But each blast was followed by a whip crack. Everett did not know what he would do if he did not hear that ultrasonic crack of monofilament. *Don't try to know*, he told himself. *Do what you have to do. Do what only you can do.*

He went into his Mathika software and was inputting his GPS coordinates when—Output . . . Output . . . Output—the signal bars wavered, then died.

"No!" Everett Singh yelled. Lasers turned the branches above him to matchwood. He hunched his shoulders against the rain of smoking wood. Full bars again. Output: a jump-gate destination

code. He exited Mathika. So slow, so slow, so *slow*. And opened the
Jump Controller. Inpoint, outpoint, aperture diameter. He dialed in
three meters. Duration. His fingers hesitated. How far away was Sen?

"Sen!"

"Omi!"

Flashes lit the night. Was there anything left of Abney Park
Cemetery? But now he knew where she was. Everett set the duration
to ten seconds.

"Sen, the white light."

"What?"

Everett hit the *Jump* button. White light lit up every angel and
cherub and weeping child in Abney Park. Everett peeped over the
edge of the tombstone. The Heisenberg Gate was a disc of blinding
white light standing among the shattered cenotaphs and mau-
soleums. He saw Sen, a blur of orange, hard to see in the glare. Had
she made it through? No time. Everett leaped from his cover and
hurled himself at the gate. At the edge of his vision he saw his
enemy come out from behind the maimed stone angel, arm raised,
fingers pointing. Everett dived into the light . . .

. . . And hit *Everness*'s deck hard. He rolled. Laser light burned an arc
across the far wall, then the Heisenberg Gate timed out and closed.
Everett fetched up hard against Sharkey's communications desk.
Sharkey was on his feet, taking a fire extinguisher to the burning line
the Anti-Everett's laser had cut in the hull cladding. A monitor dan-
gled, spraying sparks, its angle arm lased through.

"'Our holy and our beautiful house, where our fathers praised
thee, is burned up with fire,'" Sharkey said, foaming out the blaze.

Captain Anastasia was on her knees beside him. Her eyes were
wide with concern. Her hands were strong and soft and knew where
the hurt was.

"Sen, medicine chest."

"No time!" Everett winced at the pain in his ribs, his chest, his cheek. *You're alive, that's what that says.* "They can follow us through!"

Captain Anastasia frowned. Everett insisted: "Every time we make a jump, we leave a trace. We jumped from Abney Park, straight to here." Did no one understand? Was everyone shocked, or just stupid? "We have to move the ship!"

White light filled the bridge. A glowing disc hovered a foot from the ground, directly in front of the great window. Sharkey dropped the fire extinguisher and swung the shotguns from his coattails.

"Sen!" Captain Anastasia shouted. "Full reverse thrust!" Sen's hands were already on the control levers.

The white disc cleared. The ship's crew looked through a circular window into a dark, rock-walled chamber. Desks ringed the gates, lit flickering blue by computer monitors. A squad of men and woman in black, wearing black soft caps, stood at the foot of a metal ramp, weapons sloped. Behind them were figures too familiar to everyone on the bridge: Paul McCabe, scruffy in an ill-fitting suit, and Charlotte Villiers, deadly in sharp-tailored clothing and killer make-up.

"Come on my dorcas!" Sen yelled, her whole, small weight behind the thrust levers. "Come on dolly polone!" Slowly, very slowly, *Everness* moved. Two hundred meters of nanocarbon hull, cargo holds, batteries, and ballast was heavy inertia to overcome. Slowly, very slowly, the open jump gate began to drift toward the great window. *Other way around*, Everett thought. *The jump gate is staying where it is. It's the ship that's moving away from it. It's all relativity.* Charlotte Villiers realized what *Everness* was doing. Everett heard her yell a command. The soldiers hesitated. The hesitation defeated them. The jump gate passed through the great window and hung out in midair. The squad commander, the blonde woman Everett recognized from his previous skirmishes with Worldgate 10's private army, realized the mistake and dashed up the ramp to the very edge of the portal. For a moment Everett thought she might jump, then the ship separated completely from the gate. Still Sen leaned on the thrust levers, inching *Everness* away from the open Heisenberg Gate. To Everett it seemed like a group of soldiers standing in midair, ringed in brilliant light.

"We need to jump," he said.

"You're in no fit state," Captain Anastasia said.

"You don't understand!" Everett yelled before remembering the look in the captain's eye, the tone in her voice, the last time he had challenged her authority on her own bridge. "Ma'am, with respect, we need to make a Heisenberg jump. They've got someone with my mum and sister. They've got an agent."

"Him," Sen said. "It's him. From another plane. Him. Everett. But . . . zhooshed up. He's got shooty stuff."

"We have to jump out of here."

Everett forced his aching bones up from the floor. Captain Anastasia planted a hand on his chest.

"Where would you take my ship, Mr. Singh?"

Everett almost slapped the restraining hand away. Captain Anastasia felt the strength gather inside him and widened her eyes. Everett remembered what Mchynlyth had said, that she had learned French martial arts from the masters of Marseilles. In this universe, the French didn't have martial arts.

"Do you remember when we were caught between Charlotte Villiers and the *Royal Oak*?" One hundred meters off the prow, the Heisenberg Gate turned to a disc of solid white, shrank into a blinding white dot, then vanished into the clear night air. Captain Anastasia stood up. "Do you remember?" Everett asked again. "I wondered, if the same way that Charlotte Villiers can open a jump gate to the bridge here, because we always leave a trace of where we've been, maybe the jumpgun leaves a trace, too, a memory of all the gates it's opened. And one of those, one of those would open wherever my dad is." Everett struggled to his feet. He hurt. He hurt worse than he had ever hurt before, even after the toughest football games, when the other team smacked up the goalkeeper when the referee wasn't looking. He felt like he'd been in a war. He was in a war. He was still in a war. He would always be in a war, him and everyone he met and everyone he loved and every life he touched. Fifteen days ago, Tejendra had been lifted from outside the ICA, only fifteen days ago, and Everett was tired, so so tired. What had Sen said when Captain Anastasia had turned up her card *The Traveler Hasteth in the Evening*? Far to go before I sleep? "I can't do that. Mchynlyth can't do that. I need to take the jumpgun back to the place that made it."

"Where is that, Mr. Singh?"

"It has to come from one of the nine worlds of the Plenitude."

Captain Anastasia nodded.

"I don't know for certain."

Captain Anastasia raised an eyebrow.

"I think . . . I believe . . . I believe, completely and absolutely, that it comes from the plane you call E1."

Shock: it's not everyone gasping at once or reeling back in horror or throwing their hands up; shock is a thing you sense like electricity, a thing you smell like a change in the weather. Shock is a chemical thing.

"E1 is embargoed, Mr. Singh," Captain Anastasia said. "Completely, absolutely."

"We have to go there."

"From the ghouls and the frights and the dreads of our nights, the Dear and his dorcas deliver us," Sen said. She clutched the Everness tarot tight in her hand, pressed against her heart. At the same time, Sharkey said, "'So will I send upon you famine and evil beasts, and they shall bereave thee: and pestilence and blood shall pass through thee; and I will bring the sword upon thee.'"

"All inter-plane traffic to E1 was closed down fifteen years ago," Captain Anastasia said. "The Heisenberg Gates were sealed. No one knows what for. But I would hazard it's mighty dread to quarantine an entire world. And you propose to take my ship and my crew and my daughter there."

"Yes," Everett Singh said. There was no other answer. So many requests he had made of Captain Anastasia and her ship, so many demands and dangers, and he could see no end to them. And as he thought that, he knew that she had come to the same conclusion, that the only way to end this was to go through it, wherever it led, all the way.

"Well, I know we can't stay in this world very much longer," Captain Anastasia said. "Mr. Singh, take us out of here." She found an undamaged microphone. "Mr. Mchynlyth, power to the jump gate. In your own time, Mr. Singh."

Everett opened up the Infundibulum. It was a simple matter to find the point in E1 that corresponded to this position over White Hart Lane football ground. He slid it into the Jump Controller. The board lit green. He hit the button.

Voom, went Everett Singh.

12

Silence in the streets of London. On Clapton Common and Park Manor, only the sound of crows insulting each other. From Wingate Estate came the scream of cats fighting, loud as gunfire in the still air. Pigeons hooted. In the distance dogs howled, their voices strong with the wolf within. No thud of subwoofer bass from the boy racers on Sterling Way, no shriek of jets inbound for Heathrow and Silvertown. The dawn sky was clear, hard blue, pure January. Not a jet trail scored it. Nothing moved in the air or on the Earth.

Sen swiveled the brass track ball and sent the little survey drone diving down Stamford Hill. Buddleia ran rampant in the gutters and on the flat roofs, a forest of skeletal branches and twigs and the dry brown brushes of last summer's purple flowers. Grass sprouted in thick clumps from the curbstones and cracks in pavement. Tree roots had pushed up the paving slabs. Debris from fallen shop fronts littered the pavements: shards of cracked plastic shop signs, piles of broken glass. The windowless shop fronts were like the empty eye sockets of skulls. A few cars stood abandoned at the roadside. Their windows crumbled sugar glass. Their upholstery was mottled green and sprouting with moss and weeds.

Sen gave a little cry and put the drone into hover. Everyone saw what had made her stop, a glimpse of a pale limb. She turned the cameras. A doll, lying like a murder victim on the street, one arm outstretched. Her plastic hair was matted thick by the elements. Her eyes were the worst; black emptiness.

You were loved once, Everett thought.

Plane to plane, world to world, point to point. *Everness* arrived at the same geographical coordinates from which she had departed

Everett's world: one hundred meters over White Hart Lane. The two stadiums could hardly have been more different. These roofs sagged, and in places they had collapsed altogether. One of the floodlight towers had fallen. The pitch was a jungle of weeds, shrubby growth, and choking buddleia bushes through which traces of white lines and markings could be glimpsed. The goal nets were tattered. Crows perched on the crossbars. This was a dead stadium in a dead city.

"Calling London, calling London," Sharkey had repeated over and over, one headphone pressed to his ear. "'Then said I, "Lord, how long?" And he answered, "Until the cities be wasted without inhabitant, and the houses without man, and the land be utterly desolate."'"

Captain Anastasia had gone to the great window. She had clasped her hands behind her back and looked a long time out over the desolation. Empty streets, empty cars, and empty houses. An empty city.

"Tomorrow," Captain Anastasia had ordered. "No one's looking for us here, so let's get what sleep we can. We're going to need it, I think. Latties and hammocks. Tomorrow we solve mysteries."

Everett swung in his hammock for long sleepless hours. So much, too much. So many worlds, so much running and fighting. His head reeled: another him. A doppelganger. A ringer. A cuckoo in his nest. Of all the things Charlotte Villiers had done, this was the sharpest and cruelest. He did not doubt he would find his dad, out there somewhere in the Panoply of worlds. But to take another him and turn him into . . . what? Some cyborg killing machine? To think that that was staying in his house, sleeping in his bed, living with his mum, and with Victory-Rose . . .

No one can sleep in a dead city. The silence was louder than any traffic roar or storm.

In the morning, Everett scrambled the last of the eggs for breakfast. The crew devoured them on the bridge while they looked for signs of life in the dead city and answers to the mystery of what had killed it.

"Captain," Sharkey said, and the tone in his voice made Everett tear his eyes away from the scene outside the window. The fork paused halfway to his mouth. "Aft cameras." Sharkey flicked the image to the monitors. Everyone pulled down a magnifier in front of the tiny display tube. Everett felt his stomach freeze in a moment of insane dread, the dread of seeing something so different, so strange, so *wrong* that your mind is incapable of processing it, and the only safe thing is to fear it.

Everness lay over White Hart Lane like a compass needle, her prow pointed north, her tail south. To the south, behind her, lay Leyton and, beyond that, the Isle of Dogs. In Everett's world, the Isle of Dogs was a city in its own right, complete with towers and conference centers and business parks. He had flown through them with Sen. That was Everett's world.

In this world, the Isle of Dogs was dominated by a towering spire, black as oil. Everett had seen pictures of the great Burj Khalifa in Dubai, his world's tallest building. This thing—more a spike than a tower—was five, six times the height of the Burj Khalifa. It was hard to tell exactly how tall it was; it dwindled to a fine, sharp point. It was like a knife thrust out of the heart of dockland. It stabbed the sky. On maximum resolution, its surface seemed to move and catch the light like flowing liquid. A dark halo surrounded it. Everything about it was wrong: its height, its sharpness, its geometry. Everett knew—everyone on the bridge knew instantly and by instinct—that this thing rising out of the dark heart of Docklands was the cause of this abandoned London.

"Bring us about, Sen."

Sen turned *Everness* slowly on her center of gravity.

"Mr. Mchynlyth, break out the drone."

The camera lifted away from the abandoned doll. Sen took the drone up quick and fast, speeding over the weed-choked chimneys of desolate Hackney Downs and dead Dalston. *My home is down there*, Everett thought. There are shrubs growing out of the gutters and pigeons nesting in the attic and all the windows are smashed and the carpets are soaked with rain. He remembered how horrible his real home had looked that time he had come back from meeting with Colette Harte and found the door broken down, everything trashed. He knew now who had done it, and he knew what she had been looking for.

The drone flew on, homing in on the dark spire. Now Everett began to see the little differences hidden by the huge differences that made this world utterly unlike his own. Those car skeletons: they were sleek and low and streamlined, like cars from futuristic science fiction movies. Where were the power lines, the phone lines, the cell-phone towers? The closer the drone came to Docklands, the more frequently modern architecture appeared among the older buildings. The buildings were shaped like clouds, or those strange, transparent creatures from the bottom of the sea, or flowers and seeds spun from spider webs and glass. They were no less abandoned than the old buildings of brick and concrete and steel, their glass walls fallen in so that all that remained were beautiful skeletons. Everett could see beneath the ruin that this had been a hi-tech world far in advance of his own. And something had destroyed it.

"Where did all the people go?" Sen asked.

The drone came in low over the old wharves and docks of the Isle of Dogs. There were no buildings, no roads, no conference centers or hotels or restaurants or water-sports clubs. Every exposed surface was covered with what looked like an oily black lava flow, tongues and ridges and fans of something dark and half liquid. Like lava, it was in motion. The flows and tongues oozed and spread, melting into each other, forming new, short-lived shapes and patterns that existed for a moment before collapsing back into the darkness. Bubbles, spines, cubes, delicate three-dimensional fans and paisley patterns, whirlpools and spirals and things that looked like flowers or turning gears or miniature cities. Sen took the drone close; the camera zoomed in. Everett saw that the surface of the blackness boiled with movement, that the patterns that emerged and submerged were made up of smaller, similar patterns, that the whole buzzed like a swarm of insects. Minute insect motion, patterns made up of similar smaller patterns. These were fractals, like the ones produced by the Mandelbrot Set that had given him nightmares of falling forever through endless mathematics.

He thought he had been afraid before. Now he knew real fear.

Sen took the drone up and away. She flew straight for the dark tower. Now the dark, smoggy halo that surrounded the spire came into focus. Birds. They were black birds. But birds that crashed into each other and merged and split apart into two birds again or a dozen smaller birds, or the birds would merge into one great flying thing that did not look so very much like a bird at all. Birds with more than two wings, or birds with whirring helicopter fans in place of wings. Birds that did things no bird could. They flocked like starlings around the drone, dashing and swooping around it as Sen carefully took it in.

The surface of the spire came into focus. Faces. It was made up of human faces. Faces embedded in the black, buzzing substance of the spire. Faces of men and women, old and young, children, babies, millions of them. Their faces were contorted, their mouths opened wide in a never-ending scream. The drone's microphones were small and basic, but they were sharp enough to allow that vast scream, made of millions of voices, to fill *Everness*'s bridge. It blasted into every soul. Everett knew he would never hear anything worse than that.

"That's where all the people went," he said.

Captain Anastasia strode to Sharkey's communications desk and cut the transmission. The silence was like an ache ending, but Everett knew that part of him would never stop hearing that endless howl that projected out over this dead London.

"'But the children of the kingdom shall be cast out into outer darkness: there shall be weeping and gnashing of teeth,'" Sharkey said. His voice was low and soft and full of the fear of God, or something worse that God.

"Miss Sixsmyth, recall the drone and power up the impellers," Captain Anastasia said. "I want us out of this dreadful place."

13

He woke with a shiver and a cry. Fire dreams, missile dreams, laser dreams. Graves exploding, firing flaming bones into the air. Angels falling on blazing wings. Burning trees.

This was no dream. This was remembering.

"Everett?" A knock on the door. That was what had awakened him, the knock, the name.

"In a minute." Everett M tried to unscramble dream from memory. A fight. There had been a fight, in a graveyard. There was dirt under his fingernails, graveyard dirt. Among the tombstones and the trees and the weeping Victorian angels he had battled his enemy, his alter. Everett Singh. It all came to him in a rush. They'd escaped, done some smart trick with the Heisenberg Gate they'd stolen. God, it was cold. Had the heating broken? Everett M put his hand on the radiator and pulled it away with a yelp. It was on full. Cold and starving. So, so starving. He had gone through an entire box of cereal when he'd come home after the battle of Abney Park but it hadn't even begun to fill him. And the shower, to get rid of the dirt and the smoke, the leaf litter and the blood from flying stone chips that had grazed him, hadn't even begun to touch the core of ice at his heart.

The door creaked open. Laura's head peeked in.

"Everett! Someone to see you."

"If it's Ryun, tell him I'll see him later."

"It's not Ryun."

"Look, I don't want to see those two cops this time of the morning. Either they believe me or they don't."

"It's not the police. Are you going to get up? She's been here for twenty minutes."

She. Everett M dived out of bed, scrabbled for jogging pants, a T-shirt that didn't smell, and flip-flops. He was running his fingers through his hair as he went through the living room door.

Charlotte Villiers was sitting in Tejendra's chair. Laura Braiden glared at her. Charlotte Villiers ignored the dark looks. She was dressed elegantly, with lace gloves and a small hat. She had put up her customary veil. Her legs were crossed at the ankles. Her handbag was neatly aligned with her red high-heeled shoes.

"There's a Bosnian saying that if you put your handbag on the ground you'll never have any money," Everett M said. He'd gotten the saying from his friend and classmate, Alia Vedic. Alia's Dad had escaped from the siege of Sarajevo in 1992, settled in Stoke Newington's Yugoslav refugee population, married, had two daughters, and then Alia, one of Everett M's best friends at Bourne Green school. That was what had happened in Everett M's world. In this world, Alia had walked past Everett M on his first lunch break in the E10 version of Bourne Green. Alia hadn't even glanced at Everett M. Charlotte Villiers smiled, but the bag remained where it was.

"I'd like a cup of tea, Mrs. Singh. The day's not begun without one, don't you think?"

"Braiden. Mrs. Braiden," Laura said.

"Darjeeling," Charlotte Villiers said to the closing door. She smiled at Everett M. "That was an impressive mess you made of Abney Park Cemetery. Fortunately, since the riots it's easy to blame such things on disaffected local youth. Disappointed, Everett. Very disappointed." She bent down to take her compact from her little bag. She snapped it open and surveyed the state of her make-up. She seemed satisfied.

"Oh, sit down. You're not in school." Charlotte Villiers shut the compact with a loud clack and put it away. Everett M had not noticed that he was still standing. He sat down on the edge of the sofa. It was impossible to be comfortable in Charlotte Villiers's presence.

"Who did you tell her you were?"

"Social Services."

"Social Services don't dress like that."

"They ought to. That's the general problem with this grubby little world. No class. You let him get away, Everett. The Infundibulum has eluded us."

"He opened a Heisenberg Gate. He was out of there like a rat up a drainpipe."

"We know. We tried to inject a team through the quantum echo. Twenty seconds sooner, we would have had them on the bridge on their own airship."

Everett M remembered the viral video, passed around phone to phone, of the airship floating over White Park Lane.

"Are they still here?"

"Of course not. They jumped off this world immediately."

"Where did they go? You said you could follow their trace."

"E1."

In the upholstered, centrally heated living room of 43 Roding Road, Everett M felt a shock run out from the center of his spine. E1: ghost world, hell planet, place of demons and monsters. Banned. Quarantined completely and for all time. The only things that came off E1 were rumors and urban legends. Everyone knew the stories. No one knew the truth.

"But—"

"Must you question everything I say? Do you think our interdictions mean anything to these criminals? They can go anywhere they want. Your alter is clever. Very clever."

Everett felt his jaw tighten, his teeth clench. *Yes, tell me again that I'm the dumb one, the useless one.*

"He has the jumpgun—my jumpgun, and he's worked out where I got it from," Charlotte Villiers said.

"You've been to E1?"

Now Charlotte Villiers tightened her jaw in annoyance. *I can get to you*, Everett M thought. *Good. I'll keep needling you with those so-so-dumb questions.*

"It came into my possession," Charlotte Villiers said. "We have a mission for you. It will be difficult and it will be dangerous but, frankly Everett, you have much to prove."

Everett felt his stomach tighten in dread.

"You're sending me to E1."

"Yes."

"To E1."

"Yes."

"To hordes of insane killer nanobot assassins."

"Everett, whatever urban legends the over-fertile imaginations of Fifth Formers send wafting through the corridors of Bourne Green School, I assure you, they're very far from the truth. It is all arranged. I will be temporarily taking you into care—for observation. We're not convinced you've recovered from your trauma. It will only be for a day or two. Our story will be quite convincing. I have all the proper documentation."

"Who are you?" Everett M asked. "You're not the Plenitude."

The living room door opened. Laura entered with a mug of tea in one hand and a plate of toast in the other.

"No Darjeeling, Charlotte."

"Ms. Villiers."

"I hope Earl Grey's okay."

The corner of Charlotte Villiers's mouth gave a tiny twitch of displeasure at the sight of the Tottenham Hotspur mug.

"Would you like some toast, or maybe some cereal?"

Charlotte Villiers looked at the plate as if she had been offered toast spread with dog turd.

"I find the idea of eating in the morning nauseating," she said. "Thank you, Mrs. Braiden."

"Are you all right, Everett?" Laura asked from the open door, with the plate of toast in her hand.

"Thank you, Mrs. Braiden," Charlotte Villiers said again.

"I'm okay," Everett M said. "Mum." The word was not so hard this time. "Really. Can I have that toast?" Hunger was gnawing him. Laura set the plate on the arm of the sofa and closed the door. Charlotte Villiers set the tea mug on the coffee table and waited before answering Everett M's question.

"I assure you, I am the Plenitude, Everett. I am Plenipotentiary from E3 to this world."

"What you did . . ." Those words were still difficult. Everett hated the thought that his body had been taken and used and engineered to other people's wills without his consent, without him even knowing. "What happened to me, did the Plenitude order this?"

Charlotte Villiers sighed. "There are many worlds, Everett, but politics is the same everywhere. We have theories, philosophies, schools of thought, and opinions, and they naturally form groupings—not quite political parties, more like shared interests—and goals. Think of them as clubs—societies, orders. I, and my alter, Charles, are both members of one particular order, along with many others, on all the known worlds. We are even beginning to attract members on this world, even though it is still not yet an official member of the Plenitude. Therefore, their membership, and my activities beyond my official duties, as well as your presence and purpose here, are subject to a degree of secrecy. It's regrettable but necessary. Our concern is the ultimate security of the Plenitude and seventy billion human lives."

"Your alter said there are forces beyond the Known Worlds that make even the Thryn look puny."

"Yes. We have evidence of other entities in the Panoply that, if they had access to the Infundibulum, could endanger our survival as a species. But you must understand the seriousness of our mission: I am a mathematician, Everett. Does that surprise you? I am a Maestra of Ars Mathematikal and Algorithmikal from Cabot College, Cambridge. I have a set of Schinken-space multidimensional algebraic

groups named after me: the Villiers Set. Your alter would understand. Thus, I achieved mathematical immortality. But I lacked the
single-mindedness to become one of the true gods of mathematics.
Perhaps it requires a particularly male mindset, perhaps I simply
desire more from a life than chasing dusty theorems down long corridors of abstraction to the end of my days. You may mistrust me in
my role as a servant of the Plenitude, but as a scientist, believe me
when I say that opening up the Panoply of All Worlds is the least of
what the Infundibulum can do. The very least. The threat is to
reality itself."

The toast did not look so appealing to Everett M now.

"I don't know what to believe," Everett M said.

Charlotte Villiers smiled. Everett M thought he had felt cold
before, when the lasers sucked all the energy out of him. It was
nothing to the absolute zero of Charlotte Villiers's smile.

"Then we're getting somewhere. We are right, and we are good.
You'll come to see that. So, if our methods seem harsh now, it's only
because we know that, in time, you will come to see that we are
right, and work with us for the love of that." She glanced at an elegant, jewelled watch, ignoring the time that pulsed on channel display on the flat-screen television. "Your mission, Everett M. We
asked too much of you. You are, after all, very young and inexperi-
enced. But we're giving you a chance to redeem yourself. We need
you to plant a tracking device. Every time your alter makes a
Heisenberg jump, he leaves an imprint in the universal quantum
field. We can find where he goes, but not where he goes after the
jump. Airships are just such versatile devices. You will jump back to
E4, where Charles will equip you with a tracking device. It utilizes
the phenomenon of quantum entanglement. Through it we will be
able to locate your alter on any world in the Panoply he cares to
jump to. All you need to do is affix it to the hull of the airship. You
won't come into contact with your alter, isn't that a relief? My alter
will also fit you with some new equipment from Madam Moon. To

go to E1, you'll require some . . . augmentation." Charlotte Villiers slipped her bag onto her arm and stood up. She pulled down her veil, glanced in the mirror over the mantelpiece to adjust the set of her hat. "The police will pick you up here at five o'clock sharp. They'll ensure your mother isn't worried. You will be returned as soon as the mission is complete. Please thank your mother for her hospitality, and maybe suggest that she buy some Darjeeling. Good morning. Do not fail us again, Everett."

14

He woke, bolt upright, instantly awake. Gasping, staring. *What, where?* A glance at his surroundings did little to ease his disorientation. He was in his own hammock, swinging gently in his tiny latty as the wind moved *Everness* at her mooring, but something wasn't right. *A scream.* He'd been awakened by a sound that had started as low whimpering before erupting into a full-throated shriek of fear and horror. For a moment Everett thought it had come from his own throat. No, he could hear breathless, fearful panting. It came from the latty next to his. Everett pulled on warm layers and went to rap a knuckle on the door.

"Sen."

"What?"

"Are you all right?"

"Go way."

"You're awake."

"I's all right"

"I thought I heard—"

"I said, *I's all right.*"

Everett stood, forehead pressed against the nanocarbon. He felt the door being unbolted.

"No I's not."

Sen had wrapped herself in the quilts from her hammock. She looked very small and pale in the dim cabin lights. Her eyes were wide and scared. Sen's latty was the usual mess of dumped clothing, discarded equipment, ropes and lines and pieces of paper with ideas for tarot cards. She clutched the precious deck in a hand like a claw. Her beloved bare-chested rugby players looked down from the posters tacked to the walls. Everett smelled stale air, girl sweat, underwashed bed sheets, strange musks, and Sen scents.

"What is it?" She looked tiny in the faint glow of the night-lights. Everett wanted to hug her to him, but he knew she would have hated that. She was so fierce, so defiant, so independent.

"I had a dream, right? Meese dream." Sen shivered. And not because of the winter cold stealing from *Everness*'s huge empty spaces into the warm little latty. "I don't want to go back in there, no no. I don't want to go back to sleep, not ever again, no. Come with me, Everett Singh. Sit with me. Keep me from sleeping." She swept her quilt around her like a monarch's robes. Everett ducked into his latty to gather quilts from his bed and a little paper bag of his latest batch of semolina halva. With his signature dish of hot chocolate with a hint of chili heat, it never failed to lift Captain Anastasia's mood. It might do the same with her adopted daughter.

Sen led him down to the cargo deck. Everett's breath steamed. Condensation dripped from every rail and upright. Sen turned the dial on her wrist control. The loading platform lurched, then descended smoothly. The cold almost took Everett's breath away. The night was absolute, pure dark without a single light. The sky was clear, and it seemed to Everett, riding the platform down, that he was surrounded by a halo of stars. Sen stopped the platform.

"Come on, Everett Singh." She sat on the edge, her legs dangling into the dark. She pulled the quilts and sheets tight around her. "Does you have a place, Everett Singh?"

"What do you mean?"

Sen patted the deck beside her. Everett sat down. He gingerly extended his legs over the gulf. The stars were magnificent. Everett had never seen skies so dark, not even in the Punjab, when Tejendra had taken him to visit his extended family in India.

"A *you* place."

"I do, but it's not on the ship. It's . . ." The word almost choked him. The shower, under the warm water, where all the best ideas and clearest thoughts came together; the quiet sunny corner of the garden, where he could sit all summer long in shorts and nothing else and drink in the heat; the desk by the window in his room, where he could look out over the street. Gone. Not just gone, taken away by someone who looked like him, talked like him, smelled like him, sounded like him, liked the things he liked, laughed at the things he laughed at, knew the things he knew. But who wasn't him.

"Home?"

"Yes." He tried to keep his answer flat, unemotional, cool. But you can't lose your home, your family, your world to an evil double without emotion creeping into your voice and cracking it.

Sen swung her legs. "I loves it here. It's good to have nothing under you. Disconnected, like. Gravity free. I gets things clear up here. I heard them, Everett Singh. The people in the tower. I heard. They were right in my room, oh and they were calling my name and there was one voice, one among all them zillions on the tower, and when I heard it, I knew how they knew my name."

"We're miles away, Sen. It's gone."

Captain Anastasia had not ordered the impellers off Full Ahead until the black tower of faces was far below the horizon. Even then, she had driven the ship on over the empty land. They had only stopped because Mchynlyth had spotted a line of old wind turbines striding along a chalk ridgeline and had demanded that Captain Anastasia moor where he might steal some power. The land far below Everett's feet was what remained of the county of Oxfordshire.

"I'm in there, Everett. That's how it knew me. That's how it knew my name. I know it. Remember when you told me that there were many mes, out there in all them worlds. And I argued back and said that there's only one of me, I's unique. That's not true. I knows it. I heard her, Everett. She's in there with all the rest of them, and she can't get out, and coz she can't get out, she wants to die. But she can't die either."

"It was a dream, Sen."

"No it weren't. You saw those faces. You heard them. I heard her. She was there. She was me." Sen swung her legs over the darkness. She chewed her lip. Everett slipped the bag of halva out from under his quilts and covers.

"Have some. I made it. Pistachio and cardamom. Your favorite." He rattled the bag. The rustle of paper was the most ordinary, silly sound in all the universes. The madness and the darkness drew back a little. "Everett's halva . . ." He waggled the bag, trying to entice her. Sen took a piece but did not eat it.

"I heard more, Everett. I heard you."

Then Everett felt the chill that was not night or winter, the chill of something terrible and monstrous and completely beyond his explanation.

"That's why they closed this world, ain't it?" Sen said. "Do you think there's anyone left at all? I's scared if we stay too long, we end up in that big black tower, me right next to me, screaming together."

"Don't say that, Sen."

"Why did you bring us here, Everett Singh?" The anger cracked in her voice like a whip. Everett knew he would never get used to how suddenly and sharply Sen's moods changed. "I hates this world and it scares me. Why are we here?"

"We won't stay here a second longer than we have to. That's a promise."

"Whatever you's looking for, whatever you think you going to find here, it ain't here. There's nothing here."

Sen was saying everything Everett feared.

"It is. It has to be."

"Nothing 'has to be,' Everett Singh." Sen took a bite from her cube of halva. She chewed a couple of times, pulled a face. "Don't taste right."

"It's the same as I always make it."

"Don't think so, Everett Singh. Tastes like an omi with stuff in his head made it. Like you mixed in all the things that scare you and make you uptight and make you feel like you can't do anything, and sad and dark. Things that don't taste good. Bitter things." She lobbed the remains of the halva out into the night. "Sorry Everett."

"He's with my family. He's with my mum and Victory-Rose."

Sen said nothing. The condensation that had settled on the loading platform was beginning to freeze.

"He was me," Everett said. "And they did something to him to make him my worst enemy. What did they tell him, how did they get him to have all that done to him? There's no world in the Plenitude where people are born like that. And my mum, and Victory-Rose, and all my relatives, and everyone at school, and all my friends, they think he's me. They think I came back. He just walks in and takes over my life. Every single bit of it. And he beat me."

"Nah, you fooled him. That was a bona trick. I didn't know you could do that, open up a gate thingy right onto the bridge. Fantabulosa."

"He beat me, Sen. I went to get my mum and my sister. He knew I was coming. How did he know? Because he's me. He'd do exactly the same thing. I went to rescue them and I failed. And because of that, they're worse off now. They'll be expecting me to try again. They won't let them out of their sight. And you know? He wasn't even half trying. He has enough firepower to blast Stokie to slag. He could have cut us to pieces. He gave us a kicking and he wasn't even trying."

Everett felt Sen's weight and warmth against him. Her hair tickled his face.

"I never thought about that. Not really. What it's like to be you. Planesrunner, all that. You hear it and you go, wow, that's dead exciting and all, but, well . . . I still has all this. The ship, Ma, the omis. Family."

"I'll get them back." Everett's voice was fierce with determination. "All of them. Mum, Dad, everyone. You asked me why I brought us here? Because here's where it changes. Here's where we stop running. Enough running, enough being chased by navy airships and hovercraft and aeroplanes and by Charlotte Villiers and my evil assassin twin. Here's where we stop, and we find what I know is here, and when we find that, we don't run away any more. We take it to them. We fight back."

"Any more of them halva things, Everett Singh?" Sen asked. Everett presented the bag. Sen took one, bit into it. She nodded in approval.

"Maybe it was just bad in bits. This one tastes bona." She stood up and pulled her quilts around her. "I'd get up if I's you, Everett Singh. Don't want to lose your dally legs." Everett swung his legs up as the hatch began to close. It sealed out the stars and the night and the cold with a solid clunk.

"You coming Sen?" he called from the spiral staircase back up to the accommodation deck.

"I's going to stay here a bit, Everett Singh," Sen called up.

"It was only a dream," Everett said.

"No it weren't. I don't want to dream it again. Sometimes, I sleeps down here, right at the bottom of the ship, with the air beneath me. Sometimes, if it's like Amexica, you wakes up with the hull plate warm under your cheek and you can smell all the green growing things and the ocean in the air. Stay with me, Everett Singh."

"What?"

"It's all right, I's not going to charver you nor nothing. Just sleep. Don't want to go back to that latty, not tonight. Don't want to be on my own." She curled up on the nanocarbon hull like a cat in winter curled up on itself. "I's cold, Everett Singh."

Everett gingerly settled down beside Sen, pulling his quilts tight around him. Sen was right; two were warmer and cozier than one. He curled up around her, all the while wondering if this was right, if this was wrong, and what made right or wrong in the world of *Everness*, an Airish airship lost on a hostile alien Earth. Right here, right now was all the world there was, and its rules were in front of him. He folded an arm over Sen, bundled up in night things.

"Everett Singh?"

"What?" He pulled back his arm as if a snake had lunged at it.

"When you knocked me door."

"Yes."

"When you heard . . ."

"Yes, you—"

"Shut up. Listen, Everett Singh, you never hears that again. Never ever never."

15

Everett woke stiff and sore on the hard cargo deck. For one moment he couldn't think where he was. For the second moment, he couldn't remember how he had got there. Memories raced back. Sen, her feet dangling over empty space, lobbing halva out into the darkness. Sen's cry in the night. Sen warm against him, like a kitten curled up in the corner of a sofa. Sen was gone, and he was very cold. Everett got to his feet. Every bone creaked. He had a headache. He never had a headache. He tried to knuckle bad sleep from his eyes and saw Mchynlyth, watching him with amusement over the top of his mug of tea. He poured a second mug and nodded for Everett to join him.

"How long have you been here?" The tea was very strong and very hot. Everett cupped his hands around the mug—Tottenham Trojans—and let the warmth seep into his joints.

"Long enough," Mchynlyth said.

"She had a bad dream," Everett said. "She needed someone to be with her. She didn't want to go back to her latty."

"Oh, I dinnae doubt it for a moment. She's gets her own way a little too much, that polone, and because we're crew, not family, she thinks she's a lot more grown-up than she is. She thinks she don't need anyone to look after her, but she does. We all do. Sabi, Mr. Singh?" Mchynlyth slid a wrench across the workbench to Everett, huddled in his quilt and blankets. "When you've that down ye, you can give me a wee hand getting that big mill working so we can grind out some electricity. Make yourself useful."

But Everett had been too thick with drowsiness to be anything other than useless. The day was bright, but he was dumb; the sky was clear, but his head was not; the cold was sharp, but he was dull.

Then he had dropped the wrench for the third time. When he went down the tall white shaft of the wind turbine, Mchynlyth shouted down at him.

"And where do you think you're going wee lad? Send the wrench up on the line, you keep yer lally tappers firmly planted on terra firma. You're as much use to me today as willets on a boar."

A new figure was descending from *Everness*'s open charging hatch, riding the line down, coattails fluttering and the slipstream tugging at the feather in his hat: Miles O'Rahilly Lafayette Sharkey.

"You can hunt up something decent for dinner," Mchynlyth shouted. "I'm getting a wee bit weary of saag channa, nae offense."

Sharkey touched ground lightly, snapped off his drop harness, whipped a shotgun out of the coattails, and threw it to Everett. "Ever handled one of these before?"

Everett caught the gun cleanly—damn sure he wouldn't let Sharkey make him look like a handless middle-class idiot. He broke it, like he'd seen Vinnie Jones do in that old gangster movie *Lock, Stock and Two Smoking Barrels*, and hung it over the crook of his arm. Sharkey touched the brim of his hat.

"You're mighty spry around the kitchen, sir. 'And he will take your daughters to be confectionaries, and to be cooks, and to be bakers,' in the words of the Dear. But in my philosophy you ain't no real cook until you've cooked what you've killed yourself. Man cooking. Let's go hunting."

The wind turbines stood along a ridgeline. The short turf of the ridge was pockmarked white with the chalky debris from rabbit holes. Sheep, wild and scraggy, fled from Sharkey's approach. The wind that the turbines had been designed to catch was finally blowing the fog from Everett's head. The day was gloriously clear, and he could see for miles and miles. The land fell off the long ridge into scrubby valleys. To the south were further parallel ridges; to the north was open, flat farmland—or what had once been farmland. The land carried the patterns of fields, but hedgerows had grown into tangles of thorn and beech and the open spaces were rank with winter-brown weeds and scrubby growth. Roofs and chimneystacks rose from overgrown gardens. Some roofs had collapsed altogether, leaving the timber joists exposed to the air like the broken ribs of a decaying animal. Everett saw light glint from the glass of distant windows. There was not a sound. No rumble of traffic from the highway Everett could see cutting through the chalk downs. No chug of tractors or SUVs. Not even the bellowing of cows in the overgrown fields. No sound but the whistle of wind in the turbine blades high over Everett's head and the croak of rooks.

"Rabbit," Everett called. Twenty yards away, a lookout for a warren dug under the concrete footing of a wind turbine twitched its nose.

"I've a hankering for something a little more toothsome," Sharkey said. "This way." He turned off the ridge and followed a sheep path down into a narrow valley. Within twenty paces, scrub elder and sycamore saplings had closed overhead. The branches were bare and stark against the clear January sky. Sharkey held up a hand. Everett stopped dead. Sharkey motioned for Everett to stay where he was. He had seen something through the tangled branches. Everett could see nothing. Sharkey raised his shotgun and walked forward. Something exploded out of the undergrowth in front of him. Everett saw a dark object flash into the air and whirl over his head. Then he heard Sharkey's gun fire twice and saw the thing tumble from the air in a shower of feathers. Sharkey grinned. Smoke still leaked from both gun barrels.

"Now that's fine manjarry," Sharkey said. "Bring her back, Mr. Singh."

Everett found the bird in a bracken brake where the dense valley vegetation gave way to the poor grazing of the water-starved ridge top. It was a cock pheasant, its breast shattered with lead shot, limp and dead but still warm, still oozing blood. Sharkey inspected the bird, looked pleased, and tucked it into a pocket of his great coat.

"My daddy had this theory . . . more a philosophy, a rule of living, really. When we were growing up, we never ate fur, fowl, or fish he hadn't killed; he either butchered it or hunted it. And when we got bigger, that we'd killed ourselves. I reckon each of us Lafayette Sharkeys was born with a fishing rod in his hand, and when we got old enough to handle a piece without blowing our own feet off, we'd hunt most days. Must have killed and cooked near every darn thing flies or crawls or swims. You see, my daddy believed that if you eat meat, which is a critter's life, then you must be prepared to take that life yourself. To buy a piece of meat from the store, that wasn't just a dishonor to the dumb beast whose life was given for you, it was an act of cowardice."

"I used to cook with my dad," Everett said.

"Every man should know how to feed himself, or a passel of coves."

"I've cooked mussels." Chop the shallot fine and sauté them in the butter, add garlic and a glass of wine and, while it's still steaming, throw in the mussels, alive alive-o. When all the shells are open, they're done.

Sharkey smiled.

"Then you understand the principle."

"But I also think that if you do kill something, then you must eat it. It's just as big a dishonor to kill for the sake of killing."

"There's plenty of critters kill for the sake of killing," Sharkey said. He reloaded his shotgun.

The sun rose toward its full winter height and Sharkey and Everett worked down the valley into the flat lands beneath. Three times Sharkey stopped and lifted his hand when he sensed some movement, some presence, some thing in the scrub that Everett could not. He lifted his gun but did not fire again.

"Sharkey, back in your world, when we were trying to make the run to Germany, would you really have handed me over to the sharpies?"

"Yes, I would have, Mr. Singh. And I believe I owe you an explanation for my action. I am not a good man. Never have been, never will be, despite the word of the Dear on my lips and in my heart. I've done bad things, Mr. Singh. Shameful things, terrible things. Miles O'Rahilly Lafayette Sharkey, weighmaster, soldier of fortune, adventurer, gentleman. I've been all those things, and in every one of them I was sinful and faithless. I was a damned soul, cursed to wander the Earth without hope or home. 'Wandering stars, to whom is reserved the blackness of darkness forever.'"

"I heard a story that you killed your father because he slapped your mum at the Peachtree Ball."

"Where did you hear that?"

"Sen told me."

"'Deliver me from the hand of strange children, whose mouth speaketh vanity, and their right hand is a right hand of falsehood.' Do you not sabi by now that half of what that polone tells you is lies? The trick is learning which half. No, Mr. Singh, many sins may drive a man from his hearth and his home. I was a vagrant soul for many years, sufficient that you know that I can't go home again. Captain Sixsmyth found me on the streets of old Stamboul, a soldier of fortune, a freelance agent, a man with money on his head, and she gave me that home, and hope. That ship up there, that's the closest I'll ever get to heaven. And I am loyal to it, if nothing else, and I will let nothing threaten it, and I will do anything to keep it safe and free and flying. I owe it. I have my own amriya, as these people say. Nothing personal, Mr. Singh."

"Of course not, Mr. Sharkey." *And you would do it again*, Everett thought. *Without hesitation, or even a thought that you had done anything wrong. I'm safe now because we are all in danger together, but when the moment arrives when it is me or the ship, you will sell me. And it won't be personal. It'll be an act of old Deep South honor.*

"Shh." Sharkey raised his hand. They had come out from the valley onto an old, abandoned country road, so overgrown it was a

tunnel beneath overarching tree branches. No hunting here: Sharkey
turned off through a collapsed farm gate into a field. "Hare."

"Where?" Everett whispered.

"There."

Everett sighted along the line of Sharkey's pointing finger. A
hare it was, upright and suspicious, at the very far edge of the field,
where it ran up against the overgrown verge of the lost highway.

"You'll never hit it from here with a shotgun," Everett said.

"'His going forth is prepared as the morning.'" Sharkey tucked
away his shotgun. From a pocket in his coat that Everett had never
seen before, he drew an elegant, silver-handled revolver. From
another secret place he took out a long metal tube that he screwed
onto the barrel of the revolver. From the poacher pocket where he
had stashed the pheasant, he took his cigar box. With a twist he converted it into what looked like a wooden rifle stock. One click and it
locked to the handle. The revolver had become a bijou rifle.

"Eisenbach of München in Old High Deutschland. Finest damn
gunsmith in the world—or any world, for that matter." Sharkey
took a firing position, aimed, slowly let out his breath. The shot rang
out. The hare dropped cold, dead. *Rifle bullets travel faster than sound*,
Everett thought. It was dead before it could even hear the killing
shot. Everett fetched the hare. From alive to dead in a moment. He
had seen that moment, that little jerk, that tiny spurt of life stuff as
Sharkey's precision shot went clean through the hare's head. It would
not even have known. Death was not knowing. It was nothing. No
thing. The hare was still warm in his hands. Its fur was very soft.
Everett felt blood wet his fingers. Sharkey's father had been right. It
was a moral thing, to only eat what you are prepared to kill.

"Never cooked hare before," Everett called. The absence of any
machine sound was eerie. His voice sounded loud and wrong, as if
every plant and cloud and living thing took offense at it. Sharkey
beckoned Everett over. With two deft strokes from his knife he
opened and gutted the hare.

"Hang him for a day or two and he'll be bona." Sharkey walked on, scanning the hedge line, toward the chimneys of an abandoned farmhouse that rose from a tangle of overgrown garden shrubs. "Might be some layin' fowl around here. Chicken is a national passion among us Dixie boys."

The sound was low and soft and carried far and clear across this haunted England: the swoosh of blades cutting through air. Everett looked behind him. Up on the hill, the wind-turbine was turning. Everett thought he saw a figure, no more than a speck, riding up from the rotor hub toward the open power hatch in *Everness*'s belly. He waved, though he knew Mchynlyth could not possibly see him. The airship hung over the ridge like a cloud.

"You coming, Mr. Singh?"

The house had been a country retreat. A dead Audi stood on the weed-choked gravel. Moss grew in the car's grooves and sills. Storm winds had tugged at the house's loose tiles, found weaknesses, and, over successive winters, stripped most of the roof. The attic had been converted into some kind of workspace. Peeling walls, peeling paper, and sagging plasterboard had collapsed down on top of desks and office chairs. The windows were all broken; rain-soaked, sun-bleached curtains wafted in the wind. Everett smelled rotting carpet and mold. Gardens and lawns were overgrown jungles. There was something blue and bloated and luminous and very, very dead in the leaf-clogged swimming pool.

Sharkey shook his head. "Don't look like much chicken around—"

The things came hard. They came fast. They burst around the corner of the house. Everett saw them, three dark, low bodies, at the same time that he heard Sharkey shout a warning. He acted without thinking. The shotgun clacked together, the safety slid off; he leveled and pulled the trigger. The recoil almost knocked him off his feet, but the blast blew the lead creature across the yard. The other two came on. Everett fumbled with the shotgun. At his side Sharkey pulled out the other shotgun. Two flat cracks sent clouds of birds up from the surrounding trees.

"All you all right, Mr. Singh?"

"Yeah." He had fired, had killed, without thinking. "I'm okay."

"Good shooting, sir."

Everett went to examine the dead things. The sawed-off shotguns were brutal weapons at such short range. The bodies were terribly mutilated, but there was no mistaking the creatures. Dogs. They were lean and mean and hungry. One had the foxy look of a terrier, another the perky ears of a sheepdog. The third was larger and had the curly coat and long ears of a standard poodle, but they all looked halfway between their original breed and their wolf ancestry. The canine DNA pool wasn't so much a pool as a shallow puddle. Within a dozen more dog generations, they would all converge on the wolf within.

Blackness leaked from the eyes and ears and nostrils of the dead terrier and formed a pool under its head. The pool was moving, seething, as if it was alive with millions of insects. Moving, piling up, changing shape. This was not blood. Everett stepped back. Now the black was pouring from the eyes and ears and nostrils of the other dogs, forming streams that flowed across the bricks of the drive, flowing toward each other, flowing with purpose and intelligence. The streams merged with the pool of boiling black that surrounded the dead terrier.

"To me, Mr. Singh," Sharkey said. Everett stepped away from the mass of seething black. "Can you reload a shotgun?"

"Yes, sir."

"Do so, expeditiously. You will need it."

Everett broke the gun and slid in two fresh cartridges. Sharkey kept both his shotgun and his revolver-rifle trained on the black. The surface was bubbling now. Shapes appeared out of the black, then broke apart and dissolved into the liquid. Shapes like tiny hands, and fox heads, and bird wings, and open jaws, howling out of the darkness.

The black shuddered and formed into the shape of a dog's head, straining to break free from the liquid. It slumped back into shapelessness. Then the blackness shivered again and sprang into being: a dog, wolf, hellhound, black and huge, head held low and hungry.

"'Upon her forehead was a name written, MYSTERY, BABYLON THE GREAT, THE MOTHER OF HARLOTS AND ABOMINATIONS OF THE EARTH,'" Sharkey said. "Get ye to the slime pits, spawn of Siddim!"

He fired, Everett a split second behind. The hell-wolf flew apart in an explosion of black liquid. Blackness dripped from the branches of the overgrown trees and ran down the front of the house and the sleek curves of the abandoned Audi.

"'And he shall purify the sons of Levi, and purge them as gold and silver,'" Sharkey declared, putting up his guns.

The drips of black ooze ran along the gaps in the brickwork of the drive. The trickles merged, flowed together into streams, into a pool around the dead terrier. It bubbled up into a blister, patterns raced across the surface, then it spasmed and snapped back into the shape of the black hell-wolf.

"Back out of here, Mr. Singh," Sharkey said. "Slowly. Keep me between you and that hell-spawned abomination. Do not take your eyes off it."

The hell-wolf crouched. Hackles rose. It bared black teeth. Black liquid dropped from its fangs. It growled. The growl sounded like dead things being torn open.

"Slow and steady, Mr. Singh. I have it covered. I can't kill it, but I can inconvenience it. How many shells do you have?"

"Four."

"The same, and what's left in the revolver."

Not enough, Everett thought. The hell-wolf sank lower, its legs tightening to leap.

"On my word, run. Run like every devil in the nine hells are after your soul."

"But Sharkey—

"You're the only one can get the ship off this God-forsaken world. Ready."

And the hell-wolf leaped. It seemed to fill all the sky, hanging in midair. In that moment, Everett knew that Sharkey was dead and he was dead and, worse than dead, they'd be devoured, possessed; they were doomed to be meat puppets to the blackness inside, like the dogs. And then there was a high-pitched screech that dropped Everett to his knees, the sound so sharp that he was forced to clap his hands to his ears. He watched as the hell-wolf turned into a big flying splash of black that dropped in heavy rain to the ground.

The air curdled like heat haze and turned into figures in helmets and battle packs and copper-colored combat armor. Six soldiers moved to surround Everett and Sharkey, weapons raised and aimed. Sharkey carefully set down his shotgun and rifle and raised his hands. He nodded for Everett to do the same. Two soldiers checked out the splash of black on the bricks. One held some kind of scanning device. The other aimed a gun at the black stain, a gun like none Everett had ever seen before.

"No activity, ma'am," said the figure with the scanner. "It's dead. Permanently." The second figure swung the weird weapon over its shoulder into a retaining clip.

One of the soldiers stepped forward and touched its collar. The elaborate helmet unfolded like an insect's mouthparts. *Very* Halo, Everett thought. Inside the armor was a woman in her early thirties with a square face and blonde hair going black at the roots. It was the kind of face you saw at an elementary school or looking for a parking space at Tesco, not in combat armor, having just splattered some evil dark liquid soul zombie all over the forecourt of a ruined country house.

"I am Lieutenant Elena Kastinidis of Agistry Unit 27, Oxford Command," the woman said. "You are under arrest."

16

E verett sat on the ledge of the medieval stone window and looked out over the quadrangle. Evening sent long shadows out across the neat lawns and raked gravel paths, out from the great specimen trees in the Fellows' Garden. The last of the daylight caught the steeple of the chapel and the towers where the college fronted St. Giles. As the darkness deepened Everett could see the defense field flickering like an aurora against the twilight.

"Hey Dad," Everett whispered. "Made it to Oxford."

Elena Kastinidis had been brisk and brutal after taking Everett and Sharkey into custody.

"Strip," she had ordered.

"What?" Everett had said.

"Strip," the officer said again, in a voice that would not repeat the order a third time. There was no place Everett could hide himself from the soldiers, but he could turn his back on Lieutenant Elena Kastinidis. Already Sharkey had removed his hat and was shrugging off his coat.

"'Blessed is he that watcheth, and keepeth his garments, lest he walk naked, and they see his shame,'" Sharkey quoted.

Jacket, shirt, and ship shorts slipped off. Everett unbuckled his Bona Togs boots and wiggled out of his leggings. He stood shivering in his underwear. There was no warmth in the winter sun, and the wind was keen.

"Everything," the lieutenant said.

"This is child abuse, you know. There are laws about this."

The soldiers laughed.

"Take them off, or I take them off you." Lieutenant Kastinidis tapped a combat knife buckled to the utility belt of her armor.

Everett hooked his thumbs in the waistband of his underpants and pushed them down. He stepped out of them, naked and exposed. This was hell. This was the hell of the Bourne Green changing room after a game. This was the hell of the noisy guys who didn't mind taking their clothes off around others, the ones who flicked towels and jumped on their friends when they were butt naked and wrestled them to the floor and grabbed each other's nipples and made animal hooting noises. This was the hell of the showers, of keeping your back to everyone in case the pummeling hot water had started anything you'd be embarrassed to show, of not knowing when you stepped out whether the others had hidden your clothes. It was the hell of shame and exposure and being completely naked and alone.

"Hands behind head."

Everett locked his fingers behind his skull. The soldier with the scanning device worked up from Everett's toenails to his scalp, carefully, slowly, minutely, circling him. The second, the one with the hell-wolf-killing gun, held the weapon twenty centimeters from the bridge of Everett's nose. Everett tried to keep his eyes from making contact with the eyes inside the helmet. Then the scanner worked over his clothes and boots, slowly, carefully, painstakingly. Everett held himself perfectly still.

"Clean. Nahn free."

The armed soldier swept the gun up and away and clicked it into a cradle on his back. *Naan?* Everett said to himself. *Like, Punjabi bread?*

"You can get dressed again," the lieutenant said.

Everett almost dove into his clothes. He hopped as he pulled on leggings and tried to jam on boots that seemed to fight against his frozen feet. The shivers started as he was fastening the frogging on his cavalry-style jacket. Glancing over at Sharkey, he saw the American pull on his caped coat. Two other soldiers held his guns. Sharkey put on his hat, adjusted the set of its feather to precisely the right angle, and straightened his cuffs. Dignity restored. Cool under fire.

Everett envied that. But he was still burning with shame, and he was angry. He flipped up the hood of his quilted great coat and took a step toward the officer.

"What was that about? What is this? Who the hell are you?"

Lieutenant Kastinidis took Everett's anger as lightly as February drizzle.

"That's not a question you ask me, boy. I ask you, and you answer. An Earth 3 Class 88 cargo airship up on Aston Hill."

"You know—"

"We've had you on radar since you first popped up over Northeast London. We'd better go have a word with your captain. Call him, let him know what's happened."

"Her," Sharkey said. "Captain Anastasia Sixsmyth."

Lieutenant Elena Kastinidis was unimpressed.

"Move out." She waved her armored troopers forward. They carefully stepped around the shiny black stain on the brickwork of the drive. Everett noticed that Sharkey had left the hare and the pheasant on the roof of the abandoned Audi. They didn't seem good eating any more.

Captain Anastasia raged. She raged at Sharkey for being captured. She raged at Sharkey and Everett for bringing sharpies back to the ship. She raged that armed strangers were holding her crew, her daughter, and herself at gunpoint. Most of all she raged that she was being issued orders on her own bridge

"This heading." Lieutenant Elena Kastinidis touched her heads-up display glasses and information flowed down her finger onto the palm of her hand. *Cool*, Everett thought.

"Make it so." Captain Anastasia almost spat the words. Sen hesitated. "Make it so!" the captain snapped. Sen entered the heading and pushed the thrust levers forward. Everett felt *Everness* tremble under him.

Lieutenant Kastinidis bent close to Mchynlyth's homespun

engineering rig that hooked the jumpgun and Dr. Quantum together.

"This I recognize." She tapped the jumpgun. "This I do not." She prodded Dr. Quantum.

"Don't touch that. It's mine," Everett said. At once he regretted it. But she had recognized the jumpgun. She knew what it was and what it could do. *My instinct was right*, Everett thought. *My instinct is always right.*

"I'll touch what I like, son."

It must be something about uniforms, Everett thought. Leah-Leanne-Leona and Moustache Mulligan had displayed the same sense of entitlement when they had sat in his mum's kitchen and demanded tea and toast after the disappearance of Everett's father. *No, not uniforms*, Everett thought. *Sharpies. They're the same the universes over.* He was starting to think in Airish, he realized.

"Go ahead," Everett countered, "provided you're comfortable with the possibility that hitting the wrong button could send us anywhere in the Panoply."

It was a lie; a jump gate couldn't be opened without the control panel, and Everett had password locked that, but it was enough to make Lieutenant Kastinidis step back from Everett's desk. She stared at him.

"Just who are you?"

"Everett Singh," Everett said. "And I's a navigator." He remembered the pride in Sen's voice when she had announced that she was *Everness*'s pilot. It was a glow. It restored a little self-worth after the humiliation at the ruined house. Sen glanced over at Everett from her position at the flight controls. She gave a tiny smile, flashed her eyebrows. *Bona omi.*

Lieutenant Kastinidis went to the great window and stood before it, hands clasped behind her back. Everett saw Sharkey bristle with rage. That was the captain's position, reserved for the master and commander of *Everness*. The ship flew low, two hundred meters

over the ruined land. Highways, factories, villages, and estates lay
abandoned to nature—or whatever nature had become. Sunlight
winked from dead windows. Everett's breath caught. Far ahead a
faint curtain of light flickered like an aurora on the horizon. It
looked like pale lightning arcing across the sky, forking and
reforking into glowing streamers, hard to see against the westering
sun, fusing and splitting into a web of light.

"What is that?" Everett asked.

"That's the Oxford defense field," the Lieutenant said. "So far the
Nahn haven't found a way around it. I don't think they're even
trying anymore. It's been over a year since the last massed assault."

"Nahn. I heard you say that word before."

"You did, son. And you'll hear it a lot more." Lieutenant Kastinidis touched a communications panel on the chest plate of her
armor. "Unit 27 to Oxford defense grid. We're on approach. You
should have us on visuals." A pause. "Yes, it's an airship."

Now Everett could see the city behind the shivering walls, the
low light catching the college towers, the chapel spires, the cloisters
and quadrangles and gardens, the parks and the glitter of the two
rivers running toward their meeting.

"Ahead slow," Captain Anastasia said, as if to remind herself
that she could still give orders. Sen pulled back on the throttles.
Everness drifted slowly over suburbs and streets as empty and
decaying as any in London. The airship was coming in from the
southeast, over the Thames and the water meadows around
Christchurch College. Ahead, the defense grid shivered like oil on
water. Outside were buildings like snapped, rotted teeth, pieces of
skull, and dead bones. Inside was movement, life: wind turbines
standing taller than the trees across Christchurch meadow, with
cows grazing at the rushy thin winter grass around their foundations; vehicles and pedestrians and even some bicycles; early lights
in windows. And along the line where the defense field touched the
ground, Everett saw a ring of black. Glossy, liquid black, frozen into

drips and splashes. It was the same black liquid that Everett had seen earlier in the day, splattered all over the driveway of a middle-class country retreat.

"It's an EM field," he said.

"Explain, Mr. Singh," Captain Anastasia said. *Everness* drew closer to the flickering lightning.

"An electromagnetic field. It scrambles compu . . . comptator circuitry. It'll fry—" Everett almost bit his tongue.

"Fry what, son?" Lieutenant Kastinidis said. She nodded. One soldier moved between Everett and Dr. Quantum. The other deftly unplugged the Infundibulum.

"No!" Everett yelled. The soldier restrained him. Sharkey was out of his seat. *Click click click.* Weapons drawn. Lieutenant Kastinidis turned Dr. Quantum over in her hands. She spoke into the back of her hand. "We're coming in, drop the field."

The wall of soft lighting flickered and went out. Looking down, Everett could see more soldiers in power armor spilling out of troop carriers to take up positions along the inside of the black zone. *Everness* slid slowly over the colleges of Oxford. The city had always seemed to Everett like the board for some complex intellectual game, the squares and cloisters and walls of the colleges. The architecture was similar to the Oxford of Everett's world—the spires a little taller, the quadrangles a bit bigger, the cloisters somewhat darker—but the arrangement was different. There were colleges here unknown in Everett's world. Sen maneuvered *Everness* in over the dome of the Radcliffe Camera and Broad Street, descending over peaceful college gardens to the designated mooring at Museum Road.

"Clear," Sharkey said. Lieutenant Kastinidis touched the back of her hand. Behind the ship, the defense grid sprang to life again, a ghostly wall cutting across the pastures and bare winter trees of the college meadows.

Everett went to Sharkey's rearview monitor and pulled it down on its swivel arm. He dialed up the magnification as far as it would go, zooming in on the blackness splashed up like dark winter slush against the shimmering defense grid. The splatter zone; the hell-wolf blown into black ooze by what must have been a focused version of this defense field; the black, seething, boiling mass crawling across the docks and wharves of Docklands, drawn by an evil tide toward that terrible dark tower. The patterns came together in his mind.

"Nahn," he whispered. "Of course. Nanotechnology."

The light was almost gone now. *Everness*'s navigation lights flashed beyond the chapel roof, moored over Museum Green. Those lights flickered against the aurora glow of the defense field. The darkening sky behind the skyline of towers and spires and college rooftops looked as if it burned with cold fire. Even in this empty, dark-haunted world, the university city was beautiful, like a last flame in a storm or a lone voice singing in darkness. Cambridge was the best science university, but Tejendra had been sent to Oxford. He had been the pride of the family. Look, our son, our boy at the greatest university! A Singh! A Bathwala boy! An Oxford physicist! It did not matter that they didn't understand what Tejendra did there; it was where he did it. Even if his path in time led away from that city, to London and a different university, Oxford was a thing about which Bebe Ajeet and her sisters could boast. If the family was disappointed that Tejendra had not made it to be a fellow there, the edge had been taken off of that disappointment by the certain expectation that Everett would. Two Singhs at Oxford! That would ring around the rafters of the Tottenham Punjabi Community Association until the end of time.

And here he was, the second Singh. In a medieval room, in a college, looking out over a quadrangle. But this quadrangle, this college were not of Tejendra's Oxford, and the door and windows of this medieval room were locked. Everett went to the door. He rattled it. Ancient oak, firmly bolted on the outside. "We're going to have to hold you until the prefect has a chance to speak with you," Lieutenant Kastinidis had said. The old college room was comfortable, if a bit studenty. Comfortable and very secure. Everett would have kicked the door, but five-hundred-year-old timber would have done more damage to him than he could have done to it.

A noise, behind him. A tap on window glass. He whirled. Sen hung upside down outside his window, framed by the twin arches. Her legs were twined around a drop line. Everett mimed puzzlement—*how did you get out?*—then helplessness—*can't you see it's locked?* Sen grinned upside down, fished inside the flap of her jacket and pulled out a thin, flat, finger-length paddle. She slipped it through the wooden casement, just above the lock. Everett knew what to do. He went to the window and carefully slid the paddle back to the outside. The monofilament line was almost invisible in the medieval gloom. One mistake could cost fingers. Sen took the handle, locked it to the other, and tugged sharply. The monofilament sheared clean through the metal lock. Everett swung the casement open. Sen made an elegant, slow somersault off her drop line and landed upright on her feet.

"Fantabulosa or what, Everett Singh?"

"Did you steal Mchynlyth's lock-pick?"

"Steal?" Sen looked offended. "Airish never steals off each other. T'ain't *so*. Borrowed. From each according to their ability, to each according to their need."

"That's Marx," Everett said.

"No, Mchynlyth's," Sen insisted, mishearing. "Aincha glad I did though?" She put a foot up on the windowsill. "Come on then, Everett Singh." She slipped a hand into the drop-line wrist loop.

"Where?"

"Up and out. I saw the sharpies taking Ma and Sharkey across the gardens. Come on before they see us." She touched her wrist control and shot upward. Everett barely had time to slip his hand into the foot loop and step off the window ledge before the winch whisked him up two floors to the roof. Sen had fixed the line around one of the medieval stone chimneys and clipped a pulley to the end of an iron lamp bracket. How had she made it up here in the first place? The uppermost line of windows was a good four meters below him, and there was a tricky roof overhang. Sen saw Everett checking out the drop and the precarious state of the guttering as she stowed the gear in her shush-bag.

"Climbed it," she said proudly. "You're pretty fit, but you couldn't do it. Come on, Everett Singh."

She was off, running so light and lithe that she hardly seemed to touch the roof stones at all. The shivering glow of the defense field made her look like a silver ghost, a sky fairy. Everett's footing was less sure. The flickering light made the steeply pitched roof treacherous. Everett was sure he felt the slate move under his foot. He froze. Sen was a whole roof ahead of him by now. She stopped to look back at him, one foot on the sloping roof, the other on the ridge of a dormer window, tapping impatiently. *Come on, Everett Singh. Trust your body. Goalkeeper instincts. It's just a different way of using them.* Everett took a deep breath. Don't look down, that was always Sen's advice. He looked ahead at Sen, hands on her hips. And he ran. His body felt out the different slopes and structures and slipperinesses of the roofs. Just like a real-life version of the *Assassin's Creed* video game. Sen grinned, then turned and ran, and Everett ran after her. She stopped where a nineteenth-century tower butted up against an eighteenth-century roof.

"I saw them take her in here." Sen slid down the side of a dormer window, grabbed the little ornament on the peak, and leaned out as far as she could to scan the front of the tower. "There's a balcony down there. I think I can make it from here. By the way, don't try and do this, Everett Singh." Before Everett could snark a reply, Sen was halfway up the tower, quick as a pale spider. Victorian Gothic architecture was rich in hand- and toeholds, but Everett's heart kicked in dread as Sen hauled herself up by her fingertips onto a ledge so narrow that only her toes rested on it.

"Why are you going up?" Everett whispered to himself as Sen pulled herself over the stone balustrade that ran around the top of the tower. She grinned, waved, struck a triumphant pose. Then he saw her strategy. Sen unpacked the drop line, looped it around the balustrade, and locked it. She slipped foot and wrist into the loops and rode the line down the face of the tower to land lightly on the little stone balcony. "And what about . . ." Everett whispered. Sen had done all this just for him. She connected the end of the drop line with her shushbag, swung it a couple of times to give it momentum, and lobbed the bag to Everett. He caught it, untied the drop line, slipped his hand into the line's wrist loop and one boot into the foot loop, and cast off. The corner of the tower loomed with terrifying speed. Everett grazed past it, swung over the crouching Sen, and pendulumed back and forth while she worked the wrist control with delicate precision to drop him on to the stonework beside her.

"There must be an easier way of doing this," Everett said.

"Maybe, but it wouldn't be as much fun. Look." Window and balcony were a Gothic ornament, built purely for decoration. The window was high in the upper level of a great double-height hall, all roof timbers and coats of arms and portraits of former students gone on to greatness: the Victorian notion of what the Middle Ages looked like. Through the glass Everett could see a table set along a raised platform and figures sitting in chairs behind it. In front of the table, down on the floor, were two seats. There was no mistaking the close crop of Captain Anastasia's dark head, and that hat, set on a side table, could only belong to Miles O'Rahilly Lafayette Sharkey. "Mind your fingers," Sen said. She slipped Mchynlyth's lock cutter from inside her jacket and slid one end through the gap between the window frames.

"How did you get all this stuff off the ship?" Everett asked. Lieutenant Kastinidis had been as thorough with the rest of *Everness*'s crew as she had been with strip-searching him and Sharkey. Down to the skin, and head-to-toe body scan, close and very personal. Everett had an idea now of what they were looking for.

"Airish got ways of hiding stuff sharpies know nanti about," Sen said, pulling back on the monofilament. The metal parted with a musical clink. "Nor ground-pounders neither—no offense, Everett Singh."

They gingerly opened the window. Inside was a narrow wooden gallery that seemed to have been built there for no other purpose than to make the place look the maximum in mock medieval. The gallery floor was thick with dust and the sun-dried corpses of dead flies—no one had been up here to clean for a very, very long time. Everett and Sen crept forward and crouched down behind the wooden railing. On the far left was Lieutenant Kastinidis, no longer armored but still looking the soldier in a close-fitting one-piece suit. Combat camouflage patterns flowed across it like water. The effect made her look as if she were constantly fading in to and out of reality. They had phased in from invisibility at the farmhouse, Everett remembered. Light glinted from circuitry at hand and ankle, neck and chest. *This was what they wore under their bronze battle armor*, Everett thought.

Beside Lieutenant Kastinidis was an axe-faced man with thinning hair and the most skeletal hands Everett had ever seen. He too wore military dress: a sharply tailored uniform, nipped at the waist, and pants neatly pleated, in a style that to Everett looked old-fashioned and at the same time futuristic and alien. A beret was tucked under his shoulder strap. A badge on the beret and flashes on his chest displayed three stars with a crown above them. Everett was no expert on military signs of rank, but from the crown and the upright way the man sat at the table and folded his bony hands, Everett guessed he was Lieutenant Kastinidis's commanding officer. At his side was a middle-aged woman. She wore silk robes with high collars, wide sleeves, and broad sashes. She was dressed like some fantasy empress, but she looked weary, endlessly weary. All attention was turned to her. Of the fourth person at the high table, Everett could only see a pair of hands. Dark hands. Everett moved to get a better look.

"Oh my God," he breathed.

Tejendra.

17

"Six billion people, Captain Sixsmyth." The robed woman's voice was soft and husky in the spaces of the great hall. Her words were clear and terrible. "Eighty percent of humanity is . . . no, not dead. It's much worse than that. Transformed. 'More than human,' the Nahn says—as much as it has ever said anything to us. All those people changed. Lost to us. We were bright and we were brilliant, Captain Sixsmyth. We shone. Our culture, our technology, our achievements, they were the envy of the Nine Worlds, even Earth 4—because they were our own achievements. Perhaps we were arrogant. Perhaps we were dazzled by what our Heisenberg Gates showed us of how different those other worlds could be. Perhaps it was because we were Earth 1, the first world to develop the Heisenberg jump—in this very college, Captain Sixsmyth. And we were the founders of the Plenitude of Known Worlds. We had to lead by example. Or perhaps we saw how huge the Panoply was—all those billions of other Earths—and knew we could never explore them all. There would always be another Earth beyond, and another, and another. For whatever reason, we turned away from the unimaginably vast to focus instead on the very small. It would be the final industrial revolution, the one that would give us command of all matter."

"Nanotechnology," Everett breathed in Sen's ear. They crouched close to the wooden railing at the edge of the tiny balcony, up in the shadows. "It's engineering things at the smallest scale, engines made of single atoms, smart molecules, machines smaller even than the tiniest virus."

"Everett."

"There's an idea in nanotechnology—a thing called a replicator. It's a kind of nanosized Von Neumann machine—sorry, you don't know what that is. Anyway, a replicator is a nanomachine that builds a copy of itself, and those copies build copies, and all those copies build copies. Pretty soon, you've got billions and trillions of copies, doubling every few seconds. It's slow at first, but it gets faster and faster. The replicators can eventually eat up an entire planet. Exponential growth. Powers of two are pretty scary math in the real world—"

"Everett, shut up. I wants to hear the dona."

"We developed a prototype nanotechnology replicator," Empress Woman said. "We modeled it on the most successful micro-scale replicator we'd yet discovered, a virus. You don't need to know the details. What you need to know is that it was brilliant. It was more successful than we ever dreamed, but we lost control of it. It turned on us. No, that's wrong. That's giving it some kind of will, some evil intelligence. It's only purpose is to duplicate itself and to find material to convert into more replicators. And because we had designed it from a virus, an organic thing, it looked for organic matter to feed from. Us, Captain Sixsmyth. We lost six billion humans. You've seen the dark spire on Canary Wharf. That is what remains of the population of London. Paris, New York, Beijing, Lagos, Cairo: all the same, all over the world."

"I've seen it," Captain Anastasia said.

Lieutenant Kastinidis spoke suddenly, her voice full of passion.

"You haven't seen it. Not really seen it. Did you look at the faces? Really look at the faces? Everyone has someone in there. Most of the people we knew and cared about are in there. I was a kid when the Nahn came, fourteen years old. My mum, my dad, my big sister, all my family—everyone I knew and cared about and loved—they're all in there. You've seen nothing. Nothing."

"Thank you, Lieutenant," the thin officer said. *Captain Skinny*, Everett thought. He had always made up his own names for people. "We were hit hard. We were pushed to the edge. We looked extinction in the face. But we're fighting, Captain Sixsmyth. We're fighting an enemy too small to see. We're fighting an enemy that blows on the wind like dust. We're fighting an enemy that can infect a living body and eat it from the inside out. We're fighting an enemy that can take any shape it wants. We've developed new technologies, new weapons, new defenses. It's not certain we'll win yet. There are so few of us left. We're scattered, divided, pushed to the edges, to the islands and the remote places we can defend. Oxford is our advance base, our invasion headquarters. It's where we come close to the enemy, where we watch what it's doing, what it's changing into, where we try to guess its plans and strategies."

"Of course," Everett whispered up on the gallery. "All those people—it absorbed all their memories, all their experiences. When the complexity gets to a certain level, bang! It wakes up."

"Is you getting off on this, chicken?" Sen said.

"We have communicated with the Nahn once," the woman said. "Or, rather, the Nahn communicated with us once, only once, a message broadcast to every surviving human outpost. 'It is the Nahn. It is the future of intelligence on this planet. It is what comes after humanity. Humanity's time is over. You are to consider yourselves the last generation of a dying species. The age of the Nahn has come and it will last forever. You are to accept this and be joyful for the part you have played in allowing the Nahn to come into being. Its purpose is to spread itself throughout this and every other universe, incorporating all life to make itself the ultimate intelligence.' Ninety words. Twenty seconds. Nothing since. Only silence . . . and the Nahn slowly assimilating all biological life. What did you hear about us, Captain Sixsmyth? What legends do you tell about us on your world? Environmental ravagement, technological meltdown, machine uprising, plagues of zombies?"

"Nano assassins that hide behind your eyes." It was Sen who whispered the comment this time.

"The Nahn is all of those and worse," Empress Woman continued. "Now do you understand why this world is closed, completely and permanently? We cannot ever let the Nahn off this world. Out among the Nine Worlds, it could never be contained."

"So we're concerned when an Earth 3 cargo airship turns up out of thin air over what used to be Hackney," Captain Skinny said.

"It would seem your quarantine isn't as tight as you think it is," Captain Anastasia said, lightly. Her words fell like stones through water. Every eye behind the High Table fixed her. There was a silence that could intimidate even Anastasia Sixsmyth.

"It wasn't enough just to seal the jump gates," Captain Skinny said. "We practice complete planetary hygiene. We have a code override on all our gate addresses. Anything trying to jump out of—or jump into—any of our Heisenberg Gates hits an automatic redirect. Instead of arriving at its destination gate, it gets rerouted to a jump point in the convective zone of the sun. Our sun, in another universe. Positions in space are different. Five million degrees should take care of any Nahn infestation. Or anything else for that matter." The officer let the implication of his words sink in. "So, Captain, tell me, why aren't you wisps of ash inside the sun?"

Everett saw Sharkey glance at Captain Anastasia. Her head gave the smallest of nods. It said, *trust me, I'm the Captain. Trust me like you trusted me when I challenged Ma Bromley to hand-to-hand combat on the bridge of her airship over the evil sands of Goodwin.*

"We stole a jumpgun," Captain Anastasia said with simple, direct honesty.

"This one?" Captain Skinny took the jumpgun from a concealed drawer in the back of the high table and set it on scarred, polished oak in front of him.

"You know fine well it is, sir," Captain Anastasia said.

"You stole this, you say?"

"I did, sir. I stole it from a Plenipotentiary of the Plenitude of the Ten Known Worlds," Captain Anastasia said. A murmur of amazement went along the line of officers and officials.

"Why didn't you lie," Sen hissed, so loud Everett feared they would be overheard.

"What's the point? They know everything," Everett whispered back.

"The point is, it's the Airish way. Ground-pounders don't deserve the truth."

But she did tell a lie, Everett thought. It wasn't Captain Anastasia who had taken the jumpgun from Charlotte Villiers. It had been him, Everett Singh.

"Perhaps the question, sir, is how a Plenipotentiary came to have one in the first place," Captain Anastasia said mildly. "The Plenitude has come to a pretty sorry pass when its diplomats must go armed."

"For a commercial airship captain you're very well versed in interplane politics," Captain Skinny said.

"My people value education," Captain Anastasia said.

"Madam, you're hardly in a position for flippancy," Captain Skinny snapped. Empress Woman lifted her hand.

"Enough, Brigadier," Empress Woman ordered. *So*, Everett thought, *Brigadier Skinny*.

Empress Woman turned her attention back to Captain Anastasia: "Ten Known Worlds, you say?"

Everett could not see Captain Anastasia's face, but he knew she was smiling. Sen clenched a fist: a small victory there.

"Earth 10 made contact independently with Earth 2 earlier this year," Captain Anastasia said. "The Plenitude has sent a diplomatic mission to open accession negotiations."

A new voice spoke now, one Everett recognized. It tore long strips from his heart.

"That might explain this device."

Everett edged closer to the railing, straining to hear, fearful that the scrape of a boot or a pigeon feather dislodged from the ledge would attract attention. Tejendra set Dr. Quantum on the long, scarred oak table. He wore a simple dark suit and a collarless shirt buttoned up to the neck.

"Explain please, Dr. Singh," the Brigadier said.

"It's a portable computer, fairly sophisticated by the standards of the other Known Worlds, but it's nowhere near our level of technology."

"I don't see how—" Brigadier Skinny said. His voice held an edge of irritation. Everett had the impression that his dad enjoyed needling the military. *No, not my dad*, Everett thought, *never my dad*. But this Dr. Singh appeared to be doing the same thing that Everett's dad would have done in the same situation.

"The point about the jumpgun is that it's a random parallel plane." Dr. Singh said, cutting the officer off in midsentence. Still, his voice was milder than the Tejendra Everett knew, his tone more apologetic. "The odds of arriving in this universe, out of all the other possible universes, is so small as to be mathematically insignificant."

"Your point?" the Brigadier snapped. Everett thought he saw Dr. Singh flinch at the whip-crack voice.

"This was a directed jump."

"Using this . . . device?"

Again the woman held up her hand to silence the Brigadier.

"You're saying they've solved the navigation problem?"

"I believe so, Agister. The coding language is different from ours, but the interface is quite straightforward. It's a seven-dimensional topological manifold of the quantum-field matrices for several billion networked parallel universes."

The elderly woman turned to Dr. Singh and raised an eyebrow.

The Brigadier was visibly annoyed now, sucking in his upper lip. "Will someone—"

"Let Dr. Singh finish, Brigadier"

"Of course, Agister." He almost spat out the final word.

"I believe . . . I have no experimental evidence, but I believe that this device, properly constituted, would enable a Heisenberg Gate to open a jump point anywhere. Not just at another Heisenberg Gate. At any point in any parallel universe. The whole of the Panoply. Not just the nine . . . sorry, ten, worlds of the Plenitude."

"My God," Lieutenant Kastinidis whispered.

"'I will lead them in paths that they have not known: I will

make darkness light before them, and crooked things straight,'"
Sharkey said.

"Captain, is this true?" the Agister said to Captain Anastasia.

"It is, ma'am." Captain Anastasia spoke plainly and simply, one
woman of authority to another.

"How did you come to be in the possession of this device?"

Everett held his breath. Would she lie? Dare she tell the truth?

"We have a word among my people: *Gafferiya*. It means the tradition of giving haven and shelter to lost and stranded travelers. But
we can be . . . flexible. A young man came to us. He was a refugee.
His whole world was hunting him because he had that machine you
hold in your hands, Dr. Singh." There was nothing in Captain Anastasia's voice, the way she carried herself, that betrayed that she recognized this alter Tejendra. Everett could see part of Sharkey's pro-
file and it, too, was stone. "He was alone, far from home, in a strange
world with no one soul he could trust. What other choice had I?"

"Now I's crying, Everett Singh," Sen murmured.

"Sen."

"What?"

"You shut up."

The Brigadier would have cut in, but the Agister again raised
her hand.

"Your . . . singular guest. We would have words with him."

"He's fourteen years old, ma'am," Captain Anastasia said.

"You expect me to believe that the only working map of the
Panoply is in the hands of a teenage boy? God help us all."

"My word, ma'am. Whether you believe it depends on whether
those stories about what an Airishwoman's word is worth have made
it as far as this world."

"I know a story that's just fanciful enough to be persuasive."

The Brigadier would be restrained no longer.

"Agister, with respect, this is now a security matter."

"Brigadier—"

"I have assessed the risks and I have no choice but to invoke Defense Protocol 4."

"What's that?" Sen whispered.

"How would I know?" Everett saw Dr. Singh draw a sudden breath and sit up, as if something cold had crawled on the back of his neck. Lieutenant Kastinidis shot an uneasy glance at her superior officer. "But I don't think it's good."

"Lieutenant, escort the captain and her first officer into custody."

Heavy chair legs scraped on medieval wooden floorboards. Sen searched inside her jacket for the Everness tarot. She slipped a card from the deck, flipped it through her fingers, and dropped it carefully, oh so carefully, through a gap in the gallery's floorboards. It turned over and over in a fall that seemed to last forever. Then it struck the floor and time restarted. Moments later, the toe of Sharkey's boot came down toward it and at the last moment veered to one side. Quick as anything, Sharkey stopped, scooped up the card, and flicked it up the sleeve of his voluminous caped coat. He glanced up and winked.

"And you, too, Dr. Singh," the Brigadier said. Tejendra's alter sent a worried glance to the Agister. She nodded. "Leave the device," the Brigadier called out.

"Sen," Everett whispered, "give me the drop-line control. I'm going after Da . . . Dr. Singh."

Everett peered cautiously out of the window. Weather had moved in while he and Sen had spied from their hidden place. A light, fine snow was sifting down from the sky. The Airish, with their military escort, had reached the shelter of a college staircase. Tejendra's alter was crossing the quad, the collar of his coat turned up against the unexpected snow. Sen slipped off the control and deftly slid it around Everett's wrist.

"You mind yourself with that, omi. I's staying 'ere. I ain't lettin' that comptator out of my sight. I trusts that sharpy cove about as far as I could shit him."

18

The snow swirled around Everett as he followed the scientist across the college garden, bare and blasted by winter. The Oxford defense field flickered above Caiaphas College's steep roofs and turrets.

"Dr. Singh."

The scientist stopped in the shadow-filled arch to the staircase.

"Yes?" He peered through the flying snow at the figure that had called his name. "You're not as old as I thought. You're off the air-ship, aren't you? From Earth 3."

"No," Everett said. "Not Earth 3."

Tejendra's alter took a step away from the gloom of the stone staircase into the light from the iron wall bracket. For the first time Everett saw him clearly. It was the Tejendra Singh of this universe. Like his dad in every part and feature, yet at the same time different. Life and experience had weighed on his body differently, had laid different lines on his face and had salted grey in his hair and in the loop of beard and moustache. Him, not him. Dr. Tejendra Singh frowned at Everett. Fine powder snow flurried across the cone of light from the suspended lantern. Then Tejendra recognized what stood before him.

"Oh my dear God." His hands flew to his mouth in shock and horror. He looked as if he had seen a ghost. *Maybe you have,* Everett thought, *from another world. Maybe that's what ghosts are, flickers from a parallel world breaking into this one.*

"I am Everett Singh," Everett said.

"Oh my boy, you are, yes you are," Dr Singh stammered. "This can't be right. This isn't right . . . You can't be . . . You are . . ."

"My father is Dr. Tejendra Singh of—"

"The Department of Multiversal Physics, Imperial University, London," Dr. Singh finished.

"The Department of Quantum Physics, Imperial College, London," Everett corrected.

Snow eddied around them.

"Come in, come in," Dr. Singh said suddenly. "I need to . . . I've questions . . . Just come in. You'll freeze out there." He stepped into the shelter of the staircase and opened the heavy wooden door to his ground floor rooms.

"I shouldn't be here. They think I'm safely locked up," Everett said.

Tejendra Singh smiled, and Everett's heart turned over in his chest. It was his father's smile, rare and carefully portioned out, but when it came it transformed his entire face.

"The military think they run this base," Tejendra said. "I take every opportunity I can for minor acts of rebellion."

The room was like the one Everett had escaped: uneven floors, cold radiating from the stone window frames, walls wood paneled, the ceiling low and timbered with dark, warped beams. In an old stone fireplace, blackened by generations of smoke, a wood fire glowed behind a wire mesh guard. On either side of it two tall, wingback chairs faced each other. A screen glowed on the top of a small round side table. Everett could see no tablet computer, no laptop.

"Holographics," Dr Singh said, noticing where Everett's eyes rested. "Make yourself at home."

Everett let himself carefully slide into the chair. The leather creaked. It made him feel very adult. That was the way his dad had always treated him, like a fellow civilized human male. He caught the alter Tejendra staring at him. Dr. Singh tore his gaze away.

"I'm sorry. It's . . . scary. You look like . . . her. How old are you?"

"Fourteen. Fifteen in May."

Dr. Singh closed his eyes. Everett saw old, deep hurt.

"May. Nineteen ninety-seven. I remember May 1997. I was on the last squadron of tilt jets to make it out of Birmingham before the Nahn assimilated the city. Get the scientists out. The scientists and the politicians. Everyone else was expendable. The Nahn was coming at us out of everywhere on that convoy to the airport: everywhere. In the sewers, up from the gutters, out of the sky . . . That's how they got through London so fast; the rats and pigeons. Assimilate those, and you've got the whole sewer system, the U-ground, the power system . . . If you're never more than ten feet from a rat, you're never more than ten feet from the Nahn. Under the earth and in the skies. It was after the Nelson Square Massacre that we realized what we were up against and that we couldn't hope to win. Fight the birds, the rats? We call it a massacre—but can you have a massacre when no one dies? But they did die, all those people who went down to Nelson Square to see the lions and stick their feet in the fountains and look at Nelson in his memorial and take pictures of each other feeding the pigeons. The Nahn-infected pigeons. They stopped being human. That's dying."

Dr. Singh paused. He looked directly at Everett.

"But how could you know anything about this? You weren't there. You weren't born. You never were born. Nelson Square, then the attack on the London U-ground. Every single person on the subway that day just vanished. Assimilated by the Nahn and sucked into pipes and the tubes and the wires. They found the entire inside of the tunnels coated in black slime. That was the people. Dozens of kilometers of them. It seemed an unimaginable number of casualties, incalculable. Now it's just a statistical blip. The government drew up plans to evacuate London. Then the spire began to grow out of the Isle of Dogs."

Once Everett had seen a David Attenborough wildlife series on the BBC. In one scene, a rain forest became infected by a fungus. That had seemed pretty creepy to nine-year-old Everett, watching on a Sunday night. What happened next would stay with him forever. The fungus worked its way into the ant's brain. It turned the ant into a zombie, sent it climbing up to the top of the plant, where it locked its jaws into the stem, never to move again. Now the true horror began. The ant's carapace shrank and collapsed in on itself as the fungus consumed it from within. Then, under time-lapse photography, the ant's head split down the middle and a tendril wiggled out: the fungus's fruiting body. It wiggled and grew and grew and grew until it was ten times the ant's body length. A spine, a spire. At the very end, it burst, shedding spores. Spores drifting like smoke on the wind to infect new ants. Nine-year-old Everett found a thing out about the universe. It wasn't sweet and it wasn't kind, and it didn't have morals or pity. There was nothing human about it. It *was*. It was the scariest kind of horror because it was real. Then Everett saw the spire of nanotechnology, thrusting out of what in his world was Docklands, fed by the hollowed-out bodies of the people of London.

"That was when we knew we were out of time," Dr. Singh continued. "We had to move right away. Eight million people, all at once. It was chaos. Roads were clogged for miles. The railway system broke down. No one dared use the U-ground. The police couldn't move. The army was trying to ferry troops around by helicopter to organize the evacuation. It couldn't work. It was never expected to work. If anyone got out it would be a bonus. What was expected was that we'd lose the entire population of London. I had priority clearance because of the university—they sent a helicopter to get Laura out of East London to meet me in Birmingham. It was scientists and their families."

"Laura," Everett said. "My mum."

"Your mum. My wife. I was based in Imperial—we were sleeping under the desks, trying to develop something we could use against the Nahn. She was still in Stoke Newington."

"Roding Road," Everett said.

"Number 43. We'd just bought it. Hell of a mortgage. Like that matters now. The police were picking up everyone on the priority

list and taking them to an evac point up in Finsbury Park. *Evac point.*
Spend enough time around the military and you end up talking like
them. I heard later from one of the soldiers what happened. From
Hyde Park to Hackney Wick, every street was gridlocked. Nothing
moved, nothing could move, nothing could hope to move. I could
hear the car horns from Imperial. It was people trying to take things
with them. Pile it in the back, load up the trailer, throw it up on the
roof, wedge it in around the passengers; they wouldn't go without
their stuff. You'd think if it were your life or your stuff, there'd be
no decision to make? Wrong. Their stuff was their life. There was
nothing moving on Stamford Hill. The soldier said he'd never seen
anything like it. They were jammed right up to the shop doors.
When I saw what it was like in Central London I tried to call her,
tell her to get up high, get up to a roof or something. She was
wearing the color of the day—all the ones on the list had been told
to wear yellow—they would have seen her and picked her up. The
networks were all overloaded. The helicopter was coming in to the
evac when the soldier saw what he thought was the biggest flock of
starlings he had ever seen. It was like a cloud that stretched from
horizon to horizon. Couldn't be, he thought. There aren't that many
starlings in the country, let alone London.

"It was the Nahn. It didn't need pigeons or rats anymore. It had
learned everything it needed from them and had discarded them.
They were just fuel."

"We saw flying things around the tower," Everett said. "That's
when we pulled out."

"It was the last thing anyone saw," Dr. Singh said. "Black flap-
ping wings coming out of the sky. Attacking anything that moved.
Falling like black snow, the soldier said. They saw the Nahn fall on
people and take them. The eyes are the last to go, human eyes in the
blackness. They had early EMP guns and were able to clear the lift
zone for the evac. They just barely got out. Laura didn't. She was two
months pregnant."

Beyond the diamond windowpanes, the snow was piling up, flake on flake.

"With me?" Everett said.

"Yes."

Your fear was wrong, Sen, Everett thought. *It's not you in that black tower. It's me. You never even came to be in this universe. Perhaps you are what you feel yourself to be: unique. The one and only Sen Sixsmyth. All alone in the multiverse.*

Sen lay flat on the wooden balcony, pressed as close as she dared to the rail, focusing all her concentration, all her attention, on the voices in the chamber below. Perhaps they felt self-conscious of speaking loudly in such a large space. Perhaps it was the natural sense of conspiracy when two high-ranking officials talk in private. Whatever the reason, the Brigadier and the Agister dropped their voices and Sen had to strain to catch their words. Even her breathing sounded loud enough to cause her to drop a phrase or miss a syllable.

"You know who the boy is?" the Brigadier said. He stood on the other side of the table from the Agister of Caiaphas, hands on the oak surface, leaning forward in her face. His stance was close and intimidating. The elderly woman refused to be intimidated. The Brigadier did not wait for an answer. "Dr. Singh's son."

"Ah!" Sen gasped, then clamped both hands to her mouth.

"Dr. Singh's son was never—"

"Not in this world." The Brigadier touched his wrist. A window of light appeared on the tabletop. From her painful angle Sen could not see what was in it, but from the expression on the Master's face she could guess it was Lieutenant Kastinidis's security report on the crew.

"Bastarding sharpies," she whispered, then bit down sharp on her knuckle. *Hush up your screech, polone.*

"He even looks like him," the Brigadier said. "There can be no doubt. Everett Singh."

"His alter found the Manifold," the Agister said. "Does our Dr. Singh know?"

"No. I'm happy for it to remain that way for the time being."

But he does but he does but he does! Sen shouted to herself.

"Master, does it not seem scarcely credible that the Manifold—the key to the multiverse we have been looking for for over forty years—arrives in our world in a solitary E3 tramp airship?"

"What is your argument, Brigadier?"

"This, Master. If it were a genuine, Plenitude-wide breakthrough, the sky would be full of E3 airships and E2 tilt jets and E4 Thryn spiderships and God knows what else. In other words, Master, there is one Manifold and only one."

"The Infundibulum. He calls it the Infundibulum."

"And this Infundibulum is tucked into the hand baggage of the fourteen-year-old son of Dr. Tejendra Singh's alter. The E3 captain obfuscates. You wouldn't give the most valuable and unique object in the Plenitude to a teenager unless you had a very good reason for doing it."

"Dr. Singh's alter needed to keep it out of someone else's hands."

"He is in trouble. He may even be dead. Mr. Singh Junior has the only example and he is on the run from the same forces that threatened his father."

The Agister's face tightened.

"We may have been cut off from the Plenitude for the last fifteen years, but it is inconceivable that it could change beyond our recognition."

"With respect, Agister, everything has changed beyond our recognition."

"Explain please, Brigadier."

"We are not cut off from the Plenitude, or even the Panoply. We have a way through the quarantine. We can open a Heisenberg Gate and it won't drop us into the heart of the sun. We can get out. This world is finished, Agister. We can't beat the Nahn. It's too big, too smart. There are too few of us, and we're too divided. Clinging to our islands, huddling in our little bubbles, puffing ourselves up on brave stories that we will launch some grand reconquest and take back our world. Won't happen. Can't happen. The Nahn hasn't finished us because it doesn't need to. It knows we are the final generation. We will dwindle and depart and humanity will be extinct in this universe. We erected the quarantine to protect the rest of the Plenitude from the Nahn. What we did was lock ourselves in the cage with the tiger. We have the key to the cage, Agister."

"We cannot take that risk, Brigadier. If even one replicator—"

"You think I don't know the risk?" The Brigadier leaned into the Agister's face. She did not flinch even at breath-close quarters. "I live with the risk every day, every hour, every minute of my life. It's the thought I wake to. It's the thought in my head when I fall asleep—if I'm able to sleep. I see a squad come back from patrol, I wonder, when they open the helmet, will there only be black nanotech behind the eyes?"

"Oh the Dear," Sen muttered. "It was true, it was true! The nano assassins behind the eyes! I always knew it!"

"I see a fox on the streets at night," continued the Brigadier, "and I think, is that a Nahn infiltrator? Have they found a way through the defense grid? Is the invasion about to break over us like a black wave? I see a bird circling up there above the grid, I think, is that a Nahn spy? My every waking thought is about that single replicator blowing on the wind like dust, blowing out between the worlds. What keeps that thought in my head is something I see in my mind's eye. My eyes see eyes, Master. My wife's eyes. Have you ever seen anyone taken by the Nahn? Up close? So close you can see the look in their eyes as the blackness consumes them? The eyes are the last thing to hold any trace of humanity, any memory of what the victims had been, and the terrible knowledge of what they are about to become. My wife's eyes, Master."

"We've all lost someone," the Agister said darkly.

"Get the children to safety," the Brigadier went on. "That was the last thing she said. She sacrificed herself so they could escape. Get the children to safety. And I never could, not on this world, not even here, behind the defense grid. One day, the Nahn will find a way through it, and it will be like London. It will be like Birmingham. It'll be like every city in the world all over again. We'll retreat to our islands and we'll imagine the children are safe there. And one day the Nahn will come for the islands, and they'll turn the sky dark, and the black snow will fall again. Get the children to safety, Agister. We can do that."

"It would have to be just Oxford," the Agister said.

"Just us. The defense shield makes us clean. We could get out and maintain nanosecurity at the same time."

"We would have to go beyond the Plenitude," the Agister mused. "If the Praesidium found what we had done, it would hunt us across all the universes. We would need a world of our own."

"The 1969 Imperial University Survey found hundreds of worlds."

"Thousands," the Agister said. "But you could hardly call it a survey. The probe had less than five minutes on each world before making another random jump."

"What?" Sen murmured. "Oh . . . I get it. Like the jumpguns. Must have been the same kind of thing. Random jumps."

"We just need one world, Agister. The archive must still exist somewhere."

"We lost almost all the Heisenberg Gate research when we abandoned Imperial."

And you worked on it, Sen thought, pressing her face against the wooden banister to better see the look on the Agister's face. On that face Sen could read disappointment, anger, resignation, endless patience, and not a little hope under the most extreme pressure. She tried to imagine what it must be like to live in a world where everything and everyone had been taken away and all that was left was ashes.

"I know," she whispered. She was back in the soft, padded bubble of the escape pod, swinging beneath the parachute as the storm winds buffeted it. Above, fixed in her sight at the center of the porthole and forever in her memory, the *Fairchild* hung burning in the sky, moment by moment turning to soot that was whipped away on the wind. Captain Anastasia's arms were around her. "Oh, I so know, dona."

"If you can obtain the data from the survey, I will take steps to secure the device," the Brigadier said. "Under its current ownership it must be considered a security risk of the highest level. If the Nahn were to get hold—"

"We confiscate the Infundibulum?"

"You meese . . ." Sen squeaked. She caught her breath. The Brigadier had left so long a pause before speaking again that Sen became sure she'd been overheard.

"Their options are limited. And they are civilians. Of course, we could eliminate the threat entirely."

"I abhor the use of violence," the Agister said.

"Violence is occasionally necessary," the Brigadier said.

Sen had heard enough. Sharkey knew she was spying—he had the card she'd dropped to him—but she must get word to Captain Anastasia fast. Captain Annie would think of something. Sen crept back from the railing to the window and opened it stealthily. The end of the drop line lay coiled in the snow at the foot of the tower. Footprints, filling slowly with powder snow, led away from it. Sen could have climbed it easy, but why get your hands frozen on those cold stones? She hunted inside her jacket for a device and slipped it on to her wrist: a drop-line controller. A touch and the line uncurled from the drifting snow. "Never give them your only one," she said to herself with fierce satisfaction. She slipped hand and foot into the loops. "I'll show you locked in a cage with a tiger."

"Infundibulum," Dr. Tejendra Singh said. He turned the word over in his mouth, tasting its syllables, feeling the weight of its rhythms on his tongue. In. Fun. Di. Bew. Lum. His dad had come to English as a second language and liked the sound of English words, how some words were so familiar you forgot how silly they sounded. Platoon. Cartoon. Dragoon. Anything with the *oon* sound in it made him smile. Oon. Oons and Ips. Snip. Parsnip. Ipswich. Some sounds were naturally funny. Everett saw that same small smile on Tejendra's face. "That's a good word. The further in you go, the bigger it gets. What is it, a seven-dimensional manifold?"

"I saw how a simple transform could decompose the dataset to a series of prime knots in seven . . ."

"You did this?"

Everett almost bit his tongue. *This is not your dad. It is Tejendra Singh, but it is not* your *Tejendra Singh. Be careful what you tell him. You trust him because you trust his face, his voice, his smile at the sounds of English words. He probably supported Tottenham Hotspur as well, when there was a Tottenham Hotspur. But Spurs was taken, and his wife was taken, and his friends and colleagues were taken, and he has lived through things you can't even begin to imagine. And it can happen that all those Tejendra things, those Dad qualities, can lie so long in the shadow cast by the Nahn over every part of this world that everyone left here takes on some of that darkness themselves.*

But I have to trust him, Everett thought. *What I tell this Tejendra Singh can open the way to where the real Tejendra Singh might be.* Everett caught that thought. The real Tejendra Singh. They're both real.

"Yes, I did," Everett answered. *At the kitchen table at my best friend's house, on a dark night before Christmas, drinking grapefruit juice from the fridge to keep myself awake.* It felt like years ago. It felt like another person. This Everett Singh had spent all his life among the gas cells and walkways and latties and hidden cubbies and staircases of *Everness.*

"If you did this, then you would be—"

"The greatest physicist of my generation."

Dr. Singh stared at Everett.

"Someone said that to me once. If you understand quantum physics, you would be the greatest physicist of this or any other generation."

"Was it . . ." Dr. Singh hesitated over the word. "Me?"

"No," Everett said. "It wasn't you."

"It was what I was going to say," Dr. Singh said. "I dedicated my life—my professional life—to looking for that: the manifold, your Infundibulum. I was a kid in Bathwala when they opened the first Heisenberg Gate—even there, we heard about it, even if no one knew what it meant. Other worlds, parallel universes? I was five years old, running around, and all I understood was that there was another me, in another Bathwala, running around, closer to me than my own skin, yet further away than the most distant star in the sky. And that made me feel strange and cold and yet wonderful all at the same time. I started to think about that Tejendra Singh, how like me he was, how different. If I was at school I would wonder what his school was like. If I was in bed, I would wonder where he was sleeping, what he was doing, what he was experiencing and feeling, and whether that was the same as what I was feeling. I set up a Jus-Connek site for him, like an imaginary friend."

"*JusConnek*, is that like some kind of social networking site?" Everett interrupted.

"Yes, it was."

"We have this thing called Facebook, but we didn't get it until 2004," Everett said.

"Facebook," Dr. Singh said, and Everett could see him tasting the word. "Horrible name."

"It's only really in my dad's lifetime that we've had personal computers," Everett continued.

"I think I see where our histories differ. Our first practical general-purpose computer was the Babbage-Bose Analytical Engine, in 1850."

Everett's mind reeled.

"We never built the Analytical Engine," he said. "It was only ever a design. Babbage couldn't get the government to fund it." For a few months, Everett and Ryun had been part of an online steampunk ARG, stalking werewolves and battling vampires and foiling sinister cabals, and yes, flying improbable airships in an alternate Victorian London. Their crime-fighting efforts had been bolstered with the aid of Mr. Babbage, an artificial intelligence housed in a massive steam-powered Analytical Engine. It had been fun for a season, but Everett had dropped out when it turned out that the other ARGers were less interested in computer-science speculation and playing with history than they were in dressing up in goggles and stupidly small top hats. Here was the real, alternate, computer-assisted nineteenth century.

"Your Mr. Babbage should have gone to the Bengal," Tejendra said. "Kolkata was a center for computational research. Nawab Siraj Ud Daula had introduced the Jacquard loom to the textile industry. It's a short step from punch cards for looms to punch-card programs for calculating mills."

"In my world, the British destroyed the Bengal textile industry," Everett said. "The Raj was built on the bones of Bengal weavers. My dad told me that." Everett was North London born and bred, but he had always been interested in his Indian heritage and history.

"In this world, the East India Company lost the Battle of Plassey, and after dispatching the British, the Nawab didn't waste any time expelling his French former allies. For a hundred years Kolkata was a bright and brilliant jewel of learning and science and commerce."

"Dr. Singh, you know that strange, cold, wonderful feeling you talked about?" Everett said. "I'm getting it now." And this was the point where he could roll all these worlds of wonder and science and alternate history over into the important questions, the ones that required trust. "Dr. Singh, do you want to know about that other

Tejendra Singh? I can tell you. I think I should tell you. He grew up in that same village, Bathwala. His family emigrated in 1974. He was always expected to shine."

Dr. Singh smiled. *Yeah*, Everett thought. *Punjabi parents, Punjabi grandparents. I have much expected of me, too.*

"Like you, he went into science, into quantum physics. I think his mum and dad would have liked it better if he'd been a surgeon. I don't know why he chose that field of physics. Maybe because it asks the really big questions about what reality is like. Maybe because the answers it comes up with aren't comfortable. Maybe, I don't know, is this possible? Maybe the walls between the worlds aren't as solid as we think they are and sometimes things leak through. Maybe dreams and visions and having a flash of the future, maybe they're moments when you brush past your other you. Like when sometimes you stroke a cat's fur and you can feel and see the static electricity? They're like static between the worlds. But sometimes I think we can never know why anyone does anything. Really know. He named me after the man who came up with the Many Worlds Theory—well, he did in our world—Hugh Everett."

"I had thought of doing the same," Dr. Singh said. "I apologize on behalf of my alter."

"Well, there's me, and there's my kid sister Victory-Rose—she's very young. There were problems. I think she was an accident, when they were making up after a fight or something. You know how they do. My mum and dad split up last year. They're doing all right. I'm with my mum, but I see my dad a lot. I'm getting on better with him now than when he was at home."

"I'm sorry to hear about your mum and dad, Everett," Tejendra said.

I know what you're thinking, Everett thought. *If your Laura hadn't died, might you have ended like my Laura and Tejendra, just fizzled out?*

"Ten days before Christmas, my father was kidnapped on the Mall, right in front of Buckingham Palace. He was kidnapped by a woman called Charlotte Villiers. She's the Plenipotentiary from E3 to my world."

"The Plenitude kidnapped your dad?"

"I think . . . I believe . . . there is a secret organization inside the Plenitude that wants to control it, and the Ten Worlds, and the Infundibulum."

"And if it controls the Infundibulum—"

"It controls all the other worlds as well."

"Or keeps them safe."

"Charlotte Villiers said there were forces out there in the Panoply that threatened everyone. Every world."

Tejendra took a deep breath.

"The Panoply is much, much bigger than you think, Everett."

"I know. I've got it on Dr. Quantum."

Tejendra smiled at the name Everett had given his tablet. His face turned serious in an instant.

"No you don't know, Everett. You have the codes. You have the way to open a jump gate in any universe. But you haven't seen what's out there. There was a joke that went around at the time when we built the first Heisenberg Gate. 'Now we just need someone to build the second one.' It was three years before we made contact with Earth 2. In that time, we sent a series of exploration probes through our gate on random jumps. We found worlds without end, Everett. Worlds where the laws of physics as we know them don't exist. Worlds where the laws of right and wrong don't exist. Worlds where humans don't exist. Worlds where something else stands in our place. Worlds from which our probe never even returned. And with every bit of data we downloaded, we realized more and more the risks we were taking. Sooner or later we would run into something that could pick up the echo our probe left when it made its jump. And that echo, we realized, could be used to open up our gate from the other side."

"Dr. Singh—"

"Please, call me Tejendra."

"Dr. Singh, have you heard of a thing called a jumpgun?"

"I'd heard that the random jump technology had been turned into a weapon. Some people will turn anything into a weapon. But it's all right, they'd say, it's a humane weapon. No one gets killed, just sent away."

"My dad, your alter, he got shot by one of those humane weapons. By Charlotte Villiers. She's the Plenipotentiary. It was meant for both of us. He pushed me out of the way. He got hit. Sent away, just like that. We got the jumpgun from Charlotte Villiers and I found a way to hook it to the Infundibulum so we can make controlled jumps between worlds. The thing I want to know, Tejendra, is whether I'll be able to get my dad back."

Dr. Singh looked into the fire for a moment. Everett could see him calculating, making theories.

"If you can find him, you can reach him with the set-up you have. But the problem—"

"Is finding him. It could be any one of ten to the eighty universes."

"The Multiverse Random Survey was long before my time at Imperial, but I do know that we used a quantum-entanglement device to track the probes when we'd send them through the random jump—in case they didn't come back."

Everett was suddenly very, very conscious of the beat of his heart. He sat forward in his chair by the fire, gentleman to gentleman.

"I need to know, does that quantum-entanglement thing still exist?"

"It hasn't been used in years. It'll still be there, in Imperial. We had to leave most of the stuff behind when we evacuated." Tejendra's eyes met Everett's. "Don't go."

"I have to go."

"Please don't go."

"It's the only way I can find my dad."

"Don't go, son."

A tap, a scratch. Everett started. The noise was as loud as a gun-shot in the warm, quiet room. Again, tap-tappety-tap-tap. Everett looked around. Sen's face was pressed up to the tall, narrow window, pale as a ghost in the snow. She beckoned to him. Everett shook his head. Sen held up her wrist, tapped the drop-line controller and mimed a rapid ascent into the sky. *Out. Up. Now. Important.*

Everett got up from his chair.

"I have to go now, Tejendra."

Glancing back from the door to see Tejendra raise his eyes up from the fire to meet his gaze, Everett saw that Tejendra's eyes were misted with a mix of fear and despair, as if he were seeing a second son sinking into the endless black of the Nahn. The eyes are the last to go.

19

*E*verness held secrets and surprises still. A door at the top of a companionway that spiraled up from the outer dock opened into a wide, generously proportioned room. Eight high-back swivel chairs stood around a long table. Behind them a window offered a panoramic view out over the airship's prow. Everett realized that he had seen *Everness* almost completely from underneath, looking up. Looking down from above was an entirely fresh perspective. The heraldic paint job of unicorns and palaces and peers was laid out around and before him, dusted with a fine powder of snow. The room was spotless, not even a nanoparticle of dust, like everything on Captain Anastasia Sixsmyth's ship, but the air smelled shut-in and stale, with a strong tang of . . . what? Something maddeningly familiar and very, very everyday.

"Furniture polish?" Everett asked.

"Aye, and why not?" Mchynlyth said. "Nanocarbon zhooshes up bona with a wee touch of polish. Lovely grain, that stuff. Only the best for our valued clients."

"Divano in the High Mess," Captain Anastasia had boomed out over the speakers, calling the ship's company to council. As they took seats around the table, Sen whispered to Everett that she had only ever seen divano called once before. That time council had voted to take the Iddler's offer of a smuggling run to High Deutschland, for the sake of the ship.

Overhearing, Mchynlyth said, "Bona decision, that was."

Everett had been ordered to make coffee, two pots, enough to keep the ship's company awake through however many hours of argument it took to reach a decision. Hot coffee on a raw, snowy morning.

"Can they get the Infundibulum to work without you?" Captain

Anastasia asked Everett. The mood in the room was somber. The clock was ticking. By dawn, when the Oxford advance base came to life, they had to have a plan of action.

"In time, they could crack my password," Everett said. "I made it pretty strong—like it would take billions of years for one of our comptators to crack it. Okay, so they've had comptator science since the middle of the nineteenth century, but that just means it'll take millions of years, not billions."

"Or the sharpies could just stick a gun in your eek," Sen said. "Or even my eek."

"Ah," Everett said. He should have thought of that. So easy to be too clever. Too clever could be the same as not clever. He flushed with embarrassment. There was one taunt in school that always stung him. Dana McClurg, who could find anyone's weakness and devise a barb for it, had thrown it at him: "Hah, Everett Singh, you're not as clever as you think you are."

"Aye, and bugger all we could do to stop them," Mchynlyth said. "A wee smack in the screech from a thumper's hardly going to scare those sharpies in their fancy armor."

"We have more . . . efficacious weapons," Sharkey said, looking over the rim of his coffee cup.

"And the jumpgun is still a jumpgun," Everett said.

"I'll hear no more talk of weapons," Captain Anastasia said. "It's not *so*. We've always been outgunned and outnumbered. Our weapons are our wits."

"'Thou comest to me with a sword, and with a spear, and with a shield: but I come to thee in the name of the Lord of hosts,'" Sharkey said. He took another long draw of his coffee. In his seat by the window the flickering green light of the Oxford defense grid fell across his face. Everett studied that face for any sign, any hint, any clue to what the Atlantan was truly thinking. Is this the day the safety of the ship is more important than the safety of Everett Singh?

"This I know for sure and spitting certainty, if we dinnae have yon comptator, we dinnae get off this world," Mchynlyth said. "And I for one cannae wait to get my dish off this shite hole."

"Mr. Singh, your da . . . Dr. Singh was certain that this . . . quantum-entanglement device is at Imperial University in London?"

"Yes. Ma'am."

"Ah well, that's just fandabbydozie," Mchynlyth said. "If we cannae take on the sharpies, we've less than a fart's chance in a hurricane of getting into a London college, finding this device—and we don't even know what it looks like—and getting our dishes out again without them wee black nanobeasties eating our brains out from the inside. Thanks a bunch, omi, you've landed us in it again."

He was right. Hugely, crushingly right. They had no advantages. They held no trump cards. They had no smart tricks, no daring rooftop escapes, no last-moment drop lines to safety, no jumps out from under the guns of the enemy. He saw Sen shuffle the Everness tarot one-handed in her lap. She turned up one, glanced at it, then saw Everett looking and slid it back.

"All I know is, that is what I have to do," Everett said.

Captain Anastasia took a sip of coffee.

"This, Mr. Singh, is fantabulosa coffee. How did you make it?"

"I measured it," Everett said. Captain Anastasia savored the aroma swirling up from her coffee for a moment. Her eyes were closed. They opened, full of will and guile.

"We have something they want, they have something we want. Simple. We do what we Airish have always done," Captain Anastasia said. "We strike a deal." She stood up. Ship's council was over. "Mr. Singh, take that jumpgun to your latty tonight. Stick it wherever teenage omis stick things they don't want found. Keep it safe. Mr. Mchynlyth, Mr. Sharkey, double watch if you please, though Mr. Sharkey, I'll need your redoubtable negotiating skills to be at their sharpest tomorrow. We're going to have to explain that the chavvies were spying on them, and we're going to have to persuade them to trust us with the Infundibulum."

"'Through patience a ruler can be persuaded, and a gentle tongue can break a bone,'" Sharkey said.

"No need for broken bones," Captain Anastasia said. "We're traders. We trade."

She swept from the High Mess in a waft of furniture polish.

"It was like that last time we's had a divano," Sen whispered to Everett. "Talk for hours, then she makes her mind up anyway."

Captain Anastasia turned at the head of the spiral staircase and looked thunder at her adopted daughter.

"Miss Sixsmyth, to your latty. Tomorrow we fly to London, and I want you well rested. I anticipate military guests. We will look airship-shape and damn Hackney-fashion."

A full pot and a half of coffee stood on the table.

A circle of light appeared over East London. It was as bright as a new sun in the predawn gloaming. Birds and things that looked like birds rose from roofs and roosts at the touch of the alien light. The light vanished. Two figures dropped out of the hole in the sky. One was Everett M. Singh, suspended in a flying harness beneath a white hedgehopper. The other was a little old lady, all grey. Her hands were folded into the wide sleeves of her simple long dress. She flew beneath a second, rebuilt hedgehopper.

Everett M wiped thin, stinging powder snow out of his flying goggles and pushed the steering yoke forward. The hedgehopper answered. Everett M cheered silently, the words wind-chilled in his throat, as he raced west by south, toward the staggering, beautiful, dead towers of dead London. For a moment, eyes watering in the slipstream that found its way around the edge of his goggles, he could savor the pure joy of flight and speed. He could forget that those thousands of glass windows were dead eyes. Nothing behind them.

"These are clever little things," Charles Villiers had said when the hedgehoppers—one complete, the other half trashed by a nano-missile strike—came through the gate from Earth 10. "There's more to those E3ers than brass and helium." The police had found the second flying machine hidden behind the old chapel at the center of Abney Park Cemetery. Charlotte Villiers had given her contacts in the Metropolitan Police her standard answers: intelligence services, national security. Sergeant Tache and Leelee were becoming suspicious. "What are they?" they had asked.

"Experimental military drones," Charlotte Villiers had told them.

"In Abney Park Cemetery?"

Charlotte Villiers's dry-ice stare had silenced them, but her ability to contain their suspicion was weakening.

Back down the M2 to the Channel Tunnel terminal, to the Heisenberg Gate hidden in the secret boring beside the main Channel Tunnel. Through the white light and into the greater white glow and feather-light gravity of the Moon. "Yes, we can do something with this," Charles Villiers said, walking around the wrecked hedgehopper, examining its every strut and duct and fan blade. "What do you think?"

"It is straightforward," Madam Moon said.

As always, Everett M had not seen Madam Moon arrive. *Does she generate her own gateways?* he wondered.

Everett M looked over at the figure flying beside him. She hung beneath the flying machine like an angel, upright, with folded hands. Her long dress fluttered in the wind.

"This is my special protective unit?" Everett M had shouted. Charles Villiers had taken him through a door-that-was-more-than-a-door to another one of the Thryn's featureless, dead-white chambers. From the echo of his footsteps, Everett M had guessed that the blank white space was very large indeed. Standing there was the same little old lady, all grey, with the same little mild smile on her face. "This is going to stop the Nahn from eating me from the inside out?"

"What did my alter tell you about the place we are sending

you?" Charles Villiers had asked as he and Madam Moon, a different Madam Moon—though they all looked the same, they were all different—escorted Everett M away from the Heisenberg Gate from Earth10.

"She said that whatever urban legends the over-fertile imaginations of Fifth Formers send wafting through the corridors of Bourne Green School, they're very far from the truth," Everett M said.

"They are," Charles Villiers said. "The truth is much worse." And he told him.

In the cavernous white room deep under the far side of the Moon, the grey lady smiled and showed Everett exactly what Thryn technology could bring against the Nahn.

"Why not send her?" Everett M had asked.

"Do you remember, Everett, when I told you that the Thryn Sentiency is not actually sentient? It follows that the Thryn lack ambition. They simply would not see the need. The Infundibulum is as trivial to them as the football results. Humans are much easier to motivate. Also, humans have the concept of debt. For what we have given you, Everett, the Plenitude expects a return."

"The Plenitude," Everett had said, "or the Order?"

Even empty, this London took the breath away. Everett M's London had the taller towers—Thryn technology had made its way early into architecture—but these buildings had the boldness and daring and imagination of a culture supremely confident in its achievements. Tower tops opened like flowers or flocks of birds taking flight: roofs floated, atriums coiled like sea shells, buildings leaned at terrifying angles or hung in midair over the streets below. Nothing was solid and heavy; everything was light and lively and full of intention and energy. The city was like frozen ballet. St. Paul's Cathedral was surrounded by an honor guard of skyscrapers as thin and elegant as scimitars, curving in toward the great church like a military salute. Fleet Street was like a carnival of dazzling puzzles in solid geometry: fantastical buildings that suggested fish, or clouds, or rain forests, or rare and delicate mineral formations found miles underground leaned over the older architecture of bygone centuries without ever crowding it. There were parts of the cityscape that were familiar to Everett M, but whole streets and entire districts were new and strange—that viaduct had never crossed the Strand, and that was a new old Victorian railway terminus, all glass and wrought-iron ribs, at Charing Cross. Where had the grand eighteenth-century opera house come from? And what about the covered market behind Regent's Street and the graceful Georgian crescents and circles of townhouses? In every part this London showed grace and balance and the face of a city made for its citizens.

Swooping low, Everett M could see the rusting vehicles, the piles of abandoned personal effects turned to pulp by years of rain, the scrub growing from the gutters, the weeds in the cracks. Every window was blank, every building empty, every street deserted. The silence was total and terrifying. The only sounds were the soft hum of the impeller engines and the sough of wind through the architecture of dead London.

Everett M glanced over his shoulder. The dark tower of Docklands dominated the eastern horizon, a knife stabbed into the heart of the city. His course over London kept it at his back, but he could not keep himself from glancing back at it. It drew the eye even as it repulsed the heart. It made the skin between his shoulders crawl. It made his balls contract in horror. It was hideous sexy.

He flew over the tall chimneys and balconies of this world's Mayfair. Hyde Park opened before him. The Serpentine was a soggy swamp of reeds and rushes and winterkilled water lilies. The broad swathes of open meadow in the Hyde Park that Everett M was used to were in this world nothing more than weedy, rank scrublands, choked with brambles and buddleia and the tall brown wands of dead purple loosestrife. Everett M circled, looking for a landing space. It was a long flight to Oxford, further than the hedgehopper's range. Madam Moon carried spare power packs. Where she carried them and how she powered them were Thryn mysteries. Hyde Park was an open space with clear lines of sight and easy escape to the air, a good place to stop.

"Oxford?" Everett M had asked Charles Villiers.

"The Agistry has set up an advance study base among the colleges in the city. It's the logical place for them to go. If they survive long enough."

"You could just send me into their Heisenberg Gate."

"They locked the gates."

"You can unlock them. You're the Order."

Charles Villiers's long, hard, silent look had chilled even the cold place in Everett M's heart. In that look was all the cold and ambition of his alter. They were one soul in two bodies.

"Some things are impossible even for the Order. Earth 1's Heisenberg Gates have an automatic override. Dial in or out and you will be redirected into the heart of the sun."

Now Everett M kept a cold silence.

"Tottenham's fine."

"I thought so. Now, I want to test that new anti-Nahn weaponry again."

20

Everett M touched the ground as light as a creature from a dream. He pushed up his goggles, hit the harness release, and tethered the hedgehopper to a lamp post, half overgrown with grass and climbing plants. On every side rose the towers of London. Everett M was utterly alone. He stretched his arms out and spun three-sixty. He roared out his great shout of existence. "I am! In this dead city, I am! Everett Singh!" Birds exploded from the trees. Everett's breath hung in steaming clouds.

Madam Moon touched down beside him. She hardly seemed to bend a blade of grass. She did not react to Everett's great cry of himself. She did not react to anything.

The birds circled, slowly settling to their roosts. If they were truly birds. The Nahn could take many shapes, could slip inside and wear bodies like suits of clothes. Nothing could be trusted on this world. The Villiers alters had been right. The truth was much worse than any of the legends that had blown around Bourne Green Community School.

The dark tower was made up of the faces of the people it had assimilated. Everett M did not need to see that to know that those faces would visit him in his dreams for a long time to come. In a flicker of fear and doubt he went from King of London to alone and afraid and very, very cold.

"Have you the power packs? Give them to me. I want out of here."

Madam Moon did not move. Everett M was about to ask a second time, with impatience, when her head jerked, a tiny motion, a bird-like turn of the neck.

"They're coming."

Everett M felt very, very small and very, very alone.

"Who? What?"

"The airship. I have it on long-range scan. Strange. I am having difficulty obtaining a precise fix. It is as if something is interfering with my sensors. Like a cloud between myself and the airship. A moving cloud. But not a cloud, more like . . . snow. Particles. Insects. No. Not insects. Everett Singh! Everett Singh! Defend yourself. The Nahn is coming."

The argument could be heard on the bridge. No words, but two distinct voices, shouting. One was a woman's, high-pitched but hard. The other was low and full of Glasgow growling. Mchynlyth.

Everett was on Captain Anastasia's heel as she strode from the bridge. Sen was one step beside him.

"Bona! A barney!"

"Mchynlyth has what we call anger management issues," Everett said.

"Mchynlyth has what *we* call, *so*," Sen said.

From the central catwalk Everett could see the ring of soldiers on the cargo deck and the two figures at its center. One wore the close-fitting outfit of an Agistry soldier. Camouflage patterns flowed across it. The other wore a leather flight jacket pulled over orange hi-visibility coveralls. They stood face to face, eyeball to eyeball. The kind of distance at which you could taste your opponent's breath. Veins bulged on Mchynlyth's neck and forehead. Elena Kastinidis stood like sculpted ice, cold, nothing moving. Her eyes did not flicker away from Mchynlyth's. Her fists were balled.

Heads looked up as Captain Anastasia clattered down the spiral staircase to the cargo deck.

"Mr. Mchynlyth, what is the meaning of this?"

The soldiers parted as Captain Anastasia strode through their circle. Her boot heels rang like pistol shots. Everett could imagine how wide and blazing her eyes must be. She came as close to Mchyn-

lyth and the lieutenant as they were to each other. Their breath hung
in clouds. Mchynlyth did not look away from the lieutenant.

"That wee girl is stealing my power."

"Ma'am, with respect, your crewman cut off the power to the
battle suits in midcharge," Lieutenant Kastinidis said.

"Two pieces of information for you, wee girl." Mchynlyth said.
"I am not a crewman. I am an engineer. Engineer First Class, time
served on His Majesty's Airship *Royal Oak*. And the second piece of
the information is similar: I *am* a crewman. You are a passenger on
my ship."

Everett felt a tap on his shoulder. He looked around. Sharkey
stood beside him.

"You forgot something." Sharkey slipped Dr. Quantum out
from under his coattails. "'I will come on thee as a thief, and thou
shalt not know what hour I will come upon thee.' After all the
trouble I had getting it off that cove, I'd hate to see you just leave it
lying around."

"It's all right, my da—"

"But he's not your dad. And I wouldn't put it past them to engineer a little diversion."

"They still need me for the password."

"I'm sure these gentlemen are quite capable of slipping something into your comptator to log your password," Sharkey said
darkly.

"Would they do that?"

"I would."

Everett tucked the tablet under his arm, squeezed it tight
against him.

"Captain!" The Brigadier's parade-ground voice boomed out
from the upper catwalk. "I have twenty soldiers that need their
battle suits powered up and operational before we hit London."

"I hates that omi," Sen hissed to Everett. "I would knife him if
I could." The thin, pure hatred in her voice made Everett certain she

would, given the opportunity. Her passions and hatreds were very strange and troubling to Everett. They came from a place very far from the educated, middle-class, cool Singh-Braiden family. He remembered the glee with which Sen had watched the fist fight outside the Knights of the Air pub, when Mchynlyth and Sharkey had gone up against the Bromleys. She had called out for blood.

"Aye, powered up with our power," Mchynlyth spat. "Power I need to run my ship."

"Power you took from us," the lieutenant said.

"Power you gave us. Aye, give with one hand and take it back with the other."

Everett could not see the captain's face but he could imagine all too well the bottled-up rage and humiliation behind the tight jaw, the flared nostrils, the wide eyes, the tense shoulders. He had caught the edge of her wrath before, when he had questioned the captain on her own bridge the time she had taken *Everness* to the ancestral Airish dueling grounds of Goodwin. She had been made to look like an amateur on her own cargo deck.

"And a piece of information for you, Mr. Mchynlyth," Captain Anastasia said. "This is *my* ship. You are welcome aboard *Everness*, Lieutenant Kastinidis, and your unit. Take what you need to equip yourselves. My chief engineer will accommodate you. Hospitality to strangers and the needy is our way."

Everett smiled at the little barb. Unit 27 had EM pulse guns and nanotech scanners and powered armor that could blend into the background or even make itself invisible to Nahn senses, but they had no air transport. They were cargo. The Agistry clung to the remains of a once-mighty technology, reengineering and fixing and bodging it up when it went wrong or needed to do something different, but the foundations of that technology had been undermined by the Nahn. There were too few humans. There were no new ideas. The battle suits, glowing and golden like bronze samurai, were patched and scarred with rivets and welds and mismatched spare parts. Dr. Singh had been evacuated on a tilt jet, but for aircraft like that you needed engineers and tech guys and liquid fuel. There were so few humans left. They were so widely scattered. They were driven so far to the edges on their islands and highlands.

The fight hadn't been about electricity or asking permission. It had been about fear. The soldiers were scared. Mchynlyth was scared. Everett was scared. Even Captain Anastasia was scared. Every second drove *Everness* closer to the heart of Nahn-possessed London.

Mchynlyth and the lieutenant faced off for a moment then stepped back. Jaws tightened. Nostrils flared.

"Mr. Mchynlyth, with me," Captain Anastasia ordered. "Ship's company, High Mess. Divano."

Everett M froze. The cold inside reached out and paralyzed him. He could not move. His muscles were locked. His body would not answer, and he did not know what to do. The Nahn was coming.

Had he heard fear in Madam Moon's voice?

Don't freeze. Never freeze. Freeze and you end up a screaming face in the spire of souls. You do what you were trained to do. Everett M pulled off his gloves, threw off his fleecy flight jacket, kicked off his flight boots, slipped off the cold weather pants. Last of all, the hat, the goggles. The skin suit beneath was exactly what its name implied. It was thin, skin-clingy, and covered in what looked like tattooed circuitry.

"I'm not wearing that," he'd said in the ready room on the dark side of the Moon.

Charles Villiers's patience was thin and ragged now.

"Oh, for God's sake, just bloody wear it."

Once on, it did look and feel a bit like a plug-suit from the animated series *Neon Genesis Evangelion*. Exposed to the cold wind and swirling snow of Hyde park, the fabric was warmer than it looked— the Thryn were as clever with textiles as they were with any other technology—but the melted snow was soaking up from his feet.

"Help me, Madam Moon."

And Madam Moon came apart.

She split down the front. From the top of her head to the lowest point of her torso, and along her legs and inner arms dark lines appeared. Light shone out of them. Madam Moon spasmed and unfolded. Her features melted and flowed, changing from mild-faced old woman to pure anime power armor. Her inside hollowed out, Thryn machinery rearranging itself, making space, a human-sized space. An Everett M–sized space. There was now no Madam Moon. A battle suit stood on the snow-dusted grass of Hyde park, whiter than the white ground. The armor stood open, like the shell of some undersea creature. Thryn circuitry sparkled with power. The printed patterns on Everett M's skin suit glowed in reply. But he hesitated to step inside and give himself to the battle suit. On the Moon, it had been the coolest of cool manga stuff. Here, it was a boy and his alien. Madam Moon used the same technology—nanotechnology— and was made of the same stuff as the Nahn. Nothing else could make machinery flow like water, change shape and purpose, reengineer itself from little old lady to killer battle bot. When he put his head inside that helmet and it closed around him, was there any difference between his face behind that featureless mask and his face trapped beneath the black glaze of the Soul Spire? The Thryn did not eat you from the inside. They said. It's our nanotech. But was it? He and Madam Moon were the sole objects from Earth 4. This was a whole new world for both of them. What did anyone really know about the Thryn? Everyone knew the Thryn kept secrets up on their half of the Moon. The full impact of their technology would have shattered Earth society. Too much, too fast. Did they lie as well? Was the theory that the Thryn Sentiency wasn't really aware and conscious of itself just a marvelous machine, another one of their constructions? Were they clever enough to pretend not to be sentient?

Charles Villiers had strung their technology through every part of his body. How could Everett M trust that his thoughts were his own and not Thryn thinking? He had been given a word that would override the suit programming, shut down the combat systems, unlock the armor and let him step free. If that helmet closed, would it make him forget that word? Would it ever open again?

Contact with the Nahn in three minutes.

Everett M could see the edge of the nanotech like a storm front, blowing in from the northwest across the park. With a thought he could have dialed up magnification of his advanced vision. He didn't want to do that.

You're all alone in the face of a perfect storm of lethal rogue nano-technology and your only ally is a shapeshifting alien battle robot.

Put like that, the decision was not so hard to make.

He stepped into Madam Moon. She closed around him gently but completely. Everett M had seen Venus flytrap plants in the biology lab and like every young male had been fascinated by their slow horror. That was how the Thryn combat armor closed around his body. Boots locked into place, calves and thighs sealed. The seam up the belly plate melted away. Everett M gasped in sharp pain as the skin suit meshed with the armor and his implants. The ends of his fingers grew into and fused with the fingertips of the suit gloves. Missile ports along the armor's forearms meshed with the ports in his skin. The suit was inside him. The suit was him. He fought momentary panic as the helmet sealed around his face like a fist closing. For a moment he was blind and deaf, then the sensors linked with the Thryn circuitry in his nervous system and he could see and hear as clearly and freely as if he stood in his own skin. Power blazed along his nerves and muscles. With a thought he could clear those trees in one leap. With his next thought he could level all of Park Lane.

His feet were still wet.

The eastern sky was black with flying nanotech. Everett M did not need his Thryn vision to see the birds, and things that looked like birds, and things that changed shape from birds into things that could never, should never exist, let alone fly. Everett M threw his arms open to the hurtling Nahn storm.

"Bring it!"

"Two divanos in the same day," Everett said as he settled into the seat he now thought of as his own at the conference table. "Must be a new ship's record."

The cold looks froze the next smart line on his lips. He had no right to joke about the ship's history and traditions. He was crew, not a passenger, but he was not yet *so*. He might never truly be *so*.

"Sen, the cards," Captain Anastasia ordered. This was why she had called the divano. It was an *Everness* ritual, not for the eyes of passengers. Not for the eyes of smart Oxford folk, rational folk, scientific folk, who might sneer at what they saw and consider it a barbarous superstition.

Very slowly, Sen drew the Everness tarot from its place next to her heart. She kissed the deck. She whispered something to it that Everett could not hear. She shuffled it one-handed and set it on the table in front of Captain Anastasia. The Captain shook her head and slid the deck across the conference table to Everett.

Suddenly Everett was very scared. He was one of those rational folk, those scientific folk. He hesitated to pick up the Everness tarot. He didn't believe in magic. But he did believe in power.

He was scared, but pride glowed inside him. He had been given the Everness tarot. He wasn't Airish born and Airish blood, but he wasn't a ground-pounder, a load of cargo in the hold. He was from two worlds. He was the Planesrunner. He was *so*. He knew the rules and traditions of the cards. Cut the pack three times. Lay out the top six cards in a cross. Lay the final card across the card at the center of the cross. The cards held their faces to the polished nanocarbon.

"It's not magic," Sen had said, that first time, when she had used the cards on the night train to Hackney Great Port to try and trick him Dr. Quantum from him. It was looking a little up the ways, a little down the ways, a little out to the sides. It was seeing things how they really were, deep down, under everything. Yet Everett held his breath as he turned up the first card.

A struggling man entombed in rock, his arms raised over his head, battling his way through the Earth. He might have miles or millimeters to go to break free to the surface. The man trapped in the Earth couldn't know.

"*Bubbles of Earth*," Sen said. "Enemies press close and there is no clear way to victory. Something is born, or reborn. Blind hope. Next card."

A skyscraper in the classic Manhattan Empire State–style, stepping back level upon level to a sharp pinnacle. Perched on that pinnacle, a single eye, ringed with fire, inside a triangle. Very much like Tolkien's Eye of Sauron.

"*Andromeda Heights*," Sen did not give any of the card's possible meanings. The image was too recent in their memories: the dark tower full of eyes and faces. The endlessly screaming tower of the Isle of Dogs.

Everett knew these cards. He had turned them up before, on the greasy upholstery of a London Transportation Authority el-train looping around St. Paul's. The same cards would inevitably turn up in any deck, but was the magic at work here the kind he believed in? Sen was sharp with cards—he had seen the way she shuffled. Had she manipulated the deck? Did the turn of the cards mirror her own hopes and fears? Was it that her emotions shaped the cards and the cards shaped the emotions of the people around her? Was she not a magician, but rather a conjurer?

The next card. Here was something he had not seen before. A man sitting on the roof of a train. He looked out of the card, grinning. A glass of wine was held high in a toast in one hand, in the other a whole leg of ham. What he could not see, over his shoulder, was that the train was entering a dark tunnel.

"*The Jaunter*," Sen said. "The bona times won't last forever. But neither will the meese times. Do you know where you're going to? Another card, Everett Singh."

Babies hung in cocoons like fruit in an orchard. Women in eighteenth-century dresses harvested the babies and collected them in baskets on their backs. Looking closely, Everett saw that the cocoons were spun from spider silk, and the babies had insect eyes and little claws—eight little claws—that pressed through the wrapping.

Sen gave a small gasp. "*Spiderbabies.* Who can you trust? Love turns into something weird. A bijou seed grows into a strange deed."

There were only two cards now, the ones lying over each other at the center of the cross.

A stormy sea and a single bird taking off from the top of a breaking wave. Its feet scatter the storm spray. A vast beam of light fans out from over the horizon, so bright it seems to burn out of the dark, scratchy ink drawing. It was a white void. The card did not show where the light shone from—a beacon, a lighthouse, the sun, something bigger and more powerful than any of those—but the bird was following it home.

"*Shining Path.* The way is open but the destination unseen. Do you know where you's goin' to? The sun blinds us."

Sen reached across the table and slid *Shining Path* off the final card. Everett snapped it face up.

Season of the Wolf.

By pure reflex, Everett reached out to turn it face down again. Captain Anastasia's hand stayed his.

The sun, the planets, in the jaws of an all-devouring wolf. The eater of worlds. The season of darkness falls. The bad guys win. He had seen this card before. Captain Anastasia had turned it up when she'd called on Sen to summon the Everness tarot before the battle of Goodwin Sands. The bad guys who won had not been the Bromleys. They were not the bad guys. Charlotte Villiers and the Order, they were the ultimate bad guys, and they had blown Tejendra—the real Tejendra, Everett's dad—into a random parallel universe and had turned Everett and the crew of *Everness* into exiles and refugees, fleeing across alternate universes. And the season of darkness still reigned. But the light would come. That was the promise of the *Shining Path* card. The storm-struck bird was like *Everness*. Light would come and light would guide them home.

Sen hadn't given an interpretation, Everett realized. She'd given the name of the card and its individual meanings but she'd never read the spread. The cards were the words, but she had never formed them into sentences. *That's for each of us to do*, Everett thought. *Each of us finds his or her meanings and fortunes in the combinations of the cards.*

And what is your meaning, Everett Singh?

Don't do that, Everett. It's like a tiny wave on a beach that undermines the edge of the fantastic sandcastle, crumbling the whole edifice. But what I believe about reality is not built of sand. My beliefs test themselves against reality at every point, and where they are weak, where they can be undermined, the testing makes them stronger. The universe is rational, even when it seems that it is not. There are rules. *But then*, Everett thought, *there are people*. People don't obey the rules. And the futures hidden in the cards did seem to come true, in ways no one could predict.

"You see what you want to see. We make our own luck here," Captain Anastasia had said as they went into battle against Ma Bromley on her flagship.

Bubbles of Earth. Andromeda Heights. The Jaunter. Spiderbabies. Shining Path. Season of the Wolf. The cards lay on the table for a long moment. Every crewperson read her or his future into them. Then Everett gathered the cards together and squared the deck. Sen stowed it next to her heart.

"We're over West London," Captain Anastasia said. "To your posts. Clear for action."

"Captain."

Captain Anastasia hung back a moment as the rest of the crew went down the spiral staircase to the bridge and to engineering.

"Can I ask you something?"

"You can ask me anything, Everett."

Everett pressed his hands and forehead against the cold window. His breath formed a misty circle, trickling condensation. The outer edges of dead London lay under a veil of light snow. Reduced to white and black, the lines and shapes that people had put on the land showed clearly: the roads, the abandoned rail tracks, the rows of houses, the boundaries of gardens turning to jungle. He could almost believe humans still owned this city.

"Captain, when you challenged Ma Bromley . . ."

"The right of single satisfaction."

Captain Anastasia had never spoken of what happened between the moment she walked out across the air bridge to *Arthur P* and the one when Everett had seen her climbing the spire of the capsized airship. The bruises had faded; she had patched up the torn ear and balanced it by putting more rings in the other one. She had never replaced the lost coat. And she had never said a word about what she had done on the *Arthur P* with her enemies all around her.

"Yes. When you went on your own, with all the Bromleys facing you . . . were you scared?"

Captain Anastasia answered without hesitation.

"Yes I was. I was very scared. Not for me. For the ship, for you all. I was scared for what could happen to you."

Everett looked at the black-on-white cityscape, like a pencil drawing, slipping away under the hull.

"I have to go."

"Don't go Everett."

"I need to see it."

"Your da . . . Dr. Singh will know what to look for."

"I need to know it will work with the Infundibulum. I'll know if it does. He won't because he doesn't know the Infundibulum. I have to be there."

Lieutenant Kastinidis had briefed the crew on what to expect when they went down into what remained of Imperial University. It was not *if* the Nahn would come. It was *when*.

"I mean, when we fought the Bromleys, I wasn't scared, not really. It was exciting. Really. And when we went to rescue my dad, when Charlotte Villiers jumped us, it was too quick, too fast, too much going on to be scared. Even when I was fighting that other me in the cemetery, it was like playing in a football match; it was all look, understand, react, like that, bang bang bang, no time to think about it, no time to be scared. But I can see this coming, I could see this getting closer all the way from Oxford, and now here we are and it's only a few minutes away and I can't turn the ship around and I can't stop it and they will come, the Nahn, they will come. Dr. Singh told me about them. The eyes are the last to go. I can see that. I can imagine that. I can think about what that's like. Sometimes it's not good to think so much. When you think, that's when you get scared. And I'm scared, Captain."

"Of course you are. Only a fool wouldn't be. Being brave isn't about never being scared. It's about what you do with being scared. And that's why it's not bad to think. Thinking doesn't always make you scared. Thinking's the only way through being scared."

"Yeah. I thought it would be something like that. Thank you, Captain."

"Annie. You'll know when you're allowed to call me that." She opened the High Mess door on to the spiral staircase. "Your post Mr. Singh. *Everness* will have need of every hand."

"Yes ma'am."

The Nahn storm was on him. It rolled over the bare treetops like a wave and broke into a swirling flock of dark, screeching winged things.

Everett M pushed his thought into his weapon systems. The circuitry of the Thryn battle suit meshed with the Thryn circuitry inside his body. And his arms opened. He was one with the battle suit, the skin suit, the Thryn systems beneath his skin. Right down to the heart of the stuff they had put into him. Missile racks unfolded. Each branch of the rack carried ten nano-missiles.

"Go," Everett M whispered. The missiles launched. The recoil jerked his arms backward and upward, but the missiles had their own target-seeking systems. He watched the rocket trails fan out across the face of the howling Nahn wave.

Now.

Everett M brought his hands together in a power-armored clap.

The EM pulse blinded him for a moment. The radio shriek had stabbed each eardrum so high and hard that he thought for a moment that he was bleeding into the helmet.

Conventional explosive missiles were useless against the Nahn, Charles Villiers had said. They would simply reprogram themselves and re-form. EM pulse missiles would burn out their software.

"What about the battle suit?" Everett M had asked. "Doesn't that have software? Doesn't every bit of it—and me—run on software?"

"We trust Madam Moon," Charles Villiers had said.

The battle suit stood at the edge of a black-speckled field of white snow. The Nahn had dropped in a precise line that marked where the massive EM pulse of sixty nano-missiles detonating at once had knocked it straight out of the sky. Black snow. It ran as far to left and right as Everett M could see. The density dropped off the further from the front line the dead Nahn had fallen. The sky was clear. The destruction was total. Everett M surveyed his work. He took a step forward to grind the body of the closest Nahn—a four winged headless bird thing with two tiny human-like arms—beneath his white battle boot.

Targeting circles appeared in his vision. Everett M didn't want to think too hard about how Madam Moon was hooked into his eyeballs, but the HUD displays were spinning circles, like something in a first-person-shooter video game, where on-screen graphics showed which character you were meant to be watching. Five contacts, low and fast. There. In the trees. Coming.

With a thought Everett M powered up the finger lasers. His fingertips were fused with the armor's fingertips. He didn't want to think too much about how that worked either.

Five hounds of hell. They had too many legs. Black as oil, teeth white as death. Five flicks of the fingers. The five Nahn hounds fell, slashed into pieces. There was no blood; no bone; no soft, swollen stuff inside. Already the Nahn assemblers were in motion, flowing toward unity.

Charles Villiers had told him this would happen. Everett M held the palms of his hands out. Circular ports opened in each palm. It took a few seconds for the EM pulsers to power up. The lasers took them down. The pulsers took them out. There was nothing to see, not even some video-game sound effect to hear. He simply turned his hand palm out at the scrabbling half hounds and they instantly fell apart into seeping black liquid.

Everett M clenched his fists, closed the pulser ports, and let the circuits recharge. He felt like Iron Man. Tony Stark, the billionaire space explorer whose private-enterprise rocket had crashed on the Moon. Tony Stark had been rebuilt by the Thryn into a battle-suited superhero—Iron Man—who fought the forces of evil. Everett M's Thryn sense sparkled with multiple contacts. They had him encircled. The battle suit moved as easily and lightly as his own skin. Everett M spun, firing off two scythes of laser beams. Smoking chunks of hellhound cartwheeled through the air. Everett M's HUD chimed. Pulsers recharged. It was like a beautiful martial art: turn, target, hold up one hand, and fire while the other tracked the next Nahn hound hauling itself up from the trampled snow. Then they were all down and Everett M stood at the center of a circle of black splashes, like ink on paper.

Contacts. More and more. A circle beyond the first circle, and beyond that a third, racing toward him. Where were they coming from? How many reinforcements could the Nahn throw at him? The first wave exploded in a hurricane of laser fire and EM blasts. The second broke on him. At the last moment, the HUD chimed: *pulsers online*. But beyond that wave was the third, the largest yet. Here they came, racing on their six legs over the splattered remains of their colleagues. One down, three, five. Close, closer than anything. Everett M took out two in midleap, each with a full-power pulser blast. *Pulsers offline*, the HUD flashed at him. One final contact, directly behind him. God, it was fast. Everett M whirled. The hellhound was in midair. Too close to risk lasers. Jaws gaped and teeth gnashed in Everett M's faceplate, then it struck hard, turned to liquid, and smeared itself all over the chest plate of his battle armor. The Nahn stuff crawled across him, trying to find some chink, some flaw in the Thryn technology. Everett M grabbed the edge of the sheet of Nahn stuff and peeled it away from him. The Nahn flexed and coiled, trying to lock on to his hand. Everett flicked his hand and flung the Nahn away from him. It spun in midair, trying to find its hellhound shape again. Everett M stabbed his left hand forward and blew it to sludge with a pulser blast. New contacts sparkled on his HUD. Nahn. Dozens of them.

"How long until the airship gets here?"

I estimate forty minutes. The battle suit's words formed inside his head. Everett M did not like them there. They were too close. At least the suit did not speak in Madam Moon's calm, reasonable, maddening voice.

"I'm safer in the sky." He could hide out on the rooftops, among the chimneys and aerials and air conditioners and water tanks of Mayfair, swoop in stealthily onto the back of the airship and cling there like a flea on an elephant while he planted the tracking device. And once the tracking device was in place, Charles Villiers could lock on to him, open the Heisenberg Gate, and get him off this hideous world.

His hedgehopper bobbed at the end of its tether to the lamp post. Twenty steps would take him to it.

Something tugged at Everett M's right foot. He looked down. Black tendrils had burst from the ground and wrapped themselves around his boot. Everett M tugged. The tendrils stretched. He willed a touch more power into the battle suit and swung his right leg forward. The tendrils snapped, fell to the snow, dissolved through it back into the ground again.

Now his left leg was snagged. Black glossy tentacles snared him up to the calf. He heaved. The tentacles heaved back. New tendrils burst from the ground and coiled up over his knees. Within seconds he was entangled to the thighs. Everett M fed full power to the battle suit and strode forward. Tentacles strained, stretched, snapped. He almost sprawled headlong. Seventeen steps. But now his left leg was caught again, tendrils boiling out of the ground, coiling around his leg like snakes. Everett M held out his hands and opened the pulsers in his palms. But the hellhounds were closing again, hard and very, very fast. And his right leg was snared again. Everett M heaved. The tendrils stretched but did not yield. He heaved again. The tendrils heaved back. They pulled his foot back down to the ground and held it there. The ground exploded. Tentacles swarmed up Everett M's legs. Within seconds he was snared to the waist. The hedgehopper hovered at the end of its line, seventeen steps away. Seventeen steps he could never take.

Pulsers online, the HUD said. Everett M aimed his palms at his feet. Fry, you evil death tentacles. But what would happen to the battle suit's circuitry at so close a range? He closed up the pulsers and grabbed handfuls of black Nahn stuff. The tendrils coiled tighter around his thighs. Everett flexed his battle-suit muscles. Tendrils stretched, tendrils sheared. But here they came, out of the trees: the hellhounds. A wall of them. So many, so fast. Everett M blasted the first wave to slime with snap bursts from the pulsers. The second wave broke on him. Three he slashed into smoking chunks with his finger lasers, two he punched into flying blobs of Nahn stuff, a third he grabbed and tore to pieces. Pulsers recharged.

Everett M aimed at his feet. He had to make those seventeen steps, let the hedgehopper lift him away from this. He staggered to a heavy blow to his back.

I have been impacted by a Nahn unit, the battle suit said.

The tentacles were tightening around his waist now. And here came the third wave of hellhounds. Lasers seared the air, pulsers splashed dead Nahn stuff across the snow. But there were too many, and they came too fast. White teeth snapped Everett M's face and covered him with crawling Nahn stuff again and again and again. And the tendrils spiraled higher and higher, to his waist, his chest, over his shoulders, snaking down his arms. He couldn't aim. He couldn't target. Black splashed across his visor like ink. Splash by splash, splat by splat, the Nahn tech shut out the light. He couldn't see. He was blind, deaf, paralyzed.

Sensor webs are compromised, the battle suit said. Alone in the dark, Everett felt the soft thuds of more and more Nahn hounds splattering over him. *We are encased in approximately one meter of Nahn substrate.*

Entombed in rogue nanotech. From the outside he would look like one of the mummy cases he had seen in the British Museum, a rounded coffin with a head. Black. All shiny black. And more Nahn piling on top of him every moment.

Software security has not been compromised, the suit said.

"Meaning?" Everett asked.

I can maintain basic life support.

"How long?"

Until the power packs decay.

"How *long*?"

In this state, several months.

Everett M screamed then. He screamed long, he screamed hard, he screamed his throat raw. The blackness took the screams and gave nothing back. He tried to move, to kick, to punch, to even move a toe. Muscles balled. He focused power into his enhanced Thryn strength until he felt his muscles would tear sinew from bone.

Nothing. He could not move, he could not see, and all he could hear was the voice of the suit and his breath and the beating of his heart. Trapped inside Madam Moon. A metal and plastic coffin.

"Everett?"

A voice. Not the suit voice. Not his voice. No: his voice. His voice from somewhere else.

"What am I hearing?"

I am picking up a series of vibrations through the Nahn material and converting them into audible signals.

"It sounds like a voice. My voice."

Yes it does, Everett M. Singh.

The blackness lightened. Everett M's vision turned grey.

The Nahn material is clearing from the helmet visor, the suit said as tendrils of black crept back from his field of vision

Everett M blinked in the white. A shape, between him and the light. An oval shape filling most of his field of vision, blocking out the light from the winter sky. His vision cleared slowly. The spots and soft dandelion bursts in his eyes faded. He was looking into a face.

His face.

"Hello Everett," his face said.

21

Him. It was him. Standing there on the snow, among the dead Nahn things, dressed in the same battle-suit liner. His own height, his own weight, his own legs and arms and body. His own hands and feet. His own face. The eyes. That was where it fell down. The eyes were not his. They were made up of dozens of tiny black cells, like insect eyes. They caught the light and reflected it back in rainbow colors, like a dragonfly.

"Can he hear me outside?" Everett M asked the battle suit.

Yes. Now.

"Who are you?" Everett M asked. The double gave an embarrassed smile, turning his head away. Everett M would have done that. How much did it know about it?

"In a sense, I'm you—but it might freak you out talking to a double, so I won't call myself Everett."

But I have met my double, Everett M thought. *And it didn't freak me. I was cool and calm and completely rational. And you don't know. And that's one tiny advantage to me.*

"Call me what I am," the Everett M double said. "Call me Nahn."

"You look like me."

"It's more than just look, Everett. In a very real sense, I am you. We found we had your DNA in our database and used it to program this avatar. We thought you might be less hostile to something that looked and acted—and sounded—like you. We have your DNA, yet here you are before us. This puzzles us."

"Clear that gunk away from me." Everett thought *move* into the power armor. Thryn mechanisms strained, but the Nahn stuff was plastered thick around him.

"No, I don't think so, Everett. I've seen what those EM pulse weapons can do—and I've felt it too. Anything, everything done to me or any part of me, we all feel. I feel. Do you know what it feels like? Like a part of yourself being ripped out. Again and again and again. It burns, Everett. It burns."

"What do you want from me?"

The Nahn double shrugged.

"You puzzle us. Your technology resists us. It's all through you. We can't assimilate it. We thought we understood your technology. You evolve a technology to exterminate us, we use the knowledge we've collected to find a way around it. This is something we haven't seen before. There's nothing in our Consciousness about this. Who are you? Where are you from?"

Again, another tiny edge of advantage. *It doesn't know about the Thryn. It doesn't know about Earth 4. It doesn't know that I'm not from this world at all. But it can just wait, puzzling all this out, until I starve to death. I need to take a risk.*

"I'm Everett M. Singh. I'm not from this world. I'm from Earth 4."

The Nahn double blinked its insect eyes twice.

"I'm communicating this to the Nahn Consciousness. Earth 4. Yes. We have a memory of that. We have the collected memories of the six billion humans we have assimilated, but there is a lot of knowledge still to be connected. Ah, yes. Parallel universes. One moment . . ." The Nahn double cocked its head, as if trying to listen in to an interesting conversation across a busy room. "The Thryn Sentiency. This is not human biology. This is why we can't assimilate it."

Assimilate me, Everett M thought. *Melt* me *into six billion others. Give* me *evil insect eyes. And that's my third advantage: I'm from another universe.*

The Nahn double was studying him. Everett M could look back at it without horror and could see the differences, the details where the double wasn't quite perfect. The eyes, of course, and the battle-suit liner was clearly part of the double's skin: the feet were dyed grey rather than grey from melted snow. The hair didn't quite move right. It looked like the hair of CG characters in movies, like it was moving underwater. As he had scanned the Nahn, with his sensors, it must have scanned him from the outside in. Again he tried to will the battle suit to move. No. But how did it know his DNA? Unless . . .

This time, Everett M kept the cry down. And he realized a thing about bravery. Bravery needs an audience. It's for other people. When it's just you, on another world, with the collected nanotech mass and knowledge of six billion entities that used to be people— that used to be you, in some way or other—there is no brave. There's smarts, and there is survival. And as Everett M realized that, he understood that fear was the same. Fear also needs an audience. No one alone can be afraid.

The airship is ten minutes out, the battle armor said.

"You might like to know, I just got an estimate of the time it will take us to evolve a way to assimilate the Thryn technology," the Nahn double said. "Somewhere in the region of six months."

"I've a better idea," Everett M said.

"We'd like to hear it."

"I need you to release the suit."

Again, the Nahn Everett M cocked its head like an inquisitive bird.

"The Consciousness . . ."

"There's six billion of you! There's only one of me!"

The Nahn clone blinked twice. Everett M felt his neck suddenly free to move, as well as his shoulders, his arms. He looked down and saw Nahn stuff sheeting from him in a black flood. Upper body, hips, legs. The Nahn flowed away and left him standing in a circle of trampled snow and weeds.

We are no longer restricted, the suit said.

"Yeah," Everett M said. "Give me the private circuit."

We are private now, the battle suit whispered. *The airship will arrive in seven minutes.*

"Gives me time to do this," Everett M said on the private circuit. "Blue. Lambda. Oryx. Buttercup." The four code words for the override. Charles Villiers had drummed them into him, again and again and again, right up to the ramp to the Heisenberg Gate that had sent him and the Madam Moon/battle suit to Earth 1.

Without a word, the Thryn battle suit split along a seam from forehead to groin. Panels retracted and the suit opened. Everett M Singh stepped unarmed, unprotected, and alone into the battlefield of dead Nahn. He looked his double in his nanotech insect eyes.

"Let's deal."

Sen brought *Everness* in silent as a ghost over Hyde Park, over the wreck of the Albert Hall, across the dead faculty buildings and libraries and laboratories and lecture halls of Imperial University, to a dead stop nose-in to the top of the bell tower that stood at the heart of the campus. She pulled back the thrust levers and swung the impeller pods into hover.

To Everett it seemed that Earth 1 was his world—Earth 10 but with the volume turned up. The great buildings of this dead London were taller, bigger, bolder. The colleges of Fortress Oxford were more medieval, their cloisters gloomier, their gargoyles more lean and menacing. In this Imperial College—Imperial University, Everett kept reminding himself—the tower that stood at the center of snowy Queen's Lawn was a Victorian Gothic monster, taller even than Big Ben in Earth 10 London. In his world, Queen's Tower did not have four huge stone lions crouching at its base, or four angels, each bearing a different symbol of learning—a book, a triangle, a telescope, a pair of scales—at the point where the tower was capped with a dome. And that dome was not so high, and it had never been crowned with a flying angel coming down from heaven, blowing a golden trumpet, wings upraised, one foot lightly touching the summit of the dome. The same, but different. Very, very different.

"It's not if the Nahn come, it's when," Lieutenant Kastinidis had

said. Her troops were up in the out dock, armored and powered up.
The Brigadier had set up a command post on the bridge. He would
be controlling the mission from a distance.

"Some commander, as doesn't go into action with his sharpies,"
Sharkey muttered to Everett as Sen trimmed the controls to hold
Everness steady against the snow-filled gusts that swirled around the
Queen's Tower.

"Bring us into boarding distance," Captain Anastasia said. The
tiniest nudge of the thrust levers brought the huge airship within
range of the access bridge. "Full stop." *Everness* hung motionless over
the ruins of the great university. The Agister of Caiaphas College
nodded her approval. For her status, but more, Everett thought, for
her admiration of the ship and the crew who flew her, Captain Anastasia had allowed her the honored place by the great window. "Mr.
Mchynlyth, run out the ramp."

The bridge trembled as the machinery in the out dock rumbled
into life.

"Are you ready, Dr. Singh?" the Agister asked. Tejendra nodded
his head. Everett saw fear in his face and more: acceptance and peace.
Tejendra Singh had always known he must face the Nahn.

"And you, Mr. Singh?" Captain Anastasia asked.

Everett took a deep breath.

"Bona."

"Just one damn moment." Sharkey's voice boomed across the
bridge. "'Yea, though I walk through the valley of the shadow of
death, I will fear no evil: for thou art with me; thy rod and thy staff
they comfort me.'" He slipped a shotgun from his coattail and threw
it to Everett. "Everyone does the 23rd Psalm in the end. Here's some
dry shell."

Everett caught the gun and the ammunition that followed. He
had already pulled on his old North Face jacket with the glow tubes
tied to it. Visibility would be important in the lightless halls and
corridors. Now he was complete.

"'Walk on, walk on, with hope in your heart, and you'll never walk alone. . . . You'll never walk alone,'" Everett said.

"I don't recognize your verse, sir, and I am conversant with the word of the Dear, Old Testament and New."

"It's a song. In my world it's like the anthem for a football team. Liverpool F. C."

"There's wisdom in some of them worldly songs," Sharkey said. He tipped his hat with the muzzle of his shotgun, a salute to the Brigadier, and quit the bridge. See, a Lafayette-Sharkey is unafraid to walk the valley of death with his crewmate.

"Bona air, Mr. Singh," Captain Anastasia said.

"Captain, can I have a word with Sen? Alone?"

"Make it quick, Mr. Singh."

The stair foot was deserted. Everyone was above in the out dock, preparing each in his or her way. Sen threw herself on Everett like some over-affectionate animal, all hair and limbs. He almost went backward over the railing, down to the power deck below. She pushed her head hard against his chest. Her strange, warm, musky perfume was strong. It tugged at Everett's heart.

"Everett Singh, Everett Singh, don't go, don't go." She banged her head against Everett's chest.

"I have to. I'm the only one who'll know if they find the one that'll work."

"Everett Singh, no. Not again. 'Sen mind the hedgehopper, Sen mind the ship.' Sen gets told to stay behind but Sen saves your dish, Everett Singh, again and again and again. For you, it's always being on the run, for Sen it's, 'Sen you're the pilot, Sen you're captain now.' Don't go. This time, I can't save you."

Sen was as wiry as a dog, but there was the strength of steel hawsers in her grip. She was built like *Everness*: light but stronger than any storm.

"Sen, I've, uh, I've got a loaded shotgun in my hand."

"Well, let me help you with that." Her fingers were so fast. She slipped the shotgun free from Everett's grasp with the same deft touch she'd used to try to steal Dr. Quantum from him on the night train to Hackney Great Port when they'd first met. Resistance was futile.

She kissed him. She kissed like she had kissed him the last time he had gone into desperate battle, against his alter from another universe. It was full and without restraint. And it was much more intense than a girl her age should kiss. She was all energy and passion and contradiction. She went up on her toes. The shotgun fell from her fingers.

"Sen, parlamo palari."

"Of course, omi."

"The meese sharpie . . ."

"That cod fruit in the naff sharpie clobber."

"He's aunt nelling, but he don't cackle palari. Sen, if I don't troll back from this barney . . ."

"Nante parlamo that Everett Singh. Nante."

"Sen, I need a blag."

"Blag me anything, Everett Singh."

"I need to blag an amriya."

"Oh, Everett Singh, an amriya is a big blag."

"It's a bijou ask. The comptator. I've zhooshed up a code. If I nante troll back again, zhoosh it. It'll scarper you back home again. Then, Sen, do this. Remember when you told me about the Polone-queen, trolling the shush to Deutschland for the Iddler, when the lillies came? She dumped the shush in the big blue buvare and scarpered. Sabi?"

"Sabi, Everett Singh."

"If I nante the comptator, nante everyone. And Dona Villiers, she's no reason to ogle for you, not without the comptator. Jump, dump, Sen. Sabi?"

Sen lifted Everett's right hand to her lips and kissed the second knuckles of his fingers.

"I promises, Everett Singh. An amriya is made."

"Bonaroo, Sen. Fantabulosa."

He was halfway up to the out dock when Sen called his name.

"Hey. Your shooter." She threw the shotgun up to him. Everett caught it and slung it over his shoulder. "Hey, Everett Singh! Alamo!"

Everett M stepped out of the open battle armor. He looked the Nahn double straight in the insect eye.

"What could you possibly have to offer us?" the Nahn Everett said.

"A way out."

The Nahn double was still and silent long enough for the cold and wet to seep in from the outside to join the cold at Everett M's heart. The wind cut through the thin single layer of the Thryn skin suit. Everett M shivered and wrapped his arms around himself, jiggling for warmth. The last time he had been this cold was the morning of the end-of-term football game on the Bourne Green playing fields. The morning everything changed.

"The Nahn Consciousness will hear your offer," the double said. It didn't feel the cold. It didn't feel anything.

"I've got a mission," Everett M said. "I work for the Plenitude."

"The so-called government of the Known Worlds," the Nahn Everett said. "We're aware of it. It will be assimilated into a more efficient form."

"There's an airship coming," Everett M said.

"We're also aware of that."

"Four minutes," the battle armor said in the communications plug in Everett M's ear.

"It's from Oxford," the Nahn double continued. "The Agistry has an advance outpost there. We are surveying it. It, too, will be assimilated in time."

"I have to plant a tracking device on the airship," Everett M said. "That's what all this is for. I plant the device, then they open a Heisenberg Gate and take me home again."

"The quantum gateways from this universe have all been sealed. They've been set to transport anything that uses them into the heart of the sun in another universe. It's an effective quarantine."

You sound like a mathematics teacher, Everett M thought and almost giggled. It was so stupid and inappropriate and yet right.

"I'm here, aren't I?"

"Can't deny that, Everett," the Nahn double said.

"Here's the deal. I'm your way off this world. You let me plant the tracker. I call in the Heisenberg Gate. When I leave, I take a bit of you with me. Just a teeny tiny bit—nothing that would get noticed. I'm safe because you can't touch my Thryn tech, and you get . . . somewhere else."

Again the Nahn Everett was still and silent. Everett M could see the airship now, coming in from the northeast, riding on the edge of the snow. God, it was big. Bigger than he had ever imagined. It was like a cloud, or a storm, or a natural feature. And he was a big fat target out here: the bull's eye at the center of rings of dead Nahn stuff. *Come on, do you have to get the agreement of every one of the six billion you assimilated?*

"It would have to be hard for you to remove. Once back in your home universe, what's to stop you from zapping it with your EM guns? Any attempt to remove or destroy it would have to result in catastrophic damage to you."

"But it would leave my body," Everett M said.

"Of course."

"I can agree to that."

He glanced at the sky. The airship was maneuvering over Kensington Gardens. Everett M could see the impeller pods and steering surfaces swivel and flex. *You're there*, he thought at his alter. *But you don't know I'm here.* He had only moments to make the deal. It was a dreadful deal. He was letting the Nahn loose in the Plenitude.

Something worse than the worst disease. A virus with a mission to rule the universe. Had anyone ever contemplated a worse deed? But it was the only way he could save his life.

"We have a deal," the Nahn Everett said. He raised his right forefinger. The tip unfolded and refolded into a tiny black butterfly. "This may sting a little."

"What . . ."

The butterfly had too many wings. It fluttered in Everett M's face, then went around the back of his neck. Everett M turned his head and felt a sharp stabbing pain at his hairline. When he touched it he could feel nothing there. Inside. He didn't need his enhanced Thryn sense to tell him where it was. He could feel it, like a little ball of badness, wadded up tight, nestling against his spine. *What have I done?* Everett M thought. *You did what you had to do. You made a deal to survive*, he told himself.

The airship hung over the Albert Memorial and the Albert Hall, nose-in to the Imperial College tower. Queen's Tower was bigger and more Gothy in this universe than in Everett M's. But there was a Queen's Tower, and an Imperial, and there must be—or have been— a Tejendra Singh who worked there, who had discovered something that pulled people across parallel universes. The same people, the places like echoes across all the universes. He was part of it. He hadn't asked to be. He wanted no part of this. He had been the slightly geeky kid at school who could stop almost any ball when he was between the posts of a football goal. Other lives in other worlds had dragged him into a multiverse-spanning conspiracy. They had forced him to this terrible decision to save his life by betraying humanity.

He felt the Nahn thing scratch in through his flesh and sink hooks into his spine. He wanted to throw up.

"It's in me."

The Nahn Everett did not speak. Its face softened like melting ice cream; its eyes and mouth and nose and cheeks slumped and flowed. For a second it held the memory of Everett M's face, then it collapsed into a mound of Nahn stuff that merged with the mass of Nahn surrounding Everett. Like early snow vanishing under the sun, the Nahn stuff seeped into the ground. Gone. He was alone.

There was his backpack with the relay, his clothes, the hedge-hopper still tethered to the lamp post. One last thing. The Nahn Everett had said they could hack Thryn technology, in time.

"Can you still hear me?" Everett M asked the battle suit.

"I am receiving you."

Charles Villiers had drummed another set of instructions into Everett M at the Heisenberg Gate: the self-destruct code. "Pray you'll never need it," Charles Villiers had said.

"Set timer for one hour. Peregrine lamp post ultramarine harp."

"Very good, Everett M. Singh."

It was only an empty suit of battle armor, but Everett M felt he was betraying a friend. If it had still been in its Madam Moon form, he was not sure he would have been able to speak the four words of the self-destruct code.

Everett M pulled the hedgehopper down from its hover. The other would remain bobbing on its safety line until its batteries ran out and it fell to earth. Everett M strapped on the backpack. The clothes would have offered some warmth, but it would have taken too long to pull them on, so he left them on the snow. No. The goggles. He had to take the goggles. Everett M slipped them over his eyes and buckled himself into the hedgehopper harness. The steering bar was so cold that it felt like it was burning his fingers. He could barely get a grip on the thrust lever. The ducted fans swiveled, one step, two, and Everett M took to the sky with treachery in his backpack and curled up next to his spine.

22

One kick from Lieutenant Elena's power-armored boot smashed in the half-rotten door to the observation deck. The Agistry troopers were lined up along the narrow walkway. Everett squeezed his way between the bulky armored warriors and the stone parapet to his position in the line. Order was important: unit 27 could include the civilians in their Nahn confusion fields, but the range was limited. Stray more than three meters away from a suit of golden armor and you would shine like a beacon to whatever senses the Nahn used to sniff out biological material. And the dazzle fields only worked for so long. Just as the Oxford Defense grid constantly shifted frequencies in response to the Nahn constantly evolving new variants, so the Nahn found ways to see through the confusion and pinpoint the precious human meat hidden inside.

The wooden boards were treacherous with frost beneath Everett's boot soles. He landed heavily from the airship's ramp, slipped, grabbed the parapet, and yelled as a length of flaking limestone broke off in his hand and crashed to Queen's Lawn. He had never felt afraid of heights on the ship, but here everything was ramshackle and rickety and rotted. *If it's safe enough for a squad of soldiers in full power armor it's probably okay for me*, Everett told himself.

"Word of advice, sir," Sharkey said as Everett squeezed past. "Only kill what needs killing."

"Your weapons can't kill the Nahn," Lieutenant Kastinidis called back from farther up the line. The helmet speakers made her voice mechanical and anonymous, but she could be recognized by the name between her shoulders, the two stars on her upper arm shields, and the snake-haired medusa head on her helmet. *You painted that yourself*, Everett thought. *What does it remind you of, Greek home or*

Greek parents? The stare of the Medusa turned you to stone. The stare of the Nahn did worse. The stare, the eyes. The eyes are the last thing to go. Stop thinking that. Stop seeing that in your imagination.

"No ma'am, but they can slow Satan-spawned abominations," Sharkey said. "And, I hope, hurt them. Hurt them very much."

The party formed up. Two soldiers took point, then Tejendra and Everett with the lieutenant between them, then two more soldiers, then Sharkey and the rearguard of two. Tejendra looked terribly small and vulnerable to Everett. He wished he had something to give him to make him feel more powerful and in control. Not a gun. Guns did not make you feel powerful. A gun was what you used when you were out of all other options.

"We're going down," Lieutenant Kastinidis ordered. "Civilians: you only engage the enemy under my express command. At all times, you follow orders automatically and immediately without delay or question. At all times."

Everett saw Tejendra flash a smile behind the lieutenant's hulking back. Everett knew that look: the Punjabi disrespect for authority. Military bollocks.

A wooden staircase wound down the walls of the tower. The center was occupied by a heavy timber frame carrying a peal of bells. It was the same in his Queen's Tower, Everett knew. He had heard them rung on graduation days. The wooden steps creaked alarmingly under the weight of soldiers in power armor. Everett decided against trusting the hand rail. One warning was enough.

A voice called out from farther up the stairs. The helmet speakers made them all sound the same. "Hey, look. Bats in the belfry."

Dark shapes like dead autumn leaves hung from the beams that bore the bells of Imperial University, row upon row upon row, wrapped in black leather wings. Everett paused and looked more closely. Something not quite right. Something not quite mammal.

Armored left arms swung on to target. Everett's sinuses and fillings ached as the EM pulse guns charged up.

"Hold your fire," Lieutenant Kastinidis said. "The moment we let rip they'll know we're here. Winkelman, low-level scan."

The bottom-most soldier—the other woman in the squad, Everett had learned, as he waited in the out dock for the soldiers to seal their helmets—lifted up her scanner. She worked it slowly and methodically across the tower interior. The EM gauntlets never wavered in their aim.

"Inactive," Trooper Winkelman declared eventually.

"Not dead."

"Not alive either."

"Move out," Lieutenant Kastinidis ordered.

Not alive, not dead. Everett found he was holding his breath and tiptoeing past the rustling rafters of dormant nanotechnology. Were they what was left of the researchers and students of Imperial, the ones for whom the evacuation tilt jets never came? He thought about Colette Harte, his almost-big-sister, almost-friend, almost-aunt from the Imperial in his world. Had she worked with Tejendra Singh in this world too? Had she been on the genius list of those who were evacuated or was what remained of her shattered into hundreds of Nahn death bats?

The bottom of the tower couldn't come soon enough. Another kick from the lieutenant sent the door flying. Light poured into the gloomy tower interior. The soldiers trooped across the snow-dusted quad, bronze on white. *Everness* filled half the sky above them, too huge to land among the cluttered lecture halls and research blocks.

Trooper Winkelman held up a hand. Everyone froze. She turned in a circle, scanner held high.

"I'm getting Nahn activity."

Everett felt his stomach tighten in fear.

"Low-level stuff, just above background hum. I'm getting small random peaks all around us. Nothing serious. There's a big spike to the northeast, around about Hyde Park Corner."

"Reset frequencies," Lieutenant Kastinidis ordered. "Code 387."

The troopers all touched their left gauntlets. Figures flowed. *Keeping one frequency shift ahead of the Nahn*, Everett thought. "I'd be a lot happier without that big fairy airship floating up there," the lieutenant said. "Lit up all over the frequencies like a Christmas tree." She waved her squad on. Bootprints in the snow.

Cameras. Watch out for the cameras. The cameras are watching out for you. Charlotte Villiers had given Everett M a brief introduction to the design and piloting of Earth 3 airships in the car down to Earthport 1. They had cameras all over the hull. A lot of cameras. Airship design, how to fly the hedgehopper, Thryn battle suit 101, secret passwords, the brief history of Earth 1—so much to take in and memorize, but forgetting any part of it could put him in real danger.

Airships, Charlotte Villiers had said, have lots of cameras underneath and to the sides for when they come in to dock or make landfall to load cargo. They have fewer on the upper surface, since they don't need to look up as much as they need to look down. And they have one blind spot, right behind the upper tail fin. "Keep your line straight and your angle of approach true," Charlotte Villiers had said. "And hope they are too distracted by other things to be paying too much attention to the monitors."

Everett M took the hedgehopper away from *Everness* in a wide loop, climbing all the time, high over Marble Arch and Paddington. The wind was sharp as glass blades around the edge of his goggles, but the air felt clean and pure after the infected earth. Over Bayswater Everett M leaned on the steering bar and made his turn, lining up on the airship's great tail fins, like the crosshairs of a huge target. What were they looking for in there? He didn't need to know. All he needed was to get in unseen, plant the tracker, use it to call in the Heisenberg Gate, and get out. The hedgehopper zoomed down over Kensington Gardens, Everett M using his Thryn-enhanced vision to lock on to the upper tail fin. Numbers and graphics flickered across Everett M's eyeball. Keep the fin inside that circle, fly inside that cone. Five, six minutes work and it would be done. Five, six minutes and he would be off this world forever.

Everett Singh, I'm coming for you.

The last person out before the Nahn swarm hit the university had locked the doors to the Huxley Building. The lock posed no more of an obstacle to Unit 27 than it had the Nahn. The glass shattered into glittering dust. The squad filed into the lobby and spread out, covering the corridors and mezzanine, civilians safe at the center of the circle, overlapped by scramble fields.

"Dr. Singh?"

Tejendra started. He had been scanning around the reception area—the signs, the desks, the vending machines, the notice boards, the computer monitors, the architectural light fitting in the main stairwell, the leather sofas, the low tables, and the magazines from fifteen years ago left where they had been set. Dust lay thick. Cobwebs had collected in the corners and between the bars of the staircase handrails and in the intricate spaces of the designer chandelier, which had once presumably looked like a waterfall of light. But there was none of the peeling paint, the stripped wood, the lifting floor, the broken windows, and the invading mold and plants of dead cities. The place looked as though it had been entirely undisturbed by the nanotech apocalypse and the intervening fifteen years.

It was the smell that froze Everett to the spot. It was not foul, or rotting, or moldy. It was clear and distinct. It smelled of Huxley, a hundred times. Everett knew that every building has its own distinctive smell: the locker room at Bourne Green, Ryun's kitchen, his own house. You smelled it best and clearest after you had been away after term or on vacation. Smell memory is short, but it's powerful. Electricity, shiny paper, printer ink, books, overheated coffee, paper cups, toilet cleaner . . . thought. *Thought* had a smell, like electricity, but more thrilling, more dangerous. Thought smelled like a storm, like a summer morning, like unexpected snow. All these Everett smelled locked up inside this Huxley Building, and they took him out across worlds to the Huxley Building in the Imperial he knew. Colette Harte, spooning low-calorie sweetener into her coffee; Paul McCabe, when he was a smiling bumbler with a Northern Ireland accent; his dad.

"It's the same," Everett whispered.

"I'm sorry?" Tejendra said.

"Dr. Singh, which way?" Lieutenant Kastinidis asked.

"I came in at the tail end of the project. . . . I was just a post-graduate researcher processing data. When the funding was cut I moved to my own research."

"Dr. Singh, do you know where the device is?" Lieutenant Kastinidis asked.

"I think it's in storage. Down in the basement."

Everett heard Sharkey loudly murmur the word, "think."

"In my world, that's where they built the first Heisenberg Gate," Everett said.

Tejendra smiled. "In my world too."

"Move out, Dr. Singh," the lieutenant said. "After you. Don't get too far ahead."

"It needs a name," Everett said to Tejendra as he led the squad along the gloomy central corridor that still smelled of floor polish. "We always give things names in my family, me or my dad."

"It has a name: the Multiversal Quantum Entanglement Resonator."

"That's what it does, not what it is. A cool name like the Infundibulum."

Tejendra hesitated at a set of fire doors.

"Dr. Singh . . ." Lieutenant Kastinidis's voice had lost all patience. "Get it, get it quick, get out. Time for word games and making up names when you're back on the ship." *Does she even know why we're looking for this unnamed thing?* Everett wondered.

"It should be through these doors and down the service stairway," Tejendra said. "It all seems smaller than I remember."

Trooper Winkelman was making another slow scan.

"There's something going on. It's like information flowing from Hyde Park to the Dark Tower and back again."

"Your evaluation?" the lieutenant asked.

"I don't know. I've never seen anything like this before."

"'Oh Lord make haste to help me,'" Sharkey muttered.

"Okay, we're going down," the lieutenant ordered. "Cover the civilians. Lights."

Headlights sprang to life on either side of each helmet. Everett remembered an old YouTube video of Orbital playing a set at Glastonbury, the band members with flashlights on each side of their heads. It was a silly, trivial thing to think. Exactly what you would think if you were very, very scared. The lead trooper pushed open the fire doors. Wind sighed somewhere deep beneath the building. It was black down there. The helmet lamps threw double pools of light on the walls and the stairwell. Down. Everett had always hated those sections in games where you ran around in the dark, waiting for your light to touch something hideous.

The lights darted this way and that down the corridor as the lieutenant's squad checked and cleared each of the storerooms. Signs of decay down here: shelves overturned, files scattered, papers strewn, plastic boxes tipped over. These rooms had been cleared. Everything that might be useful in the war against the Nahn had been stripped. Room after room after room.

"Nahn, ma'am." Every helmet light beamed into the storeroom. Armored fists were raised. Sharkey leveled his shotgun. Long stalactites of black ooze dripped from a black patch on the ceiling. Drips on the floor were frozen into little crowns of Nahn stuff. Winkelman scanned it.

"Inactive," she said. "Been dead a long time."

"What did you keep in here?" the lieutenant asked.

"What I want to know is, who killed it?" Sharkey asked.

In the next storeroom the headlight beams glittered from metal and circuitry.

"What is that? Light it up," the lieutenant ordered.

The flashlights lit up a thick metal disk, three meters across, covered in wires and coolant pumps and heat exchangers. Webs of cable ran from it into the darkness. At the center was a hole the size of Everett's hand. He had seen that hole, this disk before. He had seen it on a wmv file on Ryun Spinetti's computer, but he knew that the real one stood in a basement like this one under Imperial College, just as this one stood in an almost identical basement under Imperial University.

"The original Heisenberg Gate."

"Lieutenant." Sharkey's voice was loud in the dark, musty, dusty room. He spoke the word with the accent of an American Confederate.

"Enough archaeology. Move out," Lieutenant Kastinidis ordered.

"Lieutenant," Sharkey insisted. "They're going to leave you."

"We don't have time for this."

"The Brigadier and the Agister. They got a plan, ma'am."

"Enough, Mr. Sharkey."

But Everett had heard power armor move enough to know what that whine of motors and shuffle of feet meant. The squad was troubled. And he knew that Sharkey had heard the rustle of discontent too.

"Once they have this device, do you know what they'll do? Open up a gate and get the hell out of this world."

"Impossible. The sun . . ."

"We got here. They made a deal with us. You help us find the device; they get a free ride to whatever universe they want. I didn't hear them mention you."

"You're lying."

"'The Lord be a true and faithful witness between us,'" Sharkey said. "Why do you think they came in the ship? Your Brigadier, maybe, but the Agister? She's surely a woman of many parts, but none of them, I think, is military. Do you concur?"

"One more word from you and I will shoot you. I mean that most sincerely, sir."

The darkness was deep, the light unsteady, but Everett thought he saw a small smile on Sharkey's face. He didn't need to say one word more. He had said quite enough. The seeds were planted.

"We complete this mission, we get out. Now, where is this thing, Dr. Singh?"

I have underestimated you, Myles O'Rahilly Lafayette Sharkey, Everett thought. Sometimes it's not a choice between saving Everett and saving the ship. Sometimes both can be done at the same time.

The storeroom at the very end of the corridor was a spooky museum of dead technology. Here stood a dozen Heisenberg Gates, obsolete dusty gateways to nowhere. The glint of helmet lights off white insect wings startled Everett, then more lights came to bear and he saw that the object was a drone. Cobwebs dripped from the fan engines in its delicate wings. Everett had seen a similar device come out of the Heisenberg Gate under Imperial College after a fantastical flight over the domes and minarets of E2 London. Similar but different.

"Gathering dust," Tejendra said. "We went from the queen of sciences to Cinderella in a single moment. Nanotech was the thing now. Nanotech would solve everything. There was money in nano-tech. There were things we could make and sell. There was never any money in the multiverse. This way."

Helmet lights struck strange shadows from row upon row of steel shelving. Cubes, boxes, rectangles, neatly arranged. They all looked perfectly anonymous to Everett, but Tejendra worked slowly along the line, checking each one carefully and thoroughly. He stopped, laid a finger on a small box the size and shape of an old-fashioned paperback book.

"I think . . ."

"It looks like a computer drive," Everett said.

"A quantum computer drive. I'll need to boot it up to find out if it's still working."

Everett's heart lurched in his chest. He had never thought that the mapping device, the Panopticon, might not work. When you need a thing so badly, you can't—you dare not—imagine failure.

Lieutenant Kastinidis stepped forward. "Give it to me." She turned the little box over in her gauntleted hands. "Looks like a standard socket. We haven't invented much in fifteen years."

"We haven't invented anything," Tejendra said.

The lieutenant popped a panel in her left wrist and ran out a power cable.

"As long as that thing doesn't eat too much power. I need every watt."

Tejendra plugged in the Panopticon and stroked the upper surface. A single blue dot woke in the center of the panel and glowed beneath the metal. Then the room was filled with glowing stars, turning slowly like the great, billion-year wheeling of galaxies.

"Oh," Everett said. "Wow."

"*Panopticon*," Tejendra said. "That's a good name, isn't it? The device that can see everywhere. I'll scale it in a little." Tejendra dragged his fingers in across the metal surface and the holographic display contracted to the size of a table top. "Yes, that's how I remember it." By the light of the Panopticon Everett could see Tejendra smiling. "All those stars, those are Heisenberg Gate events."

"That's it. That's so it," Everett whispered.

"Lieutenant, I'm getting an upsurge in Nahn activity," Trooper Winkelman said. "Increased energy levels in the hotspots. There's a huge power spike in the Hyde Park nexus and I'm getting Nahn source-code traces running right here. They may be on to us."

"I need to determine whether it's complete," Everett said. "There might be some interface unit missing. We'd have to come back for it."

"Let's see if I can remember how to get into the system files," Tejendra said. He reached for the Panopticon. A flash of light blinded everyone in the dark storeroom. When Everett could see again, a new star burned brilliantly in the holographic constellation.

"What the hell was that?" Lieutenant Kastinidis said.

"I don't know," Tejendra said. "I didn't touch anything. It's still operational . . ."

"I do know," Everett declared. "A Heisenberg Gate opening. Right here, right now."

"Whatever it is, the Nahn know we're here," Trooper Winkelman said. "Activity just went off the scale."

"Mr. Singh, completion will have to wait." Lieutenant Kastinidis ripped the power cable from her wrist. The stars died. The darkness was sudden and total. "We leave now. Standard protection formation. Go go go."

Blinking, dazzled, Everett grabbed the Panopticon and stumbled toward the door. He felt a hand in his back, urging him, guiding.

"Go on son, you'll be all right," Tejendra said. Everett tucked the Panopticon into an inside pocket of his jacket. The glow tubes on his clothing shone as if he were a man made of stars. Not bright enough to see by, but bright enough to be seen.

"Major hotspot," Trooper Winkelman said. "It's right under us."

Everett M hit the harness button and dropped lightly to *Everness*'s hull. He landed hard. He had half expected to bounce on it like a trampoline. He let go of the tether line and watched the hedge-hopper, set free, soar away until it was lost against the white sky. It would fly until its batteries ran out. No need to bring it back.

The airship was huge. Size of a building huge. Landscape huge. The upper hull curved up gently before him and away on either side. The skin was dusted lightly with snow. There was no sense that he was a hundred meters from the ground. There was no sense that he was floating on air. The only hint that he was on the back of a great machine was a gentle vibration that came up through the soles of his feet: the airship humming to the pulse of its engines.

The tail fin was the size of a house. *Stay away from the moving parts*, Everett M told himself as he squatted down to unzip the quantum tracker from his backpack. It was Thryn-tech white, sealed inside a plastic bag. Foiled by plastic packaging at the last moment, Everett M had to use his teeth to tear it open. It looked like a computer mouse. Everett M realized that he had no idea what a quantum tracking device should look like, but the idea was that you pulled the strip from the adhesive panel on the flat base and stuck it down. Simple as that. He cleared away the snow with his numb, cold hands. Two seconds. Done.

Done.

Mission accomplished.

All the fear. All the horror and the dread and the bravery, the destruction and the cold, to stick a little plastic blister to the hull of an airship. Everett MEverett M. almost laughed. He didn't because he knew that if he did he would not be able to stop, and that the laughter was right on the edge of crying, from the tension and the insanity and the sick feeling in the stomach of dread that went deeper than fear. The least thing would tip it one way or the other. And he wouldn't be able to stop.

The push button on top was the only moving part. It activated the tracker and at the same time transmitted Everett M's location to Earth 4. All they had to do was open the Heisenberg Gate.

All they had to do was open the Heisenberg Gate.

The Heisenberg Gate.

Why hadn't they opened the gate?

They couldn't. They wouldn't. They'd invested too much in him, in all the Thryn tech. He was too valuable. They couldn't leave him here, could they? He saw Charlotte Villiers's red lips beneath the net veil of her hat. Beneath the lipstick her lips were thin and cold. She could leave him stranded in this world. She could do anything.

A dot of blinding white appeared in the air in front of Everett M. In an eye blink it opened into a disk of glaring white. The white light cleared and became the white of the Moon.

"Goodbye, I hate you!" Everett M yelled. Then he grabbed his backpack, pushed up his goggles, and dived through the Heisenberg Gate. It was a good backpack. He would have hated to have left it.

Everett ran. The corridor was so much longer, the floor so much more treacherous than it had been on the way in. The grey light of the stairwell never seemed to get any closer. And the room, so many rooms . . . Helmet lights bobbed and wove crazily around him, little flashes of insane illumination. Trooper Winkelman stopped abruptly, held up her hand for the squad to stop, and held up her scanner. Reflected light played off her visor. Everett saw her helmet move and knew it was a shake of disbelief.

"Nahn!"

"Where?"

"Every bloody where!"

A soldier darted ahead to cover each open door as the squad ran down the corridor. Storerooms full of lost science and history now housed creeping horrors. Everett saw something blacker than the blackness rear up among the tumbled shelves and dead computer cases. It looked like liquid night. It had legs. Too many legs. Far too many legs. Then the soldier fired and the EM pulse blew it all over the walls.

"Clear."

"Don't look back," Sharkey shouted at Everett's shoulder. Everett looked back. A wave of blacker-than-blackness advanced up the corridor, along the walls, the floor, the ceiling, coating it like some vile vomit. Faces. There were faces in it. Ten meters, five meters. Steps. Steps up. Steps out. The light in the stairwell was blinding. Everett hesitated, dazzled.

"Up up up!" a trooper yelled. Everett took the steps two at a time. He missed his footing on the final step and almost reeled headlong. Lieutenant Kastinidis seized his collar in a power-armored steel grip and hauled him upright. As the squad hurdled through shattered remains of the Huxley Building's doors a solid column of black Nahn stuff erupted from the stairwell. It towered like a tree made up of twining snakes. It blossomed at its summit into faces, like a many-headed Hindu god, then fell and splashed all over the lobby. In the moment it took to re-form, two soldiers unclipped grenades from their belts and lobbed them into the seething lobby.

"What are those?" Everett shouted, racing for the cover of the passage under the Huxley building.

"EMP grenades," the soldier beside him answered. Everett pressed the Panopticon close to his chest. Not that it would do any good; the EMP pulse would go through him as clean as an X-ray. If it could fry the Nahn, it could fry the Panopticon. All he could do was hope that the quantum-computing circuitry was protected. The grenades went off with two flat cracks. *EMP grenades*, Everett thought. *Just like* Halo. Glancing back, he saw that the Nahn stuff frozen in the door lay like a breaking wave of oil, faces fixed forever in midscream. *Everness* hung huge above him, but black Nahn stuff was sliding out of the gutters, flowing along the Victorian fake gargoyles, taking their shape, and launching off into the air. Nahn demons stormed out of the air. Elena Kastinidis's soldiers met them with EM blasts that blew them into strange, angular kite shapes that fell to the ground and shattered like glass.

"Power down to 40 percent," Winkelman said.

Everett saw Elena Kastinidis glance at her wrist, then look up. Her fist smashed Everett to the ground. Before he could cry out, she aimed and fired. Shards of dead Nahn fell tinkling around him. He manically brushed them off as Sharkey grabbed his arm and rushed him into the passage. Elena Kastinidis paused for a moment to look at her wrist readout. She tapped it, twice. Everett thought he heard her whisper "shit" on the open channel.

From the open expanse of the Queen's Lawn, Everett glanced up at *Everness*. Sen stood at the great window, hands pressed to the glass. Even at this distance he could see the fear and helplessness on her face. This time she could not ride to his rescue on a drop line, disarm the bad guys with a well-aimed thumper shot, and whizz everyone into the sky. And between Everett and Sen, the Nahn swarmed on wings of living nanotech. But the sight of her, so far away and vulnerable, yet so strong, put fibre in his legs and iron in his spirit and a fire in his heart. *You won't ever have to make that jump home*, Everett thought. *I'm coming back.*

At the foot of the Queen's Tower now. Boots trampled the shattered door.

"In in in . . ." Lieutenant Kastinidis pushed the civilians into the tower. Everett dashed past her. A blackness slammed out of the sky. The lieutenant put up her arm, and the Nahn hit it and clung. It had the face of a two-year-old child. With her free hand Elena ripped it from her, threw it into the air, and shattered it with a blast from her pulser.

"Good save," Everett said. The steps—they went up forever. Round and round and round, up into the darkness. Then his eyes acclimated to the gloom and he saw that the beams, the braces, the struts, and the framework that held the bells were festooned with thousands of hanging Nahn.

"Just keep counting the steps," Sharkey said. One turn, two turns. Endless. Everett's thighs ached. Even Sharkey looked out of breath. And Tejendra . . . he was in pain. He was blinking, puffing, eyes bulging.

"I'm with him," Lieutenant Kastindis said. "I'm with him all the way."

And then above them, a bell chimed. A single, small high note. Clear and out of nowhere. An impossible chime.

"Oh my God," Everett said as the wooden trusses exploded with Nahn. The bells tolled and pealed as the Nahn swarmed around them.

"Arm yourself!" Sharkey yelled. Everett unslung the almost-forgotten shotgun from his shoulder.

"Civilians! Stay close to soldiers!" Lieutenant Kastinidis yelled. "Mr. Sharkey, you remember I said I'd tell you when? This is when."

Bunched tight as an ancient Greek phalanx, the squad fought its way step by step up the inside of the Queen's Tower. The bells quivered and rang with the impact of flying Nahn shards as the trooper's EM pulses shattered them. Faces. They all had faces. This was a nightmare without end. Step by step. Staircase by staircase.

"Power's low!" Trooper Winkelman yelled. Everett flinched as a Nahn bat swooped at his head. Lieutenant Kastinidis aimed at it. Nothing. It turned in midair and threw itself at the lieutenant. It had the face of an old woman. With one thought and one action, Everett swung the shotgun and fired. The Nahn flew apart and instantly began to re-form itself. LEDs lit up on the back of Lieutenant Kastinidis's gauntlet. Power. She aimed and blew the Nahn out of the sky.

"Good shooting, Mr. Singh." Then she yelled to her squad, "I'm almost out. Switching to reserves for battle-suit functions. Go go go!" She touched her helmet and it opened and retracted. "At least I can see where I'm going. Dr Singh, are you all right?"

Tejendra had stopped, exhausted, hands on thighs, panting heavily.

"Oh God . . . Oh God . . . I can't . . ."

"'And I saw a beast rise up out of the sea, having seven heads and ten horns, and upon his horns ten crowns, and upon his heads the name of blasphemy,'" Sharkey said. There was deep awe and reverence in his voice. Everett turned and looked down. The Nahn bats had all been destroyed, but now long, black tendrils were sprouting from the base of the tower, coiling up the stairs, along the beams, up the walls.

"Let's get the hell out of here," Lieutenant Kastinidis shouted. "Run!"

Everett ran. His lungs ached and the blood burned in his heart. Run. Run. There was the light of the balcony door, the white light.

Safety was the white light. Hope was the white light. *Everness* and Sen were the white light. Thirty steps. Twenty steps. Ten steps. There. The white light blinded him. The cold wind blew in his face. The soldiers were already filing across the ramp to the ship. Sen was below him, beneath the curve of the hull, but he could see the fans already running in the impeller pods. At a moment's notice, she could go.

"Get in there Everett," Sharkey shouted. He clung to the parapet with one hand, the other clapped his jaunty hat to his head against the buffeting of the ships engines.

"I have to see . . ." Everett glanced back into the tower. Tejendra had fallen behind. Lieutenant Kastinidis was with him, trying to get his arm around her bulky shoulder, help him onward, upward. Behind them, the inside of the tower was a writhing mass of tentacles, splitting into finer and finer tendrils.

"Come on!" Everett yelled.

Tejendra gave a weary smile. It froze on his face.

"Oh," he said very softly. He wore a look of mild surprise. Then a point of blackness appeared in his chest. It opened like origami, then spread over his chest. Spread, kept spreading. The oily liquid black of the Nahn.

"No!" Lieutenant Kastinidis yelled. With the last of her suit power she tore in half the tendril that had pierced clean through him. A dozen tendrils sprouted from the severed ends. "I'm out of power!"

"You know, the funniest thing," Tejendra said as the blackness wrapped his chest and sent feelers up his neck, around his skull. "It doesn't hurt a bit."

"There's nothing I can do," Lieutenant Kastinidis said, and her face was pale, as if she had seen the thing worse than any nightmare. "Nothing."

"Everett . . ." Tejendra pleaded. And Everett understood what he was asking, and he had never been asked a more terrible thing. "If you eat meat, you must be prepared to kill it yourself," Sharkey had said when they'd gone hunting in the shadow of Aston Hill, and "kill only what needs killing."

A hand grabbed the shotgun. Sharkey wrestled it from Everett's fingers.

"Go Mr. Singh."

"Tejendra . . ."

"Everett. Go."

He saw Tejendra, his brown face vanishing second by second under the devouring black. He saw his eyes. The eyes said, *I understand.* Everett turned and walked into the light. There was no rebel yell, no cry of "Dundee, Atlanta, and Sweet St. Pio." He heard Sharkey say, "The Lord bless thee, and keep thee. The Lord make his face shine upon thee, and be gracious unto thee." Two shots. Nothing more.

Sharkey was last from the tower. The ramp retracted as he ran down it. His face was like the storm of God. He did not look at Everett; he did not look at Lieutenant Kastinidis or any of her squad in the out dock. He went down to the bridge and took his place at the communications desk without a word. Everett and the lieutenant followed him.

Sen was already pulling *Everness* away from the Queen's Tower. Black tendrils erupted from the door, from the skylights in the dome, coiling around the dome like snakes.

"Do you have it?" asked the Agister of Caiaphas College in her fine robes of silk.

"I have it. It works," Everett said.

"And Dr. Singh?"

Lieutenant Kastinidis shook her head.

"Full reverse, Sen," Captain Anastasia said. Her voice was ice. "Get my ship the hell away from that thing."

Everness backed away from the tower. The tendrils had burst the dome, showering heavy chunks of masonry into the courtyard below.

They coiled together, higher and higher. Everett watched the blackness swallow the tower as it had swallowed Tejendra. It was the opposite of everything: of life, and also of death. It was un-death. Everett loathed it. He loathed it with every cell in his body. His hands shook with helpless rage.

Kill only what needs killing. The cards had spelt it out. The cards didn't care whether Everett Singh believed in them or not. *Bubbles of Earth*. Enemies press close and there is no clear way to victory. The all-seeing spire of *Andromeda Heights*. The dark tunnel that was about to swallow the *Jaunter* on his train. The hideous half-human crawling children of *Spiderbabies*. The world-swallowing darkness of *Season of the Wolf*. The bird in the endless storm, striving for the unreachable light of *Shining Path*.

Shining Path. The beam of light that pierced the darkest storm. The light from over the horizon. The light. The sun. The *sun*. Everett opened a channel on the palari-pipe to engineering.

"Mr. Mchynlyth, have we enough power to open a Heisenberg Gate?"

The Queen's Tower looked like a vile flower about to blossom. Tendrils reached out for *Everness*, coiling and twining, splitting into finer and finer tendrils. Sen leaned on the thrust levers. Slowly, so slowly, the huge ship picked up speed.

"Aye. Just about. Are you thinking of jumping us out of here? That's a bona thing to think."

"No, Mr. Mchynlyth, I'm not thinking that at all." Everett understood. Everett understood how his alter could want to kill him. Everett understood what it felt like to have every part of your life taken by someone else's hands and twisted out of shape. He understood because he had found that emotion in himself. Everett Singh understood hate. Hate was a fist of glowing iron in his chest. And Everett understood that most people are powerless in their hate, but when people have power to act out that hate, it is a terrible thing. The most terrible thing. And he had power. He had all power. He

flicked up the Infundibulum. It was easy. Dr. Quantum filled with
the slow-turning veils of the Panoply. He found the coordinates. It
was easy. The calculations, they were easy. The transforms: simple,
instinctive, right. In point, out point. Aperture. Duration. The
Infundibulum spat out a solution. Easy. He slid the code into the
Jump Controller.

The tendrils opened like jaws. Their tips, flat like squid palps,
dissolved into a storm of flying shapes. *Everness* backed away under
full thrust: the Royal College of Music, the Royal Albert Hall, the
Albert Memorial, the tree-scattered white of Kensington Gardens
slid out from under the hull. The Nahn storm whirled into a dark
tornado, leaning toward the airship.

The board lit green.

"Close your eyes!" Everett shouted. "Cover your face! Turn your
back! Do not look at the light!"

He hit the jump button. A jump gate opened twenty meters
above the Queen's Tower. The other side of the gate opened in the
heart of a sun. The lock, the override, the place those who tried to
jump into or out of Earth 1 were sent to dance for a single, searing
moment in destroying light. It worked both ways. Everett could find
it and turn it into a weapon.

He saw a flash more brilliant that anything he had ever seen
before. Then he threw himself to the deck, hands clapped over his
face. He could see the bones in his hands. He could smell skin and
hair burning. Then Everett rolled his back to the great window.

Everett had punched a hundred-meter-diameter circle into the
heart of the sun. Five million degrees of heat and light blasted down
on Imperial University and the Nahn that that had engulfed the university's buildings. Imperial didn't explode. It was flashed into a ball
of plasma. It ceased to exist. Nothing can survive even one second in
the heart of the sun. For five seconds Everett Singh blasted sun stuff
on South Kensington, then the Heisenberg Gate closed. The light
went out. There was no Queen's Tower, no lawn, and no faculty

buildings. There was a circular pit of glowing lava. Of the Nahn, not
an atom. Museums, concert halls, monuments, all the grand Victorian architecture of South Kensington had shattered and flown to
pieces under the blast. Dead cars were scattered like leaves. The Natural History, the Victoria and Albert, the science museums were
smoking shells. The Royal Albert Hall was a broken skull.
Firestorms raged out from the sun strike. A mushroom cloud of
superheated gas and smoke boiled upward from the blast zone,
insane with lightning. Two thousand, three thousand, four thousand
meters. Then the shockwave picked *Everness* up like a toy and slung
it across the sky. Everett rolled across the deck, hooked an arm
around a control desk. Sharkey gripped the arms of his seat with
white knuckles. Brigadier and Agister went reeling. Lieutenant Kastinidis's power armor kept her upright with the last of its energy
reserves. Sen clawed her way across the bucking floor to her post,
hauled herself up to the controls. Felled trees, snowy Hyde Park, the
wall of fire now spreading across South Kensington, spinning past
the great window. Sen's hands hesitated over the levers. Too heavy a
touch would tear the impeller pods from their mountings, but she
had to keep *Everness* from flipping nose over tail. The ship's
nanocarbon skeleton was strong, but a one-hundred-and-eighty-
degree somersault would snap her spine and spill her crew into the
winter air.

"I don't know what to do!"

Captain Anastasia picked herself up from the floor and dived for
the piloting station. She swung herself into the controls. *Everness*
creaked and shrieked in her every strut and spar.

"We have to run with this!" Captain Anastasia shouted. "I'm
going to turn her tail in."

"She'll tumble!" Sen cried. Mighty buffets hit the ship like fists.

"Trust me!" Captain Anastasia yelled back over the sound of her
dying airship. "On my word, full power to the impellers. I'm
waiting for a lull in the wind."

Everness screamed like a living thing, but Captain Anastasia clung to the desk, listening to the wind, feeling the vibration of the sun storm across the hull, sensing in three dimensions. Her sky sense reached out. And in the heart of the hurricane, it touched something.

"Starboard impellers, forward!" Captain Anastasia ordered. "Port, set to reverse. Full power. Now!" Sen slammed one set of thrust levers to the full length of their travel, pulled the others back. Engines sobbed. Vibrations shook Everett to the roots of his teeth. Captain Anastasia heaved the steering yoke. Everett felt the deck tilt beneath him as *Everness* went side-on to the blast wave. The deck tilted: twenty degrees, thirty degrees. Could the ship survive a three-sixty roll? *Everness* rolled, *Everness* yawed, but the huge ship turned on her axis. "Come on my lover!" The tendons strained in Captain Anastasia's neck, her eyes bulging as she wrestled the steering yoke. Then the storm caught the edge of *Everness*'s steering surfaces and spun her around, tail into the gale, and she ran sweet and straight and true before the wind from hell. Behind her Knightsbridge and South Kensington blazed, the flames leaping a hundred meters into the sky. Hyde Park was scorched bare; the snow vaporized; the fallen, smoking trees pointing to the center of the blast. The mushroom cloud had topped out into a layer of dark cloud, still flickering with electrical discharges. Sooty rain fell from the cloud layer, freezing into black snow.

"I have the con, Miss Sixsmyth." Captain Anastasia pulled down a palari-pipe. "Status, Mr. Mchynlyth."

"We're still airship-shape," Mchynlyth said. "By all that's high and holy, we shouldnae be, but we are, thank the Dear. Tell Mr. Singh he's burned out every single forward-facing camera and we've lost most of the paintjob from the nose. But we are here, and them unholy beasties aren't, so overall, it's a result. Oh, and I wouldnae hang around too long in the neighborhood. We took a pretty hefty dose of radiation there—those of you still have plans for your gonads."

"Bona speed for Oxford," Captain Anastasia said, equalizing the thrust levers. "Miss Sixsmyth, attend to Mr. Singh."

Everett stood with his fist clenched. His breath was tight in his chest. His head was very light. Everything, everyone was a distance from him. He felt loosely connected to reality. He had called down the sun. He had destroyed the Nahn. A line from the Bhagavad Gita, the great Hindu holy manuscript, came to his lips. "Now I am become death, the destroyer of worlds." Oppenheimer, the creator of the atom bomb, had spoken those words when the first test bomb exploded. Everett had called on forces smaller and more powerful than fissioning atoms—the quantum nature of reality itself—and he'd used them to open a gateway into the heart of the sun in another universe. A second image from the Gita: Krishna, in his universal form, shining with the light of a thousand suns.

Sen ran to him. Everett turned his face from her, lifted his fist.

"Sen. Leave him." It was Sharkey who spoke.

"Dad," Everett whispered.

"Impressive, Mr. Singh, but unfortunately this changes everything," the Brigadier said. "I'll take the Infundibulum. Now, boy."

"Is it ever over?" Everett shouted. "Can't you ever stop wanting something from me? Just stop needing?"

"Lieutenant Kastinidis, secure the Infundibulum." The lieutenant raised her right arm. Weaponry unfolded from her fist, but her face was featureless. She looked like a woman obeying orders, only orders. *Everness*'s crewmembers were on their feet.

"We had a deal!" Captain Anastasia thundered.

"You are traders, we are soldiers," the Brigadier said. "There are no deals in war. The Infundibulum."

Everett snatched Dr. Quantum from its stand to his chest.

"Come and take it."

"Lieutenant, as he says."

"Everett, don't be stupid," Lieutenant Kastinidis said. "I have a weapon."

"So do I," Everett answered. His fingers danced across Dr. Quantum's screen. "Oxford."

"You don't have the power," the Brigadier said. "Take it from him. Break as many fingers as you need to."

"Want to bet on that?" Everett said. "Do you really want to bet on that?"

"Everett Singh, no," Sen said. "Everett Singh, if you do it, he wins. Him, the other you. The Anti-Everett. You becomes him. Your enemy."

Everett hesitated in a moment of self-doubt. The Brigadier lunged. With a firm grasp and a fast twist, the Brigadier wrenched Everett's arm. Everett cried out in pain and Dr. Quantum fell from his fingers into the Brigadier's grasp. "You're not trained in these things, sonny." He looked at Dr. Quantum. "Well look at that. You really did have Oxford lined up. You little shit." Fast and hard, he slammed a fist into Everett's stomach. Everett gasped and went straight down. Sen gave a small, piercing cry and fell on her knees beside him. Everett retched, fought heaving pain and shock. Hit. He had been *hit*. "Well, let's get rid of that." The Brigadier swiped his fingers across the face of Dr. Quantum, erasing the code.

"If you's hurt him, I tear your heart out!" Sen screamed.

"Oh, for God's sake," the Brigadier muttered.

Elena Kastinidis's aim had not dropped.

"Lieutenant?" the Brigadier asked, his voice full of amazement.

"So were you planning on taking other ranks with you, or is it officers and bosses only?"

"Lieutenant . . ."

"Your escape plan. A way past the quarantine, right out of the Plenitude altogether. A brave new world, all yours. Planning on sharing it with anyone?"

"Lieutenant Kastinidis, where did you get this from?"

Sharkey tipped the brim of his hat.

"From me, sir."

Everett could move now, but every muscle, every bone ached. He had been hurt in football matches—goalkeeping was pretty physical, with its dives and rolls and collisions with fast-moving strikers—but this was the first time Everett had ever been hurt by personal violence. It was more than hurt. There was violation in it.

"'And ye shall know the truth, and the truth shall make you free,'" Sharkey said.

"This is mutiny, Lieutenant Kastinidis."

"It's not mutiny where she is only following orders." The Agister spoke now. "Brigadier, return the device to its rightful owner."

"You have no authority to issue orders. We are still subject to Defense Protocol 4," the Brigadier said.

"Is anyone here aware that we are under a defense protocol?"

Elena Kastinidis held her unwavering aim on the Brigadier.

"You quisling!" the Brigadier snapped at the Agister. "You were there too. You agreed with me, every single word."

"I said what I said, and it can't be unsaid. Yes, Lieutenant Kastinidis, I made a deal with the crew to obtain the device in return for safe passage off this world. But at least I have the courage to change my mind."

"Courage? Treachery," the Brigadier said.

"It's the only courage, Brigadier: to step back from what's wrong."

"You do not accuse me of cowardice. Ever!" The Brigadier's rage was as sudden and hot as the heart of the sun.

"This is my world and my home and I would rather fight than run. If we had a chance of being able to win," the Agister said. "We have that chance now. We have a weapon. The boy showed us. Everything is different. A few small modifications to our existing Heisenberg Gate technology, and we can carry the war to the Nahn. We can destroy the major nodes. Return the device to the boy. We don't need this deal, we have a better one."

For a long moment of absolute silence and stillness, the

Brigadier stood. Tension crackled like electricity on the bridge. He locked eyes with Lieutenant Kastinidis. Hers did not waver from his.

"Yes, I believe you would, lieutenant."

He briskly gave Dr. Quantum to Everett. Sen bared her teeth at him and hissed. He slipped his sidearm out of its holster carefully by the barrel and surrendered it to Lieutenant Kastinidis. She dropped her aim. Her weaponry retracted.

"Captain, do you have secure accommodation on your ship?" the Agister asked.

"My latty would be the nearest thing, ma'am," Captain Anastasia said. "No locks on airships, of course. It's not *so*."

"With your permission, Captain," the Agister said. Captain Anastasia nodded. "Lieutenant, please escort the Brigadier to the cabin."

The lieutenant stepped behind the Brigadier but gave him a respectful distance. The Brigadier gave a small bow to the Agister but did not say a word as he walked from the bridge, head high, back straight, holding on to his last threads of dignity.

"Captain Sixsmyth, we'll not be taking that deal," the Agister said from the foot of the stair. She turned to address Everett. "I wish you every success with your search for your father, but believe me when I say: the Panoply of worlds is a very big place."

Captain Anastasia straightened her belt and cuffs. Mchynlyth's voice crackled on the palari-pipe. "Would someone tell me what the hot hell happened there?"

"We won," the captain said, "Rather, we didn't lose." She clicked off the microphone. "Posts everyone. Mr. Singh, if you wish, you may retire to your latty."

"No ma'am." Everett's stomach ached where the Brigadier had hit him, hit him hard, adult to adult. He still burned with shame. Another human had used violence on him. He had never known that before. *But I beat you*, Everett thought. *I beat you the smart way*.

"Very good, Mr. Singh. The con is yours, Miss Sixsmyth. Bona speed, out of this terrible place. Mr. Singh, any chance of a bite to eat?"

23

They were dancing on the Moon, Charlotte Villiers and Charles, her alter. The room was another featureless Thryn white space, but in the low gravity they soared and swooped around it like angels. He wore a formal white tie and tails; she wore opera gloves, jewels, and a long ball gown of black and white chiffon that flew up like butterfly wings as she glided and floated across the whiteness. It was proper old-time ballroom dancing, choreographed for the Moon, to some old-time crooner tune. It was one of the most beautiful—and at the same time one of the most wrong—things Everett M had ever seen.

Charlotte Villiers spotted Everett M and Madam Moon as Charles twirled in a series of gliding steps across the white floor. She spun effortlessly from his hold and flew across the intervening space to drift down as light as thistledown in front of Everett. There was a single bead of perspiration on her upper lip. Her hair and make-up were immaculate. The layers and veils of her dress settled slowly around her.

"Mr. Singh."

"I did it."

Did he see the smallest smile flicker over Charlotte Villiers's red lips?

"Excellent. You've shown yourself trustworthy. The Order will have need of your special talents again. In the meantime, relaxation and renewal are in order. You've earned it. Now, if you'll excuse me, I must change." She flicked a look at her alter, who straightened the bottom of his tailcoat and gave a small, tight bow.

"Where are you going?"

"I have to take you back. If you recall, I am supposed to be Social Services."

"I'm not going back home?"

"Everett, no. The cover must be maintained. As long as you are there, the family is safe from your alter. You're acclimating well. We're very pleased. Young males are such resilient little things."

Charlotte Villiers swept away in a flurry of chiffons and net.

"What about my family?" Everett M shouted. "What about Mum, my sister, here in this world?" A dark circle opened in the whiteness. Charlotte Villiers disappeared into it. "Do they even know I'm alive?" The hole irised shut.

Charles Villiers looked Everett up and down in his stained and scarred Thryn skin suit. "Mr. Singh," he called from across the white space. "The battle armor?"

"My aspect was destroyed," Madam Moon said. "The Nahn was unable to overcome me. At the same time I was unable to overcome the Nahn. Self-destruction was the safest course."

Madam Moon had been waiting with folded hands when the Heisenberg Gate picked him off the back of *Everness* and brought him back to the far side of the E4 Moon. There was never any emotion in those hands, on that grey face, in those grey eyes, but Everett felt looked at, looked at from the skin in, deep looking with senses other than sight. Could she see the Nahn node nestling up against his spine? Did she already know of the deal he had struck with the Nahn? All Thryn were one Thryn. Did some weird quantum-entanglement thing bind them all together, across space and across universes? Did she know and not care? White Thryn, black Nahn, was there any difference between them? And Madam Moon was grey . . . Once again Everett M wondered whether the sixty years humans had spent studying the Thryn had uncovered any knowledge other than what the Thryn wanted humans to know.

"Welcome back to Earth 4," Madam Moon had said as she fell in beside Everett. "Please, come with me. The Plenipotentiary is dancing."

Charles Villiers carefully removed his white dancing gloves as he walked toward Everett and Madam Moon.

"Is there any danger?"

"Thryn and Nahn are incompatible," Madam Moon said mildly.

"Good job, Everett." Charles Villiers smacked Everett M lightly on the arm with his gloves as he passed him. "My alter will meet you at the gate."

Tippy-tap. Scrit-scatch.

No answer.

Louder then. *Rap rappety-rap-rap.*

"What is it?"

There was a way Everett sounded when he was doing stuff and didn't want to be disturbed. Not omi-playing-with-yourself stuff. She knew what that sounded like. This was omi-busy stuff.

"Can I come in?"

"If you like."

Sen slid open the door to Everett's latty. She let out a gasp.

"It's full of stars!"

Soft blue stars hung in the air, turning slowly, drifting like thistledown on a summer evening. The blue lit Everett's face and hands. He conducted the stars as if they were an orchestra, every movement sending whole constellations wheeling. Everett tapped the little box on his fold-down table and the stars were sucked into it.

"Aw, put them back. They was beautiful."

A stroke on the lid of the device—the Panopticon, Sen remembered, why always these big mouth-jamming words?—and the soft stars once again filled the tiny cabin. Sen pulled the little wooden misericord down from behind the door and perched her skinny butt on it.

"Wow. That's like the best Christmas decorations in the universe." She watched Everett turn the stars this way and that, dancing his hands through the light. *You moves well for a ground-pounder*, she thought. *You don't think about. You're all there, moving the stars around.* Omis looked their best when they were doing something. Omis were their best when they were doing something. All the trouble in all the worlds comes from omis with nothing to do. *All the worlds*, Sen thought. "So, what are they?

"They're all the worlds the jumpgun fired people to."

"Worlds." Sen still couldn't get her head around this way of looking at the universe. The universe was what you saw when you flew above the clouds on a night run: stars and moons and things. The universe was *out there*. To Everett Singh, the universe was nothing but Earths, like pearls on a string. Not out there, but over there. Right next to you, close as the breath in your lungs, but you'd never know. "It worked then."

"It worked, sort of."

"Oh, Everett Singh . . ."

"I've got all the locations. There they are." Everett flicked deep blue air. Stars wheeled between Sen and him. "One of those is my dad. I just don't know which one."

"But you said the Panpy . . . thing . . . that box . . . You said you could plug it into the jumpgun and it would read all the quantum echoes." She'd remembered those words. She wasn't thick—she wanted him to know that, more than anything—but that quantum stuff did her head even more than the jillions and zillions of other Earths. It must be hard to be him, head always filled with that stuff, fizzing away.

"Yes, but it doesn't tell me when. It doesn't give a sequence." Again he spun the stars. He grabbed hold of one and pulled it out to expand it into a knot of code. "This is the time we made the jump from my world to Earth 1, but I only know that because I recognize the code. It doesn't record when we make a jump, only where we go to." A slap of his hand sent the glowing worlds spinning.

"But he's there."

"Yes, he's there."

"Well then, all you have to do is go to every one of them pale blue dots and eventually you'll find him. There. Problem sorted.

Ain't that bona. And on the way, if you could take us to a world where I can get some slap and togs . . ."

"I'm scared, Sen."

She got up from her little wooden ledge, stepped through stars, and came down beside Everett on the edge of his hammock. The shape of the fabric forced them together, side by side. He was big and warm and hard, and she could feel his fear. *You been scared forever, omi*, she thought.

"I mean, I was so sure that he's alive and that he's safe and that he's got people looking after him, but I don't know that, do I?" Everett said. "The Agister said to me that the Panoply of Worlds is a very big place. I never really thought about what that means. We've seen what this world's like—there will be worlds out there worse than this."

Sen took his hand. It was freezing. Oxford snow had piled up at the bottom of his porthole. Working too long alone and not moving. That was bad for you. It was cold here, but not as cold as the last time Everett Singh had spent hours looking at code and trying to make it work. *Everness* was moored once again among the winter snow on Museum Gardens, powering up from the Oxford wind turbines. Annie and Sharkey were at dinner, guests of the Agisters of all the colleges. That's why Sharkey had double armed himself. Them Agisters, you couldn't trust them. Sen had seen how quickly they could turn. She didn't know what would happen to the Brigadier, but she suspected it wouldn't be good. They were hard people here. They had to be. That was all right. He had hurt Everett. Mchynlyth was out with the troopers, drinking. Sen hoped he didn't get into another fight. She knew what he could be like when he had been on the buvare. *Everness* belonged to her and Everett, and he had been hiding away for hours in his latty, playing with stars and universes. A polone gets bored, you know?

"But better too, Everett Singh. That's the thing, ain't it? With so many worlds, odds are you'll end up in one that's kind of bona, rather than fantabulosa or really, really meese."

"You just reinvented the Principle of Mediocrity," Everett said.

"Hey! You saying I's mediocre?" Sen felt him squeeze her hand.

"It's an important principle in science. My dad taught it to me. It says that there's nothing special about our Earth, our solar system, us. We don't have a special place in the universe, or any universe. We're not at the center of things."

"I don't know 'bout you, Everett Singh, but I's pretty special," Sen declared. "And so's you." Then she felt him catch his breath beside her. "You are all right."

"I saw his eyes, Sen. He wanted me to stop it. I couldn't do it. He wasn't my dad . . . but he was."

"I weren't there, but I seen a thing. There was an omi down in Hackney, a stevedore, ran the Dalston Number Four Dock. He couldn't fly, see, coz he had something wrong with his Aunt Nells. His balance was all meshigener—you can't fly if you can't balance. You'd never be off your dish. But he had a daughter—loved her to the death—an' she could fly, and did, on the *English Rose*. She was 'prentice engineer, and he loved her, but she died. There was this accident with the charging arm. Horrible it was. Everyone saw her. She just, like, danced, and then there was nothing, just burned stuff. Horrible, horrible, Everett Singh. But that omi, after that, the light went out in his yews. He had nothing left to live for. One day he went up the dock where she died, and everyone was shouting up, what for you doin' up there? Come down you meshigener fool, and he fell. An' he died. Oh, it was so sad, Everett Singh, because everyone knew he'd died long ago. He died when she died. You see it in the eyes. I saw his eyes too, Everett Singh. I did. I sees these things. You told me he lost his wife and everything to that black stuff. That'd kill an omi, inside. He died when she died. He was just waiting to fall over. You done nothing wrong."

She hugged Everett. He resisted. He could be so stiff and not *so*. What did they teach them in those Earth 10 families?

"I should have been able to do it," he said.

"No, you shouldn't have. How old is you? Fourteen? No. Nah. Never. Sharkey did right." The hammock swung gently as *Everness* was swayed by a rising wind. A nor'easter, Sen's weather wisdom told her. Comes the snow again. She shivered. "Everett Singh . . ."

"Why do you always call me that?" Everett asked. "Everett Singh. Never just Everett."

"Dunno. Some people, they just need two names to anchor them down. But serious, serious now: Everett Singh: back there, the sun gun . . ."

"The what?"

"The thing you zapped London with."

"Sun gun?"

"So? It's a better name than hedgehopper. Anyway . . ." She poked him hard in the ribs, then remembered he still hurt there, muscle deep. "Sorry sorry sorry. Everett Singh. When you had the sun gun lined up on Oxford—here, would you?"

"Would I what?"

"Oh, you're so *naff* . . . Would you have fired it? Melted all this to . . . glass?"

"He was right. I didn't have the power." But in the blue light Sen could see Everett staring dead ahead of him, at the latty door, and his feet were kicking in that way people do when they lie.

"But if you had—"

"Yes. I would have. I would have because I hated him. I hated the Nahn. I hated this world. I hated the Infundibulum. I hated everything because I hadn't asked for any of it. And for once I could show people what that hate looked like. Like something so bright you couldn't even look at it because it would burn the eyes out of your head. So I couldn't help Tejendra, but this fourteen year old could press a button and empty the sun onto all these people here. But you said something. You said that if I did it I would be just like him. The other Everett. But you were wrong, Sen. Don't you see? I am him already. I am him, and he is me. Everything I am, he is. That's why I couldn't beat him at Abney Park. And that's why he couldn't beat me. Because everything he is, I am too. The hate in him, I have that too. And I saw that button, and I saw the hate, and I saw what it had done to him, and I said, *I won't be like that. I won't do what he would do.*"

Sen leaned against him, wrapped her arms around him.

"Alamo, Everett."

"Sen."

"What?"

"I lied."

"I lie all the time," Sen said, leaning comfortably against Everett, swinging her booted feet. Then she realized that Everett wasn't Airish and wouldn't understand who you could lie to and who you could never lie to. "I mean, it's a *so* thing, Everett . . ."

"There was power, Sen. There was enough power. The board was green. I lied. I wanted you to think I had no choice, that there was no way for me to do the wrong thing. Because that would then make it all right. I didn't have a choice. But there was, and I almost did. I had a choice."

"You chose right, Everett."

"Yeah, I did. But I'm scared that next time—and there will be a next time—I won't do the right thing." He glanced at her "You called me Everett. Three times."

"Three times is the magic time," Sen said, sing-song. "Tap the deck three times. Oh!" She remembered why she had come tappy-scratching at Everett's latty. "Here. Something to show you." She slipped a card from inside her jacket and laid it on top of the Panopti-thingie. The stars went out. "Just finished this. What you think of it? Bonaroo, eh?"

The card showed an airship, not a sleek, streamlined sky shark like *Everness*, but an old-school one, the kind you saw in the airship museum at Cardington. One like a big silver sausage. It flew out of the card, prow pointed upward. At the bottom of the card, at the airship's tail, was a burst of sunrays. She had found the sunburst in an old magazine they had picked up on the last run to Atlanta. They had this retro-future thing going on there, like everything was supposed to look futuristic but old-fashioned at the same time. The airship came from a history book. The chest under Sen's hammock was full of out-of-date make-up and savaged books and magazines she had cut up for card ideas.

"Nice," Everett said. "I like the sun. Really 1920s."

Sen tutted in exasperation.

"That's not the sun. It's a gate. An Ein . . . Heisenberg Gate."

"Oh, wow," Everett said. There was light in his eyes now. Bona. "What's it called?"

"Oh. I haven't finished that bit yet." Sen took a pen from her pocket and carefully, slowly wrote one word in silver ink. She waved it and blew on it to dry the ink. Stars briefly filled the cabin, then vanished as she set the card down again. *Everness*. "There. Said I was good with names."

Everett reached for the card. Sen slapped his fingers away.

"You got yours. This is for me. My card." She kissed it. It smelled of ink and just-dried glue and old newsprint and futures only guessed at.

"What does it mean?" Everett asked.

"Don't know," Sen said. "I'll find out." She took the deck from her jacket and folded the card into it. Once again the latty filled with the stars that weren't stars, but points of hope in the Panoply of All Worlds. "Everett, can I?"

"What?"

"Move the stars around."

He smiled. He did not smile much, but he was one of those omis who, when they did, lit up rooms and hearts and lives.

Sen put her hand into the glowing star field, moved it this way and that way, pulled it in and pushed it out, eyes wide as the soft thistledown balls of light that spun around her.

"So where are you taking us next?" she asked.

"Like you said, don't know. One place's as good as any other. You choose."

"Me?"

"Why not?" Everett's breath steamed in the chilly cabin. "Pick a world. Any world."

The car was black, polished, shiny as oil. A Mercedes S-class. He was learning about these Earth 10 cars. The S65 AMG, with a 5,980 cc biturbo rocking 604 horsepower. Hydrocarbon engines might be resource-guzzling environment trashers, but when they let rip they made a mighty noise you could feel all the way to the pit of your belly. The car was black, polished, shiny. Like Nahn.

Tearing up the motorway from the Heisenberg Gate at Folkestone, now crawling in evening traffic down through Edmonton and Tottenham. A thaw had set in during the two days he had been on other earths. The Mercedes splashed through black slush. Grey snow was piled up in the gutters; pedestrians picked careful paths over half-melted slicks of rotting ice. Welcome to planet Hackney.

The lights were going on down Stamford Hill. The plastic shop signs were bright and gaudy, the bus windows steamed up. A woman with five dogs on leads was leaving Abney Park Cemetery. The dogs all pulled in different directions. The woman was fighting to keep her beanie hat on and keep the dogs under control. Here, in another world, he had run out of this gate for a number 73 bus and a car like this had run him down. The woman beside him had been sitting where she sat now, in the back seat, smartly upright, hands demurely folded in her lap. The man behind the wheel of this Mercedes S-class had probably been driving the one that had cut Everett M down.

As the car passed the bus gates, Everett M felt an itch at the back of his neck. A tickle that he could ignore at first, but it grew fiercer and fiercer. He had to scratch it. It would kill him if he didn't.

He tried to ease the itch on the collar of his school blazer. No good. Finally, he reached up and scratched until he felt his skin must tear, his fingernails splinter. As the Mercedes swept past the gates of Abney Park and the struggling dog-walking woman, he felt something slip from his neck into his hand.

Charlotte Villiers shot him a disapproving look. *No way are you ever going to convince Roding Road you're Social Services*, Everett thought. Not with an S-class and a real fur coat. He waited until she looked away to glance at the thing in his hand.

It looked like a tiny spider. Black, of course, shiny oil black. Nahn black. Too many legs for a spider, and no real front end or back end. It clung to the palm of his hand. The tiniest invader.

For a moment he thought of slapping it onto the back of Charlotte Villiers's hand. There was a tiny oval of exposed skin where her glove was buttoned over. He would enjoy the look of surprise in her eyes as she felt it sink through her skin, her eyes going black as the Nahn ate her from the inside. No. He needed her to get him off this world, back to his real family. The driver had a beautiful five centimeters of targetable skin between the collar of his chauffeur's jacket and the bottom on his chauffeur's cap. No. He was driving. Two car accidents outside Abney Park was too many. Wait. A whole world was his.

Everett M closed his fist as the black car turned onto Northwold Road. Left into Roding Road, up between the bright houses with the melting snow shushing beneath the wheels, and the Nahn spider in his hand. He was still cold, so cold. He knew he always would be.

PALARI

Palari (polari, parlare) is a real secret language that has grown up in parallel with English. Its roots go back to seventeenth-century Thieves Cant in London—a secret thieves' language. It's passed through market traders and barrow-mongers, fairground showmen, the theatre, the Punch and Judy Show, and gay subculture. Palari ("the chat"—from the Italian *parlare*, "to talk") contains words from many sources and languages: Italian, French, *lingua franca* (an old common trading language spoken across the Mediterranean), Yiddish, Romani, and even some Gaelic. It's taken in words from Cockney rhyming slang—"plates" for *feet*, from "plates of meat" = "feet"; and London back-slang—"eek" is short for "ecaf," which is "face" backward. Many words from palari/polari have entered London English. In Earth 3, palari is the private language of the Airish. In our world, polari still survives as a secret gay language.

GLOSSARY OF PALARI:

ajax: nearby (from adjacent?)

alamo: hot for her/him

amriya: a personal vow, promise, or restriction that cannot be broken (from Romani)

aunt nell: listen, hear

aunt nells: ears

barney: a fight

batts: shoes

bijou: small/little (means "jewel" in French)

blag: pick up/beg as a favor/get without paying

bod: body

bona: good

bona nochy: goodnight (from Italian—*buona notte*)

bonaroo: wonderful, excellent

buvare: a drink (from old-fashioned Italian *bevere* or Lingua Franca *bevire*)

cackle: talk/gossip

capello: hat (from Italian *cappello*)

carsey/khazi: toilet.

charper: to search (from Italian *chiappare*, to catch)

charver: to have sex

chavvie: child

chicken: young male/boy

clobber: clothes

cod: naff, vile

cove: friend

dally/dolly: sweet, kind.

dinari: money

dish: ass, bum, arse

Divano: an Airish ship's council.

dona: woman (from Italian *donna* or Lingua Franca *dona*), a term of respect

dorcas: term of endearment, "one who cares." The Dorcas Society was a ladies' church association of the nineteenth century, which made clothes for the poor.

doss: bed

drag: clothes, especially women's clothes (from Romani *indraka*, a skirt)

ecaf/eek: face (back-slang). *Eek* is an abbreviation of *ecaf*.

fantabulosa: fabulous/wonderful

feely: child/young/girl

fruit/fruity: in Hackney Great Port, a term of mild abuse

gafferiya: Airish tradition of hospitality and shelter for travelers (from Thieves Cant).

gelt: money (Yiddish)

kris: an Airish duel of honor (from Romani)

lacoddy: body

lallies: legs

latty: room or cabin on an airship

lilly: police (Lilly Law)

luppers: fingers (Yiddish *lapa*, a paw)

manjarry: food (from Italian *mangiare* or Lingua Franca *mangiaria*)

measures: money

meese: plain, ugly, despicable (from Yiddish *meeiskeit*: loathsome, despicable, abominable)

meshigener: nutty, crazy, mental (from Yiddish)

metzas: money (Italian *mezzi*: means, wherewithal)

naff: awful, dull, tasteless

nante: not, no, none (Italian: *niente*)

ogle: look, admire

omi: man/guy

omi-polone: effeminate man or homosexual

onk: nose

Palari-pipe: telephone/in-ship communication system ("talk pipe")

palliass: mattress or place to sleep.

polone: woman/girl

riah: hair (back-slang)

sabi: to know (from Lingua Franca *sabir*)

scarper: to run off (from Italian *scappare*, to escape or run away)

sharpy: policeman (from "charpering omi")

sharpy polone: policewoman

shush: steal

shush-bag: hold-all/backpack

slap: make-up

so: to be part of the in-crowd/Airish (e.g. "Is he so?")

strides: trousers

tober: road

todd: alone (from rhyming slang *Todd Sloanne*—alone)

troll: to walk about looking for business or some kind of opportunity

varda: to see/look at (from Italian dialect *vardare* = *guardare*—look at)

yews: eyes (from French *yeux*)

zhoosh: style, make a show of, mince (Romani: *zhouzho*—clean, neat)

zhooshy: flashy, showy

ABOUT THE AUTHOR

Ian McDonald has written fourteen science fiction novels and has lost count of the number of stories. He's been nominated for every major science fiction award, and has even won some. Ian has also worked in television in program development—all those reality shows have to come from somewhere—and has written for screen as well as print. He lives in Northern Ireland, just outside Belfast, and loves to travel. *Be My Enemy* is the second part of the Everness series.